THE PALACE OF PLEASURES

'As for Ula, she's like many around here. She is ambitious and, luckily for her, pretty. I think she sees the role of the Companion as an honour and a way to rise up the social scale.'

'Would she take the discipline?'

'As she said, she comes from the diamond ports. The schools there are very traditional, set up by the eighth Sultan. Even now, the undergraduates wear breast weights for even the most trivial things. She would seldom get into trouble and accept whatever devices you have with ease and as fair punishment.'

'I'm not too sure anyone can take some of our punishments with ease.'

THE PALACE OF PLEASURES

Christobel Coleridge

This book is a work of fiction.
In real life, make sure you practise safe, sane and consensual sex.

First published in 2003 by
Nexus
Thames Wharf Studios
Rainville Road
London W6 9HA

Copyright © Christobel Coleridge 2003

The right of Christobel Coleridge to be identified as the Author of this Work has been asserted by her in accordance with the Copyright, Designs and Patents Act 1988.

www.nexus-books.co.uk

Typeset by TW Typesetting, Plymouth, Devon

Printed and bound by
Clays Ltd, St Ives PLC

ISBN 0 352 33801 6

Contents

Part One – Arrival   1
  1   The Rules   3
  2   A Discreet Shop   14
  3   First Lessons   31
  4   The Fitting   42
  5   Inspection   59

Part Two – Schooling   71
  6   The First Chamber   73
  7   Default and Correction   86
  8   An End and a Beginning   100
  9   Temptation   106
 10   Plans   122
 11   The Rope Room   133

Part Three – The Palace of Pleasures   139
 12   Humiliation   141
 13   The Hunt   149
 14   The Sultan's Room   166
 15   The Trial   181

Part Four – Ordeals   195
 16   The Monkey Room   197
 17   The Prancing Horse   212
 18   Butterflies and Beetles   222
 19   New Arrivals   233

Part One
Arrival

1

The Rules

J'nie adjusted her waist-belt and chains of rank: the gold chains running from a wide white leather collar down to similar cuffs and back to the high waisted belt where they were fastened. The chains were long and slack, with plenty of loose links. In her position it was unlikely she would ever suffer the indignity of losing any of the fine links, but she kept with tradition and wore the traditional costume of a Companion with some pride.

For the last three years she had been the Sultan's Mistress, his only acknowledged full-time partner, and had been accorded the privileges of that position and the honour of being untouched by any other. She had her own suite on the ground floor of the palace, her own servants and complete control of all of the Sultan's other Companions.

Today had been an uneventful one. After a pandering from the maidservant and a formal visit to the Sultan, J'nie had spent much of the rest of the day writing letters. Lying sprawled across the silk of the bed, she had almost fallen into a sleep when one of three tall glass tubes beside the bed – the blue one – started to shine, and the dyed nightingale caged on top started to sing, announcing a punishment ceremony.

Rising from the bed, she slipped on a short dark blue pleated skirt and checked the fastening on her heeled boots. The bedroom led on to a large octagonal entrance hall, panelled from top to bottom in small octagonal mirrors. Three doors, each a different colour and each encrusted with jewels, stood inset into three of the walls, with the door to the bedroom making a fourth. One door – the blue one – led to the school, the yellow to the Sultan's old trusted Retainer and the controller of the ways to all the levels, and the red one to her private rooms, her maidservant and a special room for her own entertaining. In the centre of the octagon stood a fountain which brought a soothing quality to the atmosphere. She splashed her face in the pale rose pink water of the fountain and, checking herself in one of the tall mirrors one last time, she made her way to the yellow door.

She rang, then the shuffling Retainer appeared and led her through his maze of corridors to the school entrance. Descending the winding stairs in the heels she wore was an art, but one she had learned, as all graduates of the Sultan's school had, to walk with a still and elegant deportment. Soon the air grew colder and even the last beam of sunlight from the day faded. Another door was opened and, passing into the torch lit subterranean school, she passed the Companions' guards in their fine shiny black costumes glinting in the dancing torch flames.

Down here there was no lavender scent as the palace had, but more earthy, sensual fumes filled the air. She reached the ornate formal entrance to the school with its emblem of a whip, the motto *Freedom Through Discipline* proudly etched into the stone.

In front of J'nie a familiar figure approached with a wild mane of red hair, almost as red as her own. 'I'm sorry, but one of the new girls has lost the last link on her chain. She needs to be punished.' Helena, the trusted headmistress of the school, wasted no time with pleasantries.

J'nie studied the short, athletic woman. She was dressed in the same uniform as J'nie, but this time the heels were shorter, as was the skirt, giving her the look of a woman who spent a lot of time in physical pursuits and was proud of the fact. Her blue eyes betrayed no indication of guilt, and J'nie dismissed the notion that Helena's enthusiasm for punishments had overstepped the mark again. No, this was a ceremony that she had no need to stop.

'Is it Yvonne? What happened?' J'nie asked, without surprise. That girl had already run the gamut of lesser punishments, and this would only be fair, despite the pain that the girl would suffer.

'Oh, she was down to her last link and then a guard caught her attempting to bribe a maid to pleasure her in the bathing room. The maid claims she is innocent, but I've sent her to have her lower chains tightened anyway, just to be sure. As for the girl, of course, without any more links to lose she has to be punished. She's in her cell now.'

'Then,' J'nie sighed, Helena could be so cruel, 'We must make sure that this will at least set a good example for the other girls. Lead on, headmistress, and don't spare her any of your skills. That girl will cause me inconvenience and I want her to pay.'

Helena nodded and turned back to the gateway into the school. J'nie followed the flowing red hair until the two women reached a large, tiled chamber, inside which a raised podium dominated the centre. Around this the entire school of three women sat, all dressed in the uniform of a junior grade two Companion, the collars, wrists cuffs, belts and skirts in a light blue. In the centre two half circles of steel touched each other at their apex and then spread their ends apart.

Beside this contraption there stood an old wooden rack, with twelve different canes and whips displayed in tailor-made compartments. Each was numbered and named with the dates, frequency and explanations of their use.

J'nie took her place at the back of hall, while Helena walked over to two black and purple plumed guards and spoke a few quick words. The two stern-faced women immediately left, returning moments later with a young woman in a tight leather corset, that pinched her waist, her wrists held close to her waist belt. She looked nervous and walked in a slightly off balance way, in part due to the very high heeled boots that were laced to her legs.

Each of the guards held her shoulders in a tight grasp and marched her to the podium in synchronised steps. As their charge came closer to the steel structure her balance seemed to go completely, but the strong hands on her pushed her to the centre of the stage.

Helena carefully started to tie the victim to the metal frame, starting with the ankles, which were spread apart by the guards. The girl tried to stay upright but, with a final surrender of dignity, she fell forward onto the curving bars in front of her. Helena placed thick black straps around the girl's boots and pulled them, fastening them in position with silver buckles.

Helena gently pushed Yvonne's back, making her bend lightly over the cold frame, and Helena whispered some words to her captive, coaxing her. More straps were placed on her thighs and finally her waist, pulled with gentle firmness by Helena. Finally Helena took her wrists and pulled them down to a ring in the floor.

Yvonne was now helpless, the curving frame, heels and the corset conspiring to make her buttocks a large round target of flesh held by black leather in subjection. Suddenly Yvonne seemed to recognise her predicament and, even at the back of the room, J'nie could see the woman give a little shudder of fear and embarrassment as she realised that there were, in total, seven other women watching her as she exposed her most intimate reaches of her body.

Helena took off her skirt, folded it neatly and placed it carefully onto the ground and, revealing her powerful legs, squeezed into a small pair of panties. Everything that she did was accomplished with a sense of unhurried ceremony, designed to prolong the ordeal for her victim. Next she walked over to the rack and selected two instruments, a short whip and a cane, which she weighed in her hands before noting down their use on the rack and presenting them to J'nie to inspect.

J'nie could see the emotions of fear and shame in the woman's face, which mixed with the cold to give her a startled expression. Helena approached the centre of the raised platform and touched the girl's hair, brushing it while telling her to be brave, then checking the straps a final time and finding just a little more give in one. J'nie noted that it may seem vicious but the tighter the girl was tied, the easier it would be to endure the pain. If there could be no movement at all then her body would accept it with less complaint and, more to the point, Helena's expert aim would not be upset. Then Helena left the bound body bent in a smooth arc, with her buttocks taut and exposed, and walked forward to address the audience.

'Good evening, girls. As you are all aware, there is a strict code in the school as to behaviour. There are punishments laid down for every offence and, as the headmistress, I am the tool of justice.

'This young woman has dishonoured the school through her sexual greed. Her selfishness cannot go unchecked, and she has already lost every link on her uniform.

'There are some basic rules here, and each of you has seven chances to fail. But it is clear that that isn't enough for some of you. Losing a chain isn't shame enough. A public beating isn't enough.

'So for those that fail,' and Helena looked at one woman in the audience who had lost all but two links, 'retraining is needed, and in order to retrain from a fresh start one must be purged of the stain of failure, of letting the team down, of letting the school down.'

'Mistress.' Helena looked straight at J'nie. 'Will you release me to make the punishment?'

'I do.' J'nie nodded and felt a fresh burst of heat inside her. She had never once suffered herself in the school, but there was something that made her feel excited by it. She really wanted to be beaten by Helena. But she was in no position to experience this. However, each punishment she saw gave her a renewed urge, and here she was, imagining herself tied to the frame with the powerful and practised head-mistress standing in front of her helpless body. She shook herself free of the picture and concentrated on what was happening, which appeared to be going painfully slowly. She almost wanted to scream to Helena to get on with it but, at the same time, she knew the pleasure was greater from being teased. J'nie found herself breathing in slow, deep breaths as the two tall and black-clad guards unlocked Helena's wrist chains. Released, Helena practiced long arching strokes of the cane, making swishing noises that had the effect of sending Yvonne into a fresh set of shivers.

Helena walked to the front of the frame and, pulling her victim's long raven hair, made her look up to her captor's eyes. 'Do you wish to become clean, Yvonne? You know you can quit at any time: just say. All I have to do is undo the straps and you can walk away. You know that, don't you? So I ask again, do you want to stay? Are you willing to be purged and made clean? Are you ready to be punished and forgiven?'

'Yes,' the girl mouthed in a hoarse voice.

'And what are you now?'

The girl whispered something, but the confession wasn't enough for Helena.

'Tell them all. They can't hear you from the back. Tell then what you really are,' Helena commanded as she strode to the back of the frame.

Her face flushing with anger, fear and desperation, Yvonne sobbed, 'I'm dirty, a slut and an animal.' And as the last word forced its way from her lips, Helena's arm came down and landed a blow from her cane, making a harsh crack on the exposed arse. Yvonne didn't respond for a second, then let out a long moan, but it was too late. A second blow landed, expertly aimed to create a cross of red.

Helena waited, patient and practised. She twisted the whip in her hand and made a few practice strokes that caused the air to whistle over Yvonne's buttocks. But Helena was an expert. She was aware that it was the waiting that was the most exquisite part of Yvonne's torture, the inability to predict when or where the blow would land; that was what made these punishments so effective. Helena gently started to stroke Yvonne's backside with the tip of the cane, raising the sensitivity of each nerve end and preparing her so the pain would be increased, and the mental torture complete.

Her body now gently shook, from fear or cold J'nie could not be sure. She felt sorry for the girl, but also she could not help a rush of sexual pleasure spreading through her. There was something about the way Yvonne's soft flesh was being held by the cold rigid steel that turned J'nie on. Helpless, she would have to wait until Helena released her. J'nie felt the same anticipation; only Helena had the power to control the situation and the Sultan's Mistress would have to wait until her employee started the punishment before she too could feel a sexual release. Gently she resettled herself on her seat and unconsciously started to bite her lower lip.

Helena worked the whip hard until she glistened with fresh sweat and Yvonne was a whimpering form, quietly moaning for mercy, which Helena had no intention of giving.

Yvonne, her head buried between her outstretched and bound hands, began to whimper and take short sobbing breaths. Helena timed the next stroke as Yvonne exhaled, causing her to take a sharp intake of breath. It was a clean, powerful blow across the buttocks, and Helena allowed a few moments to pass, admiring the red welt as it formed.

Even the strong Helena was now visibly tired and shaking from her efforts, but Yvonne was to be given no time to rest. One gasp for air was followed by another as the whip came down and down again, forming a steady rhythm of blows, which seemed to carry on for an eternity. When Helena stopped it only got worse for Yvonne whose body now expected the whipping and failed to stop her feeling the blows even as the whip and cane ceased. Phantom whips tore at her backside until the message from her nerves was accepted by her numbed mind, and then, without the distraction of fresh sensation, Yvonne's body understood itself and, listening to the dull aches and quick stings as the pain swelled inside her, she let out another low moan, followed by an unfettered series of sobs.

Finally Helena stooped down behind the frame to admire her work. Yvonne's body was now covered in sweat too, rolling off her back and making her hair damp. Helena, finding herself content with her work, walked to the front of the frame and, this time coaxing the girl's head up with her palms, gently started making soothing noises with the care of a lover. Wiping away the tears that streaked Yvonne's face, Helena leaned down and gently caressed the sobbing woman, brushing her wet hair away from her face.

'Be brave. Only two more strokes and you will be free, free of your guilt, free to start again. You know that the binds that hold you are there because you want them to be. They are yours not mine, and the tighter the bonds the freer you are. You have been bad and that must be punished, then you will be a whole girl again, at ease with yourself.

'It's all right, just two more strokes across your most sensitive area. That is what got you into trouble, and that must be beaten. It must be taught that although it commanded you, it cannot rule you can it?'

'Oh no, not that!' Yvonne started to plead, repeating the word no over and over, but Helena had heard these pleas a hundred times over and would not be swayed. The cane came down with its very tip hitting its target, once and once again onto the now raw and swelling orifice.

Yvonne's body pushed itself over the frame, somehow finding a little extra length from its already extended and bound form, then slumped over its steel restraint. Helena warned the assembled girls of the dire consequences of failing the rules of the school. J'nie, sitting at the back, scanned the crowd – one uncomfortable at the thought of what could become of them if they were bad, two aroused, as she was. But her mind was already back in her bedchamber where she thought that a long relaxing shower was in order before changing for the night. She shifted on her seat again, finding her now damp panties were clinging to her.

Before she could satisfy her carnal urges, J'nie had to bring herself mentally back to the school. As the guards untied the disciplined girl and she virtually fainted into their arms, J'nie motioned her head-mistress over, who made sure that she had been locked into her wrist chains before approaching, but did not bother to put her skirt back on, giving J'nie another warm feeling as she watched the muscular frame sway toward her in her tight thong. It was such a shame that rules of the palace forbade any sex between the Companions in the school, and that Helena never left it, J'nie mused, especially now that the Sultan seemed to have lost interest in his Companions.

She sighed. There was nothing that could be done: the penalty was to much, as she had just witnessed, and for a woman of her position to be publicly whipped? There was no question of that happening. And Helena of all people, the headmistress and enforcer of the Sultan's law. J'nie had to be careful: it was much safer to vent her desires outside the palace where she could be discreet.

Helena kneeled before the Sultan's Mistress and waited until spoken to before rising.

'You punished her well, headmistress. I wouldn't like to be in her position,' she lied. 'But it is a pity. She was nearly ready to graduate to the second grade too. Just a few days off and she could have worn her skirt. Still, this might teach her to be more careful. After the first grade she'd get the Device, and that can hurt.' J'nie winced at the thought of the strange machine that she and Helena had maintained ready to be activated but not actually used in their time. Still it waited for the wayward in the deepest room of the palace.

'I seem to remember.' Helena again seemed to take a lot of pleasure in thinking about its delights.

'Still, there is the problem that she must start training from the start again – that is if she decides to stay.'

'Oh, she will. Her problem was too much appetite too soon. Where else could she hope to get her desires filled? I've already had the maid polish up her training harness.' Helena smiled. 'And if she was prepared to go through a public whipping . . .'

'Good, but you know that this still leaves me a girl short. There's that new one, Zena, and if all the others pass I still need one more. If any leave, well, I'm not sure the Sultan will be happy with this. These are not reliable girls. It would be all too easy for a girl like Yvonne to transgress again and then it'll be another season before we have a full number of graduates. I can't afford a dropout.'

'The rules are the rules, mistress. If one doesn't make it, then they must go,' Helena explained.

'Then let's hope I only need one more! Do you have any suitable girls? Or have your agents corrupted any from the town?' J'nie smiled a knowing smile but Helena shook her head.

'Then I suppose I'll have to get one in the harbour tonight and see our friend and what he has to offer. A new ship has come in this week and there will be a party tonight. It will make a good cover and there may be a few fresh girls. Tell my maid to have my clothes ready.'

Helena nodded, and J'nie was sure she caught a faint smile on her lips.

2

A Discreet Shop

The palace stood like a tall needle, sticking up in defiance of the large, flat island of Estra. Within the palace successive generations of Sultans had done their best to outdo their forefathers in acts of perversion and decadence and, at the top, the current Sultan taunted the gods with his perversions. Below him there were rooms for every kind of pleasure a man or woman might enjoy, elaborately decorated with friezes, lit by soft lights, with music and scent piped through grills to accentuate the pleasure.

No two rooms were alike: each had a unique light that shone through the glass walls, and each had an exquisite and unique perfume piped into it. Only the Sultan and his retainer knew how to find them as each was placed along a winding multi-level corridor that was itself a mechanical maze, changing daily. No one even knew how many floors there were; only that the Sultan lived on the top and that below were the rooms of the Sultan's Companions, the most beautiful women in the land, trained to obey the Sultan's every wish and highly disciplined, and granted power and almost complete freedom in return. Trained in the lower levels of the palace, and made conversant in every kind of sexual activity, but kept chaste for the Sultan's pleasures, and for his close friends. Each year two fresh Companions joined, and two retired to their own pleasures, leaving twenty to fulfil their master at any one time.

Estra was the first of the five wonders of the Empire, and as impressive as it was sensual. But even the dreams of the Sultans had to be paid for, and away from the pomp of the palace and its court, the harbour of Estra busied itself with the loading and trade of the rare spices that the Empire needed to power its pleasures.

Coming into port, the sailors on the trade ship the *Seahorse* shouted for joy, as much in relief at having kept their lives on the long and hazardous journey as for the money they could make, and spend in the taverns and whorehouses. Amid the drinking and jesting that always accompanied a ship's docking, a tall and slender figure in a cloak was almost unseen, slipping quietly off the *Seahorse* and disappearing into the hot summer's night.

Each ship that actually completed the dangers of the journey was a cause for celebration, and each celebration could last for weeks. It was a perfect time, J'nie assured herself, to sneak out from the palace and enjoy the common delights of the town.

J'nie lay in her bath, scented bubbles rising gently to the surface, as she reran the events of the day over in her mind, and shook with little pleasures as she imagined herself being disciplined by the headmistress, spanked across her knees then made to kiss her. She felt a sudden urge to the tension from herself again and, with the Sultan brooding over his politics, she felt no shame in rubbing herself, just a little to bring a small smile to her face.

By time night's dark velvet had descended, J'nie had finally dressed herself in the long straight dresses, stockings and platform boots that were the town's fashion that season. Running her hands over the loose folds she straightened the dress and wondered how the women ever walked in these things that held her legs so close together. Still, she had to admit they did hide nothing of her well toned body. Adding a wide brimmed hat of the townswomen, she completed her disguise and slipped unseen out of the palace using the old tunnel that had been the secret of each mistress. The warm night air, carrying the faint saltiness of the sea, hit J'nie's face like a welcome blast. It had some charge to it: an electricity that put J'nie's nerves on edge, bringing a tension to her as she walked through the crowded port.

She pulled the hat over her eyes to be sure that she would not be seen: it would not do to be recognised here, among the common people of the port. For that reason she had dressed in the common clothes, although it felt strange dressed in the long dresses of the harbour people. It was odd to be deprived of the sensual feelings of the air playing directly onto the skin, and the air here was neither as perfumed and sweet as the palace, or as athletic and close as the school. Maybe it had been too long since she had been into the harbour. Had it really been a whole month?

One twisting alley led to another, but guided by instinct J'nie made rapid time to a dark and deserted alleyway, in which a single small shop resided: one that she knew so well. On the outside it appeared much like any other merchant's house with a small glazed front for wares, and massively overhung offices above, making the whole thing look like an inverted pyramid. But the ramshackle shop revealed, on closer inspection, that what it offered was far from usual. Set into the stonework that defined the large red wooden door were two very old stone pillars with rusted iron rings set into them at regular intervals. To the unknowing this was just an architectural quirk, but to J'nie, and those who shared such interests, it was one of the ancient whipping posts from history, the well worn rings testament to the first Sultan's reign. There was also the fact that the windows were filled with panes of dark red glass that allowed no glimpse of the inside. Glancing around to be sure that she had not been seen, J'nie knocked.

The maid received her, and instantly recognised the Sultan's Mistress. Her bright innocent eyes immediately fell to the floor as she invited J'nie in. The maid kept her eyes averted as she gestured for the visitor to sit down, and flushed a little as J'nie thanked her. Everything in the room spoke of softness, the walls covered with the finest silks, exquisite tapestry depicting scenes of decadence and depravity, the dim red light that the windows let in, lightened by luminous bars of slowly changing fluids in the ceiling. The soft red velvet furnishings were made to make clients feel at home and held deep red rubies in complex gold mounts, and the the whole room held a slight smog, generated as the slowly rotating fans of ostrich feathers swirled the deep scented fumes that were piped up from ornate brass dragons on the walls. The whole room gave a feeling of being perpetually very late at night or very early in the morning, a place that many had come to in order to pass the time in quiet expectation. Waiting was, as J'nie knew, an inevitable part of being in GaJa's brothel.

'Ah, my lady, how good to see you.' The owner did not enter as much as breeze into the room, taking J'nie by surprise and when she looked up it came as a surprise to her to be reminded that he was so good looking. His dark and handsome good looks had come in very useful to his trade, but she had forgotten

17

how much she felt for this strange and disreputable merchant.

As usual his clothes were as flamboyant as he was, and he stood before her in strange long slippers with ends that pointed up and back over themselves. His muscular body spoke of years labouring but was now covered in the finest silk, his legs were in baggy rubber pants, tied at the knee, and around his neck a silk scarf completed a picture of expensive and fashionable tastes.

'Hello, GaJa, always a pleasure to see you.' J'nie held out her hand.

'Ah ehm, my lady, the pleasure is mine.' He took a deep theatrical bow and kissed her hand, lingering with his lips on her delicate skin just a little too long. 'Are you here for pleasure or business?'

'Purely business, of course. You know better than that. I have no pleasure outside of the Sultan's.' J'nie smiled a full and sincere smile at the man who responded with a curt nod, but the irony was not lost on him. 'I have lost a girl from the school and, although she will retrain, I want another, to be sure that the next graduation will please my master.'

'Ah, I understand. Let us discuss this in my office. Fenu.' GaJa clicked his fingers at the young maid. 'Please collect the girls from their lodgings and get them ready for inspection. Now, my lady, this way to the office.'

The office was on the first floor and projected out with a bay window that looked over the bay where the fishing boats and one large trade vessel lay at anchor. J'nie walked to the window and waited for the lock on the door to fall into place. As she heard it scrape into place, she began the feel the man's coarse hands start to undo the tricky clasps that the townswomen used. Standing still, her arms resting on the sill, she waited till the last vestige of clothing had fallen from her before turning.

'You know,' J'nie spoke softly, as if someone might overhear, 'the Sultan could kill you for this.'

'Ah, ahem, yes, but will he know? You only ever come here because he is paying you too little attention, yes? I provide a service: girls for the sailors, boys too sometimes, but for you it is not business. This is pleasure for us both, no?'

She felt his hot tongue kiss the small of her back, then descend with aching slowness until she felt it probe the tops of her thighs. J'nie turned her back to the sea and, while the sounds of the gulls rang in her ears, GaJa started to kiss her, taste her and tease her. She, naked except for the stockings and high platform boots, looked down with a tender expression. With his head level with her stomach he began to gently kiss, inching his way up to her pert breasts.

J'nie made one last attempt to stop, by pushing his head away, but it only encouraged him to kiss lower and more sensitive areas, and her will melted. After all, she had come here, and deep down she knew that this was what she wanted. But it was wrong. She had the sense again that she wanted to be punished like poor Yvonne for her crimes, but she was losing control, and already her thoughts were drifting. Suddenly a passion overwhelmed her and her legs felt like they should collapse as they shook with her excitement. The office couch with its velvet and jewels looked so inviting, and the night was only beginning.

When J'nie opened her eyes the sun was going into the sea. She nestled closer to her lover, her senses overflowing with the shared glow of fulfilment. Her skin was glistening with fresh sweat, her hair flayed out on the satin, redder and brighter than the sinking sun.

She looked over at GaJa. He was quietly sucking on a water pipe, which gave off gurgling sounds and a foul smell, and seemed unaware of anything going on about him.

'GaJa, I will be missed. We must stick to business. The girls will be waiting.'

'Ah, erhm, yes, the, ah girls.' Yes.' He straightened his clothes and helped J'nie back into the clumsy city clothes. 'You had better wear this: it is best they do not know who you are.' He offered her a black mask and helped her fit the tight fabric about her so that the whole of her face was covered from the mouth up, and her red hair fell like a horse's mane from the top.

'And you, erhm, will want these?' He handed her a pair of long thin black rubber gloves, which J'nie put on with some difficulty as they were so tight.

J'nie gave the mask a last small adjustment and followed GaJa to the red reception room. She felt herself lose her balance a couple of times on the stairs. Blast these ungainly shoes, she thought. Why can't they wear heels as the palace does? And the bloody clothes: so hard to do anything with the dress clinging to me. I guess the ladies aren't as active as I am.

J'nie was led into a small antechamber, where a spy hole in the wall afforded her a view of the red room, which now contained three young women, each naked and well groomed, their hair combed back and all other traces of hair removed. He knows how to present his merchandise, J'nie thought. Two blondes, one with long hair, the other with loose curls, and a short-haired brunette. They all looked good, but the taller blonde had something else. Was it that she was from off the island, as she clearly was with her blue eyes and dark complexion? Or was it something else, a sense of defiance, or determination? Still, it was too early to judge. After all, would any of them stand the scrutiny that the palace demanded?

The blonde's tall elegance was enhanced by her pinched waist and well toned buttocks. Her long legs matched a set of thin ankles, and her pert breasts settled on her young body as if defying gravity, well rounded and topped with large brown nipples. J'nie looked up, following the curve of a slender neck to a face with well set cheek bones. Her dark, almost burnt ash skin contrasting with those blue eyes.

The second girl carried a more voluptuous form: large rounded buttocks, a large and generous chest, a stomach that was as flat as the plains of the East. Her short brown hair counterpointed her round and determined face, leaving a set of hungry green eyes and large red lips defined against her pale skin.

The third girl she paid less attention to. There was nothing special in this one. She was pretty enough, but held no promise of sexuality to J'nie's well practised eye.

As J'nie entered the room the women lined up and stood to attention. In silence J'nie walked around each in turn, carefully checking over the condition of the skin, the hair and eyes. Then, checking her gloves, she started to inspect each mouth, the firmness of each breast and the condition of every orifice. J'nie returned to where GaJa stood, watching the proceedings with half a mind to profit and half to the thrill of watching J'nie's expert fingers perform their checks on the nubile bodies.

J'nie whispered in his ear and he beckoned the maid Fenu. Issuing a curt instruction to her, he smiled back at J'nie. Moments later Fenu had led one of the girls from the room, who appeared upset not to have been picked, and hung her head as she exited the room.

J'nie whispered to GaJa again and, clapping his hands, a wall slid upwards, revealing three slumped mechanical figures. Another clap from GaJa and the figures began to whirl and creak, then they lifted instruments to mouths and a slow, hypnotic tune filled the air. Fenu walked up to the girls and told them to dance for the masked lady.

With slow, careful movements, the two women started to dance, self-conscious and humiliated by the request at first. They finally relaxed, letting the music dictate their actions, pushing their bodies in time with the beat. Then they were lost in the music, crouching and leaping, unaware that anyone was in the room but themselves, getting faster and faster, until they were both swaying to the music with vigour. J'nie turned to see GaJa mesmerised by the two women's breasts and a broad dirty smile on his face.

J'nie waited until they were both covered in sweat before allowing Fenu to stop them. As the music ceased the two girls became aware that three people were looking at them, most critically the woman in the black mask, and suddenly the embarrassment made them flush. Had they lost all their dignity? Feeling like they deserved nothing more than to be treated like cheap dancers they stood back to attention. J'nie, experienced in the training of young women and having gone through this herself, knew what they felt like and could not resist giving them the final humiliation of smiling at their discomfort. There was a warm feeling inside her, and she had the strange sensation for a trained and experienced Companion of a dampness between her legs, which made her feel sexual and a little dirty. She focused back on the selection. They were both very good dancers, both beautiful women. It was hard. She decided that the decision would need to be one of the mind rather than the body.

She instructed GaJa to ask the questions, which he did with relish, as he always did when decisions like this had to be made.

'State your name and place, then tell this lady how, if you were chosen by her –' he gestured to the masked woman '– how would you serve the Sultan's Mistress?'

The brunette answered first, full of confidence: 'My name is Ula, I come from the diamond ports to the west, I live here, and work the best trade that comes in. I would serve her with the respect that the position deserves; a Companion must carry the traditions forward and must observe them. If the lady picks me I shall serve as my conscience dictates and with pride to wear the uniform of the Sultan.'

It was a good speech. J'nie detected nothing in it that would prevent her being a good Companion, if a little rigid – perhaps a future guard? Yes, she could do that. She would undergo the training and accept its strange ways for duty. She would be fine.

'And you?' GaJa gestured to the blonde.

'I'm known as Carria. I arrived from Far Island this week. I arrived because I have always wanted to be a Companion. I have no reason to serve the Sultan or his mistress. I wish to do so because I want to.'

J'nie nodded, and gestured for GaJa to follow her back to his office. Carria: what sort of strange name was that – didn't it mean something on the Far Islands? What was that girl doing here? It was a long way to come, and very dangerous a journey to make for a single woman. Yet in her there was a strength. There was something that made J'nie sure that she would have something of spirit.

Dismissing the girls, and throwing the gloves and the mask back at GaJa, she sat down on the couch and pushed away his clumsy advances. The dancing had certainly worked him into a frenzy but J'nie froze him with a single look.

'No, you have had pleasure, now business. You want the same for both women? Well then tell me more about each.'

'As for Ula, she's like many around here. She is ambitious and, luckily for her, pretty. I think she sees the role of the Companion as an honour and a way to rise up the social scale. She would rise rapidly, trust me. Some of your Companions might find some competition, which may not be a bad thing. Lucky for you, you are in a position that can't be undermined.'

'Would she take the discipline?'

'As she said, she comes from the diamond ports. The schools there are very traditional, set up by the eighth Sultan. Even now, the undergraduates wear breast weights for even the most trivial things. She would seldom get into trouble and accept whatever devices you have with ease and as fair punishment.'

'I'm not too sure anyone can take some of our punishments with ease. The other one, the Far Island girl, what of her?'

'I don't really know. She came off the boat that came in this week and took a room above the harbour tavern. Next thing she's here, wanting to know how she can become a Companion. She must be lucky to have come when she did. It is some coincidence that you came tonight also.' GaJa shrugged. 'But lucky for her and maybe lucky for you. I have the impression it's all she wants, and would have waited until the next intake if this hadn't happened. Other than that, she's a mystery.'

'Let me think about this. Send the girls home, can you?' And with a final kiss she pulled the hat back over her eyes and made her way into the night.

* * *

It was almost midnight when Carria sneaked out of the red door of the brothel. Hot and exhausted from her show for the stranger in a black rubber mask, she had taken the owner's offer of a shower, but had the feeling that her washing had been watched through a spy hole by him. Little matter. She did not mind others looking at her body, or rather it was something she was determined to get used to. She even managed to smile back at him as she left, knowing that his eyes would be staring right at her tight arse as she swung her hips. She walked out with a defiant stride, and didn't check the street. She had the air of someone who was not ashamed of being in a brothel, or who cared if she was seen there.

Her boots made a small clicking sound on the worn cobbles of the street and once or twice she heard them echo across the night. The streets were still filled with the remains of the celebrations from the *Seahorse*'s docking and once or twice Carria had to carefully step over couples fornicating in the street or lying in post coital bliss. She was anxious. Why hadn't she heard? She needed to be a Companion. It was all that she wanted. She had humiliated herself in front of the GaJa and his strange masked Companion, and yet he had refused to tell her, or that other girl, which one had been chosen. That woman, Ula, she had given Carria such a dirty look then. Oh well, she could wait. She stopped to check her way. The streets were still unfamiliar and she was sure that she could hear her steps echoing a fraction too long. She turned, but the street remained empty, and anyway, why would anyone follow her? No one here knew who she was.

Finally she made it to the seafront tavern, and climbed the rotten wooden steps to her small room. Below, a drunken sailor wolf whistled, but was quickly escorted away by a night watchman and a prostitute trying to get the trade and convince the watchman the sailor would be better off with her. In the end all three went somewhere together.

A small cheap room drew no attention, and the wooden shack on top of the noisy bar certainly met that requirement. There was hardly enough room for the four poster bed, and Carria had wondered why such a large bed had been placed in the tiny room until she realised that each of its four stout posts held the roof on. Other than this, the room contained a small shower and toilet, and a chest of drawers. There really was no more space.

Downstairs a few badly sung sea shanties crept up through the floorboards, and she decided to take a small drink before going to bed. The bar was filled, but strangely quiet. Carria guessed that a week of drinking had left only the hardcore and the desperate. The figures in the bar looked fairly rough, and on each table groups of men either rowed or slept. None of them remotely of interest. Carria was just about to leave and forget the drink when a woman's voice cut the warm, summer air.

'If you have nowhere to sit, why don't you come here?'

Carria turned to look at a very attractive woman calling from a private snug. Clearly this was not the sort of woman who drank at a rough seafront bar normally, yet she seemed well at ease. Carria was intrigued, and couldn't resist the temptation, always a failing in her she had been told. She walked over and took her robe off, revealing a short dress made of the smallest discs of silver, each linked with the finest thread to give the appearance of a single wet piece of cloth, hanging to every part of her body. The woman was older, but not by much, and dressed in a long robe that was clearly of the highest quality. Carria noticed that the woman kept the robe tightly tied, even though the air was sultry.

Carria seated herself opposite. There was something familiar about her, but she couldn't be sure what. 'Hello.' Carria smiled and helped herself to wine from the table fountain, that make an artificial 'thank you' sound as the wine filled her goblet. 'And thank you too. I didn't want to be stuck on the table over there.' She gestured to where a group of men had started to play drinking games with the forfeit of having their farts ignited.

'No, I'm glad to be of help.' J'nie returned the smile and looked into the young girl's eyes. She had meant the evening to be a gentle investigation of the girl, but now that feeling she had had in the red room was clearer; more certain. Yes, the girl had spirit and confidence, she had a bearing that was above the usual harbour scrubber, but she had one more thing: she had sexuality. Something animal; something that told J'nie that the evening may go another way than the one she had intended.

'Have we met?' Carria was transfixed by the woman. Her deep brown eyes kept her captured. Could she be making a sexual advance? No, that was silly, wasn't it, but there was something. It was like playing cat and mouse, but who was the cat? She sipped the wine.

'I don't think we have. Still, pleased to meet you. The wine here is a little poor. Can I offer you something better, eh?'

'Carria, it's Carria. Yes.'

The woman pulled a round bottle from her cloak and poured it into their glasses. It was simply the most wonderful drink that she had ever tasted. It was also the strongest.

She didn't remember the conversation, or how she arrived back in her room, but she remembered delicate and strong fingers pulling at the ties of her clothes. She would always remember the willing domination she felt as she was firmly pushed onto the bed, and with her back on the silk sheets feel those fingers work their way over her body, pushing through her pubic hair until they found the wet and engorged soft mass of her pussy. Then all her thoughts concentrated on the little part of her body. It seemed hungry to take all of her senses. All that mattered was those strong figures pulling and pushing, gently pulling and pushing, massaging and then, just as Carria had found a rhythm, they slipped with ease into her.

There was a powerful urge, a desperate need for something, but she couldn't find what. She was wriggling and convulsing with pleasure. Strong hand held her. Then she felt herself turned over, her legs wide and kneeling, her hands trying to grasp the two top posts for support, while all the time below, her body was being played. She shook and groaned, and she thought she begged and cried, but nothing could be certain.

She felt kisses, then her attention was on her left breast as the fingers worked their magic there, then the right but no, the left too as the sucking sensation began. She was confined, there was nowhere to go. She desperately wanted to repay this kindness – she needed to – but her protests were drowned. She should, she was bad, she did not deserve this pleasure. She was a fake, she wasn't what she appeared to be she was ... no, her concentration was lost, her breasts were throbbing but unattended, she could feel the saliva cooling her nipples, but suddenly all her energy was concentrated in her pussy. Strong, regular licks were administered and one by one each of her limbs joined the rhythm. It was taking her, and she had no control of the destination until it was there. It was coming fast, she wanted to slow, she knew this was bad, but it was too late. With a final scream she surrendered to the inevitable and let the rhythm take her whole mind and body.

But there was no release Carria felt the familiar massage as her mouth was pulled onto the lips of the woman below her. She felt the strong tongue push into her mouth and could taste the strong scent of her own body. This time it was quicker. She came with a loud groan and rolled over onto her back, her body still making small convulsions.

She shouldn't be enjoying this, this was only a part of the game, something she had to do, but it felt too good.

'I'm in heaven,' Carria whispered.

J'nie was silent for a whole minute before answering: 'It was good, but we can be better. You move too much.'

'I can't help it,' Carria protested.

'Next time I'll bring silk ropes, then I'll be able to stop you from squirming about.'

Carria didn't reply. She simply raised her head over higher and kissed her lover's mouth, then slowly drew her tongue down onto her neck and kissed with gossamer lightness.

'I've got to go back.'

Carria stopped. She looked up imploringly. 'Will I see you again?'

'Oh, I think you will. Tomorrow for a start, but then? Well, if you do it would be best for you to not acknowledge it.'

'Who are you?' Carria asked, but found the woman's finger placed on her lips, and a slight shake of her head telling her to be quiet.

J'nie got out of bed, and started picking up discarded garments. 'You might never know. Wouldn't that be fun? You'll just have to be good and wait. Maybe you will find me, but things might be different. Was it the first time with a woman?'

'It was the first time with anyone.'

'I see. Well, I wouldn't have known. You just need a little more training.'

'For what?'

J'nie continued, without acknowledging the question. 'Tomorrow, here, I'll bring some wine and a cane. Make sure it's a good strong one.'

'The wine or the cane?'

'Both.' J'nie smiled and smoothed out the creases from her dress. It wasn't until a long time after J'nie had left that Carria realised that she didn't know anything about her except that it slowly it dawned on her that she had seen that dress before, and she smiled to herself.

3

First Lessons

The Sultan was in another of his sulks. He brooded for hours over maps and drank wine until dawn. The finest court poets failed make him laugh. Even his favourite could not raise his spirits with a paean to drinking. The musicians failed to soothe his soul, and for yet another day J'nie had had to perform only the most menial duties for him. Even her recounting of Yvonne's spanking had not revived him, although J'nie could feel herself get excited again by its telling.

J'nie left the topmost apartment and was led through the ever changing and complex system by the Sultan's old and bitter Retainer. She knew that every second either her breasts or arse were being watched by the filthy man, and he insisted that she walked ahead so, he claimed, she could not see his map to the winding routes that literally changed all the time, due to the complex machines that constantly rearranged the connections between doors and passages.

Only the old Retainer knew all the possible routes, as his great-grandfather had built these marvels, a set of long iron boxes with doors along their sides that wheezed with steam pressure and rattled with ancient cogs as the pair walked up and down, or left or right or whichever way they were going, for there was no indication of direction. Just as it had been designed to do.

Finally, the Retainer told J'nie to stop, and he opened a door straight into her chambers. The corridors must move up and down too, J'nie mused, because she certainly hadn't walked down forty stories. Funny, she'd never thought of that before. Then she felt a clammy hand smack her lightly on the bottom, under her skirt. The filthy bastard had lifted it. She turned but already the old man was walking away from her, chuckling to himself.

J'nie fumed and stormed into the bedroom. She opened the glass valve on the red glass tube, alerting her maid. Minutes later she scurried in in her short tunic and curtsied. She was a pretty girl, J'nie thought, but was never going to be suitable as a Companion. Perhaps she would bed one of the court officials. The picture of the Retainer came back to her and she shuddered.

'I'm off to the town again, to get the new girl.'

'Mistress, you know you are not allowed into the town. You went there last night too. Helena's maid told me so, and you know if you get caught what might happen. The Sultan will be mad.'

'Helena's maid talks too much. I have a mind to have her whipped for telling tales, which are untrue, aren't they? And the Sultan won't find out, will he? Or the Sultan might find out that you've been playing in my private red chamber on your own, mightn't he?'

The maid turned redder than the furthest part of J'nie's chamber and started to obediently unfasten the buckles on her mistress's leather uniform in silence.

'Oh yes, I am quite aware when my private pleasure rod has been in someone else's panties. I hope you enjoyed it, because if I find you playing with things that don't belong to you again I'm sending you to the Device. It needs to be used once in a while to keep it running well.'

After that the maid was silent, but made sure that J'nie was particularly well washed and shaven that night.

This was to be the final test. If this strange Far Island woman was receptive to tonight's treatment J'nie would take her to the fitters and get her ready for schooling – damn the fact that she had been out the night before. In fact, damn the whole palace rules. She would have fun tonight. And so what if she had gone a little far and actually bedded the woman? No one would ever know, and by the time she realised who J'nie was, she would be completely under her control. And she was the most talented recruit she had ever had, better even than the other mistresses the Sultan kept in the palace, whose bodies she had shared in orgies for the Sultan, or occasionally in special private shows for him.

Once at the inn, J'nie climbed the timber stairs with anticipation. She was sure Carria would accept her dominance, sure that she would join her at the palace. But the tests must be conducted, and J'nie must have her fun. She checked the small leather bag she carried one final time to be sure that it contained everything she needed and knocked.

Carria opened the door a crack. Cautiously, she peered around.

'It is you.'

'Yes. Were you expecting someone else?'

'No, just you.' And Carria opened the door, revealing the reasons for her caution. She stood proudly naked in front of J'nie. J'nie had that feeling again: who was being seduced? Still it was clear the girl wanted to have some pleasure, and J'nie was not going to stop that. Without thinking she kissed the girl, fully on the lips and held her body close to her, so that her stomach and breast pressed onto her. Carria did not fight, but let herself be led kiss by kiss to the enclosure of the bed.

Carria lost herself to animal instinct. She sucked and licked and kissed, she held and groped and massaged, until the two bodies were one then, unexpected and welcome, she felt deep skilled rubbing in her groin and came. She lost her thoughts, and recovered them to find herself sprawled on her belly and one of her arms being gently pulled to a corner of the bed. Something soft twisted about her wrist, but she paid it no attention. Then the other arm was lured across the bed.

Her body was being pulled down to the end of the bed. She wasn't sure why. She tried to pull her arms back to raise herself but there was a force stopping them.

Now her legs were over the edge of the bed and Carria began to wake herself up. Something very odd was going on. There was a feeling of soft and strong material at her ankles, then a firm grip to her thighs, and that soft material being pulled between her legs. She started to panic, but it was now clear what the woman had done: her wrists were tied by silk scarves to the two top posters, her thighs and knees bound to the bottom legs of the bed, her ankles tied tight across each other, and her arse was neatly and firmly trapped on the edge, exposed and flexed.

'I told you I'd stop you wriggling about. Now are you going to be a good grown up girl and accept what's coming in silence, or do I have to gag you?'

'What are you going to do?' Carria remembered the joke about a cane. It was a joke, wasn't it?

'I'm going to teach you.' The woman laughed and began to gently caress Carria's bottom. Carria felt herself aroused. She was trapped and defenceless. She

34

wondered about the cane, and all this was beginning to make her feel very sexual. She strained against the silk bindings, more to feel the thrill of their strength than to attempt escape, which was clearly impossible.

All the time her most sensitive skin was being stroked, and she felt the blood rush about her body for the second time that night. She started to feel her womanly damp, and there was a hot flush, she was sweating. Between her legs the silk stuck to her body in comfortable creases. She could feel the material under her thighs getting damp and sticky. She felt guilty but the tight bound of silk holding her spread-eagled stopped her from being able to do anything about it. She just had to wait and enjoy it; wait until the woman released her.

J'nie stood over her, and Carria could feel her skin pricking under the other women's breath. She tried to give a shudder as something cold dropped into the small of her back.

'Only wine, don't worry. There's nothing you can do.' J'nie purred in the distance. How true, there was nothing at all. J'nie started to drink the wine, lapping it up with small quick movements of her tongue. Occasionally she sucked a little up and wetted Carria's exposed bottom with a kiss.

'I couldn't get here earlier, so what have you been doing for the last twenty four hours? Nothing bad I hope?'

How could Carria deny it? She had spent the afternoon playing gently with herself. She should have been doing more important things. Yes, she had been bad. She deserved whatever this woman was going to do.

'So what did you do?' J'nie repeated.

'Nothing' Carria whimpered, although she did not even convince herself, and now these woman's fingers were running in gentle circles over the rim of her sex.

'I don't think you did. In fact, I think you abused yourself, and that's very bad.'

'I'm sorry.' Carria moaned.

'Not only that but just tried to lie about it.' J'nie withdrew from her cunt and using only the lightest of pressures began to rub Carria's exposed buttocks.

'You know what I have to do?'

Carria felt very tense. What the woman was doing was going to drive her mad: that soft repetitive motion with her hands, drawing her fingertips down under each stroke to the delicate and sensitive area in her crack.

'When you're good and ready,' J'nie added. She slid her hand down lower and Carria shivered as a finger pushed its way inside her.

'Oh, you are ready, aren't you,' J'nie said in a wicked voice.

'Yes, yes I am.' Carria said through clenched teeth.

Carria felt the sheet under her getting very wet. She was dripping and yet she felt so bad, so guilty about what she was doing, about not returning anything to the lady she knew nothing about. She was having all the pleasure but with the frustration of not giving anything back. It was almost a relief when one of her fingers pushed home, yet the waiting was a pleasurable torture.

Then it stopped. How could it stop now? When every part of her body was alive, when she was on a path and could not turn back? Carria tried to turn her head around, but her arms prevented her from seeing anything. Her eyes strained to look down over her shoulders but she could see nothing, then the first stroke hit home.

There was silence for a moment. Then there was the sound of the second stroke whistling through the air. It sounded home with a THWACK and her cheeks burned. The fist stroke had taken her by surprise, the second hurt. It had hit her squarely on the buttocks and she could feel the sting. But it felt so good.

She felt alive through the pain. A pain given in love and received the same way. A pain she deserved for all sorts of reasons, including not being faithful to this woman and waiting for her. A pain of liberation, from the guilt. A pain of passion.

J'nie changed the angle of attack and Carria suddenly felt the soft parts of her body being hit. Every sensation came to her at once: the pain brought tears to her eyes and a small gasp from her mouth while the warm feeling brought so instantly to her sex took her to the edge of orgasm.

When J'nie stopped Carria was in tears, but tears which contained release too. An exhausted but satisfied smile played over her as J'nie kissed her cheek.

'Now you have no fear, no guilt. Now you only have a more sensitive body and are free to give yourself to pleasure. I have taken your inhibitions and now –' she paused to wipe Carria's tears away and kiss her once again, but now on her lips and deeply using her tongue '– now will you give yourself to me?'

Carria couldn't help herself. Before she could think, she heard herself screaming 'Yes' over and over, and only stopping when she felt an overwhelming convulsion of pleasure inside her body.

J'nie began to untie the silken bounds, allowing Carria a moment to ease her stretched body before she obediently allowed herself to be rebound, this time face up. Her legs were pulled wide, wider than last time to the point where they were only just comfortable. Her hands were bound together and pulled back, high over her head so that her body formed a triangle. She felt the soft and enclosing fabric of the bed soothing her smarting buttocks.

Had she been like this before she would have felt embarrassed but now she felt natural, ready to receive what was to come. To be passive having earned it. She felt sexual in a way that she had never before, each part of her was alive, and the way she was tied up made her breasts and sex stand out and open to view. She felt proud.

J'nie stood at the foot of the bed and looked down at her in admiration, then without a word she kneeled down. Stretching her hands up and gripping Carria's waist she began to lick around her lips. Carria moaned softly with each stroke of J'nie's tongue, feeling the hot wet mouth on her in a way she had never dreamed. Her newly sensitive body responded and struggled against the tight restrictions, but even this attempt was quickly abandoned, as every part of her succumbed to pleasure.

Strong rhythmic probes kept Carria in a state of ecstasy. She had thought earlier that she could get no wetter but now she had abandoned herself so completely each expectation became a distant dream, pale and wraith like next to this reality. Again she tried to move, to shudder, but to her delight the bounds held her too tightly, and made her more wild and her pleasure greater.

She reached a plateau quickly. Suddenly she was lost and, without the ability to move, all her energy concentrated itself. Carria felt as deeply as anyone had ever, a pleasure that was profound, and she knew she was exploding. She could not contain the pleasure in her fragile body. She tried to jerk in climax but the silk held firm and for an eternity the conflict between her need to move and her constraint made her ride a mad and powerful wave of joy. Finally her body stopped straining against the knots and she relaxed. Now she knew her body could contain all of this, all the pleasure and pain. She was alive in a way she had never been before.

J'nie untied the silk scarves and let them fall to the ground. She smiled at the girl on the bed. Carria propped herself on one elbow and smiled back:

'I love you.'

'No you don't love me. You don't know what that word means. Pleasure and love aren't the same thing. One day soon you'll learn that.'

'But you care about me, you do don't you?' Carria looked straight into the woman's deep eyes seeking some confirmation desperately.

'Yes.' J'nie sat on the edge of the bed and held Carria in her arms. 'Yes, I care a lot about you, I like you and I hope it goes on for a long time.' J'nie kissed her with a featherlike brush of her lips.

'I want to pay you back.'

'Hush, now I've got half a bottle of wine left here,' J'nie noted, then poured two goblets. Then sighing, J'nie slipped her dress off and embraced the girl, passing mouthfuls of wine to the girl in her own mouth. Relaxing, they lay side by side. Carria's right hand index finger idly made swirling motions in J'nie's pubic area, then casually pushed the palm of her hand underneath and pulled the warm body to its side. Her fingers ran over the hard toned body. Her fingers touched something. She traced the outline of a mark, the ridges making a complex and mysterious shape. Bending over she found she was examining a curled whip shape etched into the flesh.

'What's that?' Carria asked innocently

'Oh nothing,' Then J'nie thought that the time was right. This girl had passed the tests, and surely was keen.

'Would you like to learn even more about your body, about how to heighten its joy?'

'I can't think of anything better.' Carria giggled, and her faced reddened a little.

'Well, I can arrange for you to be taken to the palace, but if you agree you must leave all this –' J'nie gestured around the room '– and accept the rules of the palace absolutely. You will have to obey me without question; you will have to be my willing slave. You can leave, you can always walk out, but if you want more pleasure than you can have ever experienced or ever want to, then you'll stay.'

'I accept . . . are you one of the Sultans schoolmistresses?'

'I scout out for the Sultan, for mistresses can only play with the Sultan' said J'nie quickly, wondering if the lie would suffice, and if her reaction to the question had been too fast. She also caught a glimpse of her maid's warning.

'Oh, so if I go I will not see you again?' Carria looked downcast.

'One last time, the day after tomorrow, in the evening and after . . . well after something, then? Maybe you will, one day. But tomorrow we will not speak of such things. We must enjoy the moments that we have.' J'nie smiled. 'By then things will be different. Perhaps we can even spend more time together.' J'nie wondered if she had gone too far. This was dangerous ground, but she felt something for this woman. She had the sheer animal attraction that she felt for Helena, but there was more: a real feeling of wanting to like her. Was it love? How could she feel that. Her whole life was dedicated to pleasures, love had no place in her body. But, already her mouth had betrayed her, she had made illegal plans for the future where they could spend time together.

J'nie turned her face to Carria's and, looking directly to her eyes, merely stated, 'I am here to get you to the palace, and you have accepted. I'm pleased, and in a way you are now mine'

'Yes, you are my saviour too.' Carria kissed J'nie. 'Tell me, what exactly happens in the Sultan's palace?'

'You will be trained and, if you pass the schooling, become a Companion. Everything you will learn will be in order to have and give the greatest pleasure. But it is strict, you must obey, and the punishments for wandering from the past are very severe. You will learn to serve, and to sacrifice your personal pleasures for the greater pleasures of the palace.

'But before that, I will have to get you ready for the induction. You are not yet ready to start schooling. Do you still want to follow me? If you do, go to this address tomorrow.'

J'nie reached into her bag and handed over a small pink card. Then she poured the last of the wine into their glasses. The two women drank, and Carria fell into a deep and relaxing sleep listening to the seagulls, and holding J'nie. Outside the sounds of the harbour floated through the air on a hot summer night. The port bells rang in the distance signalling another barge safely returned to the city, its precious cargo of spice having made the long journey around the island and now needing men to unload it. The bell called them to employment and for the merchants sounded a reassuring beat to the commercial hustle upon which the city thrived.

4

The Fitting

Struggling to keep hold of her dream, Carria awoke. She had dreamed about being taken prisoner by bandits who had tied her to a tree. However, J'nie had arrived and she felt so relieved and thanked her. But J'nie had not untied her. She had started to kiss her legs, moving upward, lifting Carria's dress. Caressing her thighs J'nie had started to bite her soft lips.

Carria had pleaded with her to stop, but at the same time knew she really wanted this to continue. Then as she came toward climax she awoke and couldn't finish the story in her mind. She tossed on the sheets, finding herself already wet and excited, but so cheated that she couldn't bring herself off. It then it dawned on her that it was light outside. She pulled herself up off the bed and looked out of the window, to the time mast that displayed time with large golden balloons. It was nearly midday. She had slept almost ten hours, and still felt like she could sleep more.

She realised that something was different. She caught sight of a small leather box by her bedside. The box was of heavy dark blue hide, embossed with flowers and buds. On its front there was a small silver catch which was designed so that it required both hands to open it, while the box was held still. Carria sat back on the bed, gripped it with her knees and finally wrestled the box open. Inside there was a layer of blue silk and resting on it a highly polished metal and wood tube. Circular but elongated. Like a long pear with a necked top. Carria shook it. Inside something moved and the fatter end of the tube revolved in off-centre circles, producing a ribbed pattern of thin but smooth discs. Carria looked closer at the machine and discovered a small opening at the bottom. In it was a miniature key, a note tied to it, in elegant and refined handwriting. 'A gift for you, it will help you train for the school. Use it wisely and, with this and the pleasures of your fitting today, think of the pleasures to come. This device is self-winding, but after periods of non-use use key.' It was signed by J'nie.

Carria took the key out and laid it on the bed, then she lightly kissed the metal. She turned her attention back to the box. Shaking it over the sheets she discovered that what she had taken to the box's lining was in fact a pair of silk panties and under them a vial of scented oil.

The panties were made of supple leather and finest silk. The front contained a pocket into which the glass vial could snugly fit. On their back was a lace for tightening.

Carria needed no instructions and her wetness returned while fingering the device. Taking the vial she spread an even layer of oil over metal tube and worked it over the shining surface. She took a long intake of breath and relaxed. She eased her legs open, feeling the cool air replace the hot, moist atmosphere there. She took the metal object in her right hand and fingered herself open with her probing fingers, then very carefully she began to push the tube inside herself. She found it difficult to fit and brought it

back to her face for inspection. Finally she found she
could turn a collar near the base so that all the discs
lined up smoothly. Sinking lower on the bed she
started to push again. It still wasn't an easy fit, she
had to bear a small pain before it would give, but
then it slid in with ease. Carria sighed as the cool
metal entered her body. Then it was over; the thing
was fitted. It felt comfortable and strange. Carria
inserted the key and wound the device until the spring
was stiff. The gentle vibrations of the winding sent
thrills through her, and brought a few small whim-
pers of delight.

Finally she took the key out and stored it in the
box then, lifting her legs, slipped the panties through
her feet and pulled them up. At first she wondered if
J'nie had got the right size, for they seemed very tight
and it was only with difficulty that the waistband
could be pulled over her buttocks. A wide a leather
band ran between her cheeks, and when Carria pulled
the laces tight they squeezed her waist and she felt her
body held in a tight embrace. But they did not hurt.
In fact, they fitted so tightly that Carria was barely
aware of them. So fine was the material they felt like
they were another layer of skin.

She placed the vial down in its pocket and got up
to walk around in these presents. She almost fell back
on the bed in delight. As she walked she could feel the
disc move in and out like a thousand delicate fingers
inside her. Massaging her most imtimate secrets. And
then the whole device seemed to thrust inside her too
and she realised why her panties had been made so
tight. They kept this thing in the right position,
stopped it from dropping out of position, and kept it
thrusting deep inside. Not only that but in the panties
she could feel small ridges next to her clitoris and
anus that rubbed with each movement she made.

Quickly she discovered that if she stayed still nothing happened, but as soon as she took a single step her entire lower body was subjected to the most intense pleasure and she felt wildly aware of her own sex. A long walk or run would bring climax; a short walk to the street, excitement.

Carria dressed for breakfast and walked gingerly down to the harbour's local cafe. There she took a light and late breakfast, and found herself sitting at a table across from a couple of foreign merchants. She struck up some small talk, while all the time she talked politely and smiled she was crossing and uncrossing her legs below the table and thinking about the device that was giving her such pleasure.

Carria pleased herself with this new toy for a few hours. She found out how she could walk in such a way as to minimise or maximise the device's effect. She also experimented so that she could control which part of her was stimulated most. She also found, to her dismay, that achieving orgasm was not easy and required a good deal of effort.

She wondered what J'nie could be doing at that moment. Was she tending to the Sultan? Sleeping with other members of the court? Why wasn't she there? Why did she have to wait? Then she remembered the appointment. It was nearly sundown, she had to get across town too. Carria ran back to her flat, the motion making her stop several times to enjoy the intense pleasure before eventually getting back to her bedroom. Quickly she slipped off her morning dress and found another evening gown, she brushed her hair and changed into heeled shoes, there was no time to change anything else. Then she dashed toward the other side of town, to the address on the pink card. Carria found the heels made her walk quicker and in small steps. The effect was so intense that once she had to duck into an alleyway to vent her excitement.

Flushed, she arrived in the clothing area of Estra, where the shops on each side of the street were full of the finest and most expensive fashions, the most expensive gold and silver thread decorated the thinnest and finest rubber. Lace and leather tooled to the highest skill of any craftsman discreetly spoke volumes about the money clients had.

She found the sights of the busy town seemed vague and unreal against the deep physical pleasure that throbbed within her, and she wandered without any real aim around the narrow streets, pausing to get her breath now and again.

At the top of the street the old and elegant palace shop stood, with a tall copper dome and clean white marble. Live models paraded in the windows and door attendants scowled at anyone daring to try and enter. Carria presented the pink card, and to her amazement the door attendants immediately held the large oak doors open for her and saluted.

Once inside a small shrill little man with a shocking pink wig and rouged cheeks guided her to the back of the store, to the inner sanctum of the shop, decorated with the most expensive gold leaf and having the air of something old and decayed. Pretty young assistants, both male and female, scurried about the sales floor exchanging knowing glances at their customers.

A young woman, not much older than Carria herself, approached and the shrill little man introduced this newcomer as a 'personal assistant' then promptly hurried away. Normally this would have scared her, being here in such strange circumstances, but something had happened to her the previous night. She was alive. To the outside world she was the same girl, which was good – she wanted to appear that way – but inside she was stretched, enlarged, filled by adventure yet hungry for more. She was a woman.

The assistant, who was eager and attractive, also seemed to possess an air of knowing. She dressed in a short plain tunic, which indicated that she was very junior. She asked Carria how she could help, and even such a common openly seemed out of place in this environment, Carria paused before she replied:

'I've come for a fitting, for the clothes. I'm going to the school.' She held out J'nie's card, then blushed and dropped her eyelids, half expecting scorn from the assistant.

The assistant wagged her finger in an enticing way and led Carria to the fitting rooms. Carria was taken behind a set of heavy velvet red curtains, to a set of rooms, mirrored on all sides, roof and floor as well as walls. A frosted glass door allowed the soft glow of lateens to filter through and allowed Carria to make out the shapes of various garments hung in order in the passageway. Each design was suspended from a long marble wall on silver chains and around this sales floor worked a different set of assistants wearing matching clothes and, to Carria's amusement, these assistants too were chained to the wall by thin silver links.

The young girl left and Carria spent minutes alone, taking in the strange surroundings that left her reflected a thousand times over from every angle. Finally the door opened and a new assistant entered, clearly more senior.

'While within the fitting rooms I'll be your guide. My name is Fleaniful and I am the chief assistant, for your pleasure.'

Carria looked at this woman, as young as herself. She had dark hair and full red lips, white skin and a pair of blazing brown eyes. But the main thing that

47

attracted Carria was the clothes she wore: a short satin corset that shone in the light, stretched by the tension of keeping her large breasts inside. The corset ended with a lacy frill above her navel and attached from this were four taut black lengths of leather. Keeping these in position Fleniful had a pair of tight satin panties. Attached to the end of these leather straps were a pair of leather boots that reached up to her thighs. These emphasised her slender legs and made them appear to be two-thirds her height. On the ends of these were the highest heels Carria had even seen, and between these there was a chain, with a large 'O' ring in the centre from which a new length was attached. This final length was anchored to the marble wall.

'I'm here for the fitting as a Companion for the school. And I'd also like something else, something exciting, for a friend, but I've got to be able to hide it under a normal dress. I want to really surprise her you see.' Carria suddenly realised what she'd said. Flushing at the thought of the assistant knowing her lover was another woman, she fell silent, but the assistant only smiled.

'I know just the thing. I've worn one myself.' The assistant looked back at Carria with a smile. Carria realised that this woman had been eying her for a while. She was flattered that someone as attractive as that took an interest in her.

'Come over here, madam.' Fleaniful walked over to a hanging space, her chains making a slight rattling sound on the leather floor. Carria found herself looking at a simple black dress with two clasps at the shoulder. Fleaniful reached up and undid them letting the fabric fall to the ground.

Underneath there was a spider's web of thin straps. The girl's form gave it a strange shifting look, and Carria stood hypnotised by the thing.

'It's made by the finest craftsmen in the land, and each strap contains fluids that react to your body. You get excited and it follows, pulsing both you and your partner with the slightest electric shocks, that drive both of you, or more if you are so inclined, wild with the most animal passions. You can really see how it works like this,' Fleaniful said. 'Let's go and try it on. Now, madam,' Fleaniful whispered, 'take your clothes off.'

Carria felt odd at this mixture of respect and command, but automatically she responded and dropped her dress.

'Ah, I see madam already likes to enjoy herself,' the girl stated in a very matter of fact way. Carria looked down at her tight panties. In her excitement she'd forgotten what she was wearing. Now she instinctively placed her hands over her crotch in a protective way and reddened.

'Now let's get these panties off,' the assistant calmly instructed, carefully avoiding the issue.

Carria felt a thrill through her as Fleaniful stepped behind her and gently pulled at the cords behind her back. Fleaniful tugged at the sides of the material, freeing it inch by inch until they fell around her ankles. Automatically she stepped out of them, then spreading her legs a little she put her hands down between her legs. Fleaniful pushed her hands away and started to pull the device from her, slipping it down with caressing motions. Carria had become very wet and the metal device slid free without much urging. Fleaniful let it fall onto the mirror glass with a thud, but she kept her hands behind and under Carria's sex, gently but forcefully massaging her labia.

'I know you've been looking at me, madam, so before trying the costume try me.'

All Carria could say was yes. Had she been looking? She didn't know, but all the same she was liking this very much and wouldn't say a word to break the spell.

Against her will Carria let out a sigh. Fleaniful's hands were strong and sure, her motions the opposite to J'nie's gentle probings. She felt the palm close around her, squeezing her and holding her. She swayed forward and back on her feet. She could feel hot breaths on the back of her neck then a kiss, as light as a butterfly landing. Carria took a deep breath and threw her arms back behind her head, pulling that moist mouth closer to her, stopping it from escaping.

'Is madam happy?' Fleaniful whispered, her voice causing gentle waves of warm air to tickle Carria's inner ear. Carria paused. Would J'nie approve? But of course she must know what happened in this place. J'nie had probably ordered it. This was a mere assistant a servant. And she was to be in the Sultan's school, a Companion! So now she would feel the power of command for the first time.

'No, I'm not fully happy. My breasts are exposed but neglected.'

She did not have to say more. Fleaniful bought her hand up, moving her other hand over Carria's crotch. Her right hand, now wet with Carria's excitement, started to fondle Carria's breasts, one after the other. The wetness of her anticipation made the fingers glide in smooth arcs over the satin skin, while Carria's neck received the attention of Fleaniful's tongue.

Carria ran her hand down Fleaniful's shoulder, moving down her arm pulling it closer then, grasping the wrist, she pulled Fleaniful's hand to her upturned face and sucked her fingers, tasting her own juices on them.

'Now lick me out,' Carria commanded.

'Yes,' the assistant replied willingly. She kneeled on the ground while running her tongue down the length of Carria's back, giving her crack a quick flick of her tongue.

At this Carria shouted 'Again' and was obeyed.

Finally Carria felt a hot probing tongue force itself inside her and flick its hot point at her clitoris. The motion was hard and forceful. Carria had never found herself aroused as quickly. She rocked in response to the forceful thrusts of the tongue. She clenched her teeth to prevent herself from screaming, but the screaming inside her went on nevertheless, pushing her quickly to climax. When it came she had to hold on to Fleaniful's hair to stop herself from falling over.

'Now let's fit your costume.' Fleaniful spoke with her head down, still kneeling on the mirrored surface. Carria still trembled, sweat running off her and breathing hard. She ran her hands through the tangled hair below her, drawing the pale head forward. Slowly Fleaniful got to her feet and walked out of the room with the tiny jingle of her silver chains.

When she returned bearing a bundle across her arms Carria was leant against one of the cold walls, tired. She smiled back at the assistant.

'I must recommend your service to your employer.' Carria retained her position of superiority even when naked and exhausted. The joys of being in command were not to be relented upon, even when in reality the other girl had controlled every part of the seduction. Carria smiled to herself. 'And now you must show me the Companion's school uniform.'

Fleaningful held the bundle up. All Carria could see was a tangle of leather straps held together with metal hoops. But Fleaniful showed her where to put her legs and gradually the tangle took form on her body. There was a high leather belt which clinched her waist from which straps passed down past either side of her sex forming hoops around her thighs, which were pulled tight and secured with another set of straps at the back. Likewise, straps also passed up between her breasts to a thick leather and silk collar, kept in place by a lock at its back. Finally the assistant fitted the wrist cuffs, also locked into place, and secured to these, running up to the collar and down again to the waist, the chains of gold.

'Once the collar, wrists and belt are locked in place there is no way to remove the costume without a key,' Fleaniful explained as she made chalk marks on the materials for the final fitting. 'Only the Sultan himself, the Sultan's own Mistress and the headmistress of the school has a key.'

Carria felt confined by the costume, as if being in a private cage. The idea of another person having the key, of being jailed, appealed to her.

'This feels about right. Can I pick it up tomorrow?'

'Ah no, you must return tomorrow for the final fitting. It must be right for you will wear this at all times, until you leave or are promoted to the next rank. It will be very uncomfortable if it is wrong. Then, when we are sure about it, it will be delivered to the school. You will be given it after induction. Tomorrow I must also find you suitable boots, and the other items that madam will require. All of this will be explained.' Fleaniful started to take the costume off. With a slight jangle of her chains on the floor, she took it away and helped Carria dress again, taking care to insert her present into Carria and giving her pussy a kiss before enclosing it in the silk and leather of the special panties.

As Carria left the shop she allowed the device within her to lift her passions and work its way deep into her. She thought about the assistant, and the thrill she had got from ordering her about. Maybe she should go back tomorrow and order the girl to lift her skirt and be beaten. By the time Carria arrived back at her chambers she was feeling victorious in anticipation. The device responded to her feelings, giving her firm thrusts that made her make whispered sobbing noises under her breath. Once within the sound security of her room she turned on the ornate nozzles at the corners of the room that produced scented spray in diffuse squirts from a selection. She chose a rose scent and breathed in the mixture straight from the cherub shaped brass outlet. She let her dress fall to the floor and laid down on her silk bed. With a few tugging motions she freed her constraining panties and threw them away from the bed, then gently slid the device from herself so that she could finish herself off with deep strokes of her fingers.

She lay on the silk, her back arched and her right index finger probing inside her, her left hand pulling her own hair in jerks of excitement. She allowed herself to moan, thinking about the fitting, and what lay in store for her once she was within the palace. The anticipation turned her on, and she thought about the last time: tied and unable to do anything but wait for her punishment, and just thinking of that she climaxed.

Carria's heels made a distinct tapping noise as she walked back to the shop. Everything seemed tense and amplified, the street made more noise, the garish colours of the shop signs seemed to leap out of the rough side streets. Almost as soon as she got inside the rain started in earnest, making hard drumming sounds on the roof as the staff hurried about lighting the gas lights. Fleaniful approached her and took her to the fitting rooms, her chains making the now familiar tinkling noise on the mirrored surface.

With the curtain drawn Carria undressed, leaving only her heels on. She stood watching Fleaniful for a second. There was a spark of passion between them.

Carria had a moments guilt about J'nie then with an angry force pushed Fleaniful up against the cold smooth surface of the room. Fleaniful, taken unaware, attempted to push Carria away, but then gave up any suggestion of resistance and pulled Carria closer. Their mouths met and Carria pushed her tongue deep inside. Fleaniful responded by opening her legs wider, and Carria automatically responded by scooping Fleaniful's sex in her hand and squeezing. She made the girl kneel and kiss her, then kissed her on the mouth, tasting the lingering scent of her own excitement.

'Enough!' Carria stood up straight.

'As you wish, madam.' Fleaniful gave a little bow, but her eyes looked back with a pleading innocence. Carria felt powerful and dirty at once, and from that uncertainty of her own feelings came a streak of cruelty.

'No more. Fit me. I must be gone soon.'

Fleaniful smiled weakly and fetched the costume. It fitted like a glove. A tight and restricting glove, but the alterations had been done well. Carria felt the padded collar, wrist and waist bands encapsulating her. With Fleaniful's help she choose a pair of high, thigh length heels, laced down the back, that could be hooked onto the belt by lengths of specially tailored leather. Carria took great care on the size of skirt, and that the pale pastel green pleats fell high enough to allow her to move unrestricted, but just long enough to hide her straps from view when she sat.

Just as she was leaving the shop another young woman walked in: a short-haired brunette with a confident stride.

'Ula, what are you doing here?' Carria asked innocently.

'I'm here for a fitting. One of the girls in the school was caught trying to sneak out at night. Poor thing was lost in the corridors for days, then couldn't face the punishment. Anyway, she left, and I'm joining you. It's good to be chosen. Still, not like being the favourite, is it?' Ula ventured.

Carria smiled and said she would enjoy seeing her at the palace, but there was something about the way she had talked, something bitter. Carria did not think they would ever be likely to be friends. There was something hard about this woman, something that reflected itself in her stern features. Something that warned Carria away.

She walked back, now anxious, hoping for a message. Her expectations were met when she found a small silver envelope under her door, and eagerly she tore it open, but all it contained was a formal notice to attend the palace on the stroke of evening in six days time. Carria flicked the card over to see a handwritten note wishing her luck and cheekily telling her to use her gift, and reminding her to be ready for a visit. Carria smiled, but after this visit a long wait, a whole six days to go, she wasn't sure if she could stand the wait. For the first time ever she was fulfilled, well fulfilled in part and that was so good, but even better she has accomplished the first part of her mission, and would soon be very close to her goal.

When a knock finally came on the door, Carria hurriedly checked that her dress concealed her surprise from the shop. She smiled and said something, but Carria forget the small talk as soon as it had dissipated upon the air. There was no name, no background, each of them had good reason to hide there real selves, and it was refreshing after the long line of suitors that Carria had had. Boys who proclaimed love, but didn't know the first thing about it. They talked and quoted sonnets, but none had done what this woman had done to her in a few days. This lady had taken her virtue, and she had given it readily, and enjoyed doing so. They looked at each other for a long time, and then as the sun descended Carria dropped her dress, and the woman hers. Carria was struck that the woman was also wearing the spider harness, and knew that the shop girl must have told her, but it was a fleeting thought as she became aroused by the naked body standing in front of her. Then the spider's straps on her started to glow a dull orange, and the effect was true of the other woman too. There was a feeling of great well being all over her, and she was sure that some force was pulling her to the lips of her lover.

The first kiss swept over her, her whole body was one, every part was equally responsive, and the slightest touch caused her to moan in a low primitive way. There was no way to tell which part of her was doing what. She was wet. Was it her mouth or her pussy now having a tongue traced around it? Falling back on the bed, she knew she was feeling both her experience and the other woman's. Guilty she rolled over and started to kiss the vagina that was offered to her with a sharp drawing up of her lover's legs. Now the sensation was incredible, like melting, as their tongues worked in unison, each being both giver and receiver of the short, sure licks that were making them both writhe and push harder.

As one they steadily climbed, holding and sucking, licking and gently biting until there was no other place to go and they jumped off that high place together, clinging together and both crying with one voice.

'That was truly amazing,' Carria finally managed to whisper. 'I was you. I felt me in you. What is this thing?'

'This,' Carria exclaimed, 'can be a very dangerous thing. It amplifies you, your presence and emotions, so tonight it was pleasure, but it can be used for pain too. And you need a skilled operator. They don't let normal women have these.'

'But I got one!' Carria protested.

'Yes, but I let them show you one. It is my parting gift to you, for this is the last time we shall meet for a long time, and possibly the last ever like this.'

Carria didn't mean to but she started to cry, and was comforted with reminders of how strong she had been when her dedication was tested by the whip. Then night fell and sleep came. The morning brought a lonely bed, and all trace of the amazing garment and the red headed woman were gone.

After that the days seemed to drag on for Carria, whether she waited in her room reading, or idly tried to waste time in the harbour coffee shops. Even walks around the shops wearing her present and the subsequent rush back to her room to complete her pleasure did not distract her for long, and she felt unfulfilled without her lover and mistress. And then there were the sexual secrets that she now hoped the palace would bring. Five whole days during which she felt the anticipation grow – what new and strange delights would she be introduced to? She had arrived in the town less than a week ago, yet in that time she had discovered so much about herself that she had never imaged. It would not deflect her from her course, but it would make this whole mission more enjoyable. There are, she reminded herself, things more important than mere enjoyment. She had a purpose. Yes, a purpose, and that could not be abandoned, whatever she was beginning to find out about her emotional and physical needs.

5

Inspection

The sixth morning came, and Carria awoke to find herself fresh with energy. She packed everything she had into a case and paid off the innkeeper well before the harbour clock had called midday. Finding herself wandering the streets, attempting to avoid thinking about the evening, she took herself off to a small café.

She sat and drank, and attempted to think of anything but what was coming, but it was no use. Her mind drifted to the nights that she had spent with the woman: nights where she of all people had submitted, and enjoyed it. Her mind raced – who was she? She never had prised a name from her. She must have been from the palace. Then she realised – it must have been the woman in the mask! It had to be to her, but why the mask? Why was it important that nobody saw her in the house of GaJa?

The woman must be important then, but she had been naked in the same bed as Carria. But she remembered that she had always left carefully so as not to be seen. What was going on?

She had lost herself too well in thought. The half hours were chiming and she realised that the day had gone. It was time to present herself at the palace gates. Hurriedly she left and walked up the town steps to the towering form of the palace.

A small bald man came out to greet her once the guards had undressed her with their eyes and sent a message into the dark mouth of the main gate. The bald man was kind, but firm. All her possessions had to be left with him. She could collect them if she left but until then they would be locked away, and anyway, why would such a pretty girl want to leave the palace? It was a place of pleasure and she would have more than enough of that.

She was shown through to a small cubical and told to wait. She did as she was told, and with a mixture of fear and anticipation. Hours seemed to pass. She heard a noise to her left as the bald man's voice issued a similar instruction to what could only be another recruit. Then one more time, and the same instructions to her right.

Finally a small grill in the cubical door opened and a female voice instructed her to make herself undressed, which she did, and pass her clothes out of the grill. More waiting and she was beginning to get cold. Then the grill opened and the same female voice commanded her to turn to face the back wall. Behind her she could feel the rush of cold air as the door was opened, and she felt strong but feminine hands pull her hands back, while the voice kept telling her to look forward or suffer.

Carria felt pressure on her skin, then realised her wrists were being laced into some form of glove. The same expert hands were now holding her hair up, and then pulled a blindfold over her eyes, looping two bands over and under her face and covering her ears making it difficult to hear anything. The blindfold worked well, and not a pinprick of light alleviated the dark. But just as she felt that this was an indignity too far she felt a large rubber ball being pushed into her mouth. At this she instinctively rebelled and attempted to shake her head, but those firm hands held her and grabbed her nose. She waited as long as she could but it was only putting off the inevitable, and with a long gasp for breath her mouth opened with the predictable result of the gag being inserted and tightly secured.

Silence. Suddenly Carria knew that she was alone again. She twisted her body around in an attempt to hear any sounds better, but there was only a faint metallic jingle of a chain, which she deduced hung from her bound wrists. With nothing to do she stood as before, afraid to try and move and now, for the first time, unsure if she wanted to go on, but determined anyway.

After a long time she sensed the cubical door open and a hand placed on her shoulder urged her to follow. It was an open place, a courtyard, perhaps the one she had been in before the cubicle. Carria was halted by a strong tug on her bound wrists, and left to stand as the faint jingle of chain met her again. More time passed, and then she felt the chain being passed between her exposed thighs. There was a pause, then a pull on the chain, and Carria started to walk forward, feeling her own wrists held back for a second before whatever was holding it gave way. In this way she felt herself led across cold stone floors, then suddenly she crashed into a body in front of her. Beginning to right herself she was pushed from behind. So that was it, she was in a line, each new recruit blindfolded, gagged and chained together in such a way as to prevent any unexpected movement. She concentrated hard. It seemed like four sets of bare feet, but she could not be sure.

Listening carefully to any clues that might help her retrace these steps, Carria recorded each type of noise, whether the sharp staccato of the guards' boots was echoed by stone or plaster, but it was impossible. They walked over a hundred different floors, felt a hundred different environments, from open to deep inside the building. Even though the blindfold muffled any sound, Carria was aware that they passed other palace personnel on this long trip from the odd snatched comment about part of her body, or how the Sultan would enjoy that one. Others, she was sure, ignored this procession, or were silently looking at her with greedy eyes.

Finally they stopped. Carria felt herself being led off, away from the others, and then alone. She waited, but there was no sound so, with aching feet, she tried to sit, but the chain bit up into her tender pussy and, realising she was chained into a standing position, she firmly planted her legs apart and waited. She could tell that the atmosphere was damp, and the air must have been mechanically circulated for it carried a sweet scent, and her only conclusion was that she was deep underground, but how she had got here was a mystery. She realised that she was completely lost and that from here on there could be no rescue, only failure or victory.

It must have been an hour, but Carria could feel hands working on her restraints, and one by one the gag, blindfold and wrist straps were removed. Strangely she felt more naked now, without anything to prevent her knowing that she was exposed to anyone's gaze.

'You are now in the palace,' a soft voice intoned from behind her. 'You may now look about you.'

Carria slowly took in her surroundings. It was a room of glass, and at the centre was a pool from which all of the light came. Beside it was a large padded table that reminded Carria of an operating table in a way, and this hissed a pneumatic hiss while steam pipes at its side merrily whistled. At the far end there was a large carved door with a whip carved into it and an inscription that Carria could just make out: *Freedom Through Discipline*. Turning, she found herself looking directly at a middle-aged woman in a nurse's uniform, with sharp creases to her tunic and a cap with the whip emblem again.

'I am the Sultan's nurse, and this is the inspection room. You are between two places. There is a door into the school, where you can learn to be a Companion, and behind you is the way back to your previous life – whatever that was. You can leave, now or at any time, but once you have gone you cannot return.'

Carria nodded and, in so doing, she realised that she was committing herself both to the school, and also to her destiny.

'Very well then, we'll get you ready, for none can enter the school incorrectly dressed, not even I. First, however, you need to be examined. The Sultan can only have perfection.'

She was told to wash herself in the pool, and then once the nurse was happy that she was clean, Carria was made to lie on the padded table on her back. The nurse inserted a long and curved rubberised bar into her mouth and fastened it with a click behind her. This held her tongue down and, although it was more comfortable than the ball gag, it still made Carria feel like a scientific specimen. The nurse then positioned her carefully, pulling her legs wide apart and her arms at ninety degrees to her. Bending down the nurse fiddled with some levers on the side of the table, and suddenly Carria felt her body being sucked down onto it. Small holes in the table hissed as air was drawn through them, gluing Carria's helpless body to the table. Any attempt to struggle was futile, and soon she gave up as from underneath the nurse produced a bottle of lightly smelling oil, which she dripped over Carria, then worked over her body. Carria let herself relax as the warm liquid formed a layer over her. The nurse paid particular attention to her pubic hair and legs, and the reason was soon clear as the nurse produced a shiny blade and started to shave Carria of all her body hair. When finished Carria was made to lie on her stomach and the operation was repeated, until not a single hair remained.

On her back again, she glanced down the table to see that a set of shiny steel rods and pistons were being set up. She wanted to protest, but no sound could come from her mouth, then she felt a latex gloved hand start to push cold greased steel objects inside her as the nurse carefully worked the oiled pussy. The strong fingers probed and pushed, checking and measuring. Carria attempted to raise her head to see what was being done to her, but the bed held her firm, and she instead closed her eyes and began to enjoy the sensation of the smooth medical instrument being gradually forced into her. If she could not stop this, then she must learn to like it, and the inscription on the door came back to her – freedom through discipline.

When the nurse was content, the machine began to spit and hiss steam, and slowly the pistons started to pump, pushing and withdrawing with their machine timing deep inside, gathering pace as if driven by a demon.

Occasionally, she could just make out the image of the nurse writing down a set of figures, as her eyes flicked open and closed, fighting and giving in to the sensation. Sometimes the strokes would soften, only to start again, deeper. The oils mixed with her own juices, filling the air, and she recognised her own scent as the fingers worked upon her, now rubbing her clitoris with strong, regular movement. It was no use, she wanted to come. She experienced the sensation of her legs trembling, but even these well practised fingers kept missing the exact spot she knew must be attended to. Carria tried to move, but her increasingly frantic efforts had no effect. She tried to shout, but the bit in her mouth held her tongue so that all that came from her was a feeble groan. It was unbearable. She was so close but there was nothing that she could do. Her mind raced back to the room above the inn, but this was not the same. Where there had been careful and gentle love, this was harsh and clinical. There were no soft bonds, only the mechanical table and the steel fingers of the examination machine as it probed her, and the detached nurse noting when and what pressure was being used. The machine whirred and let out a puff of steam as it shifted gears and Carria found that it was now vibrating in time to her body. She wasn't fighting the action now. Her body was in tune and she felt the sensation of riding a deep and pleasurable wave, which was carrying her inextricably towards the shore. As the wave crested it plunged into the rocks, sending the wave higher and higher as her body attempted to shake with climax, but the table held her still in its vicelike grip and made all the forces concentrate themselves back to her point of pleasure, and the waves broke once more against the shore, finally throwing her on to a mental beach, where she lay exhausted and spent.

She awoke to find herself back on her stomach, but the table still held her firmly, a wet patch next to her mouth where the bit gag had made her dribble, and a wetness further down her body. Steam still hissed about the room, and as she fought off the desire to sleep again, Carria experienced a strange pressure on her anus as something smooth and round was inserted into her, then a rush of water in short rhythmic bursts, drumming her so that she could not resist giving out a little sigh of pleasure. Then she felt a second nozzle pushing into her pussy, this time throbbing in time and forcing her to bite down on her bit gag to avoid making more noise. Then it was over. With a final satisfied hiss the tubes withdrew themselves from her, and the vacuum was released. As she turned over she saw the long steel arms fold themselves back down below the wheezing table, while the nurse stood over her and instructed her to bath again. This time Carria was aware that the water had changed and carried with it a light scent.

As she dried herself for the second time the nurse brought her the harness she had been fitted for in the strange fitting room in the town, except now it seemed even more complex. The nurse, noticing her confusion, explained:

'These are your Companions' clothes, that you will always wear, but as a new girl there are also some extra things that are needed.' The nurse smiled, but Carria remained in some doubt as to how sincere it was. She felt the thick and constraining belt about her waist, the long straps pass between her legs, pulled tightly to their fastenings behind her, then the smooth material rolled up her front until the collar was fitted shut with a distinct click. The wrist bands followed, then the light but strong chain that prevented her from raising her hands beyond her breasts.

'Ah, you are nearly ready, but you are not a Companion yet, so as a new girl there are other things,' the nurse informed her as she delved again under the padded table. Carria was told to stand still as she felt a chain again passed under her, but this time it was drawn tight and locked into place, attached to hoops on her belt.

'As a new girl you must be protected from yourself. There can be a temptation to try and masturbate, or even have another pleasure you. You must remember that you are here by consent and that consent means that all of you, your mind, your body and your pleasures are now the school's.

Turning her attention to Carria's pert breasts, the nurse pinched her nipples, swelling them, and then with care she pulled the right nipple while clamping a circle of ornate silver around it. Carria let out a small gasp of pain, but the nurse continued with the left breast, then threaded a fine linked chain through eyelets in both of the devices, which she then passed up to a steel loop in the collar and attached to a thicker chain.

'This is your lead, and be sure to follow where you are lead or your breast will become very sore.' The nurse chuckled and turned her attention to Carria's legs, where she fitted long black boot with heels that were so tall that they made Carria lean forward slightly to catch her balance. Looking down Carria noticed that these too were chained so that it would be impossible to do anything more than take small steps at a time.

'Now,' the nurse addressed her. 'You are almost ready. I expect that you feel rather naked; vulnerable, in fact. That's good, you should as a new girl. In time you will get used to the uniform, and it will feel natural. By then you will have progressed to the next grade. Now go through the door!'

Commanded, Carria gingerly took a step forward, feeling for the chain to pull tight, then lifting her other foot. She was used to wearing heels, but these were different, so tall that her feet were forced to be on tiptoe inside the elegant patent leather. Her body swayed, making her aware of how tight the corsetlike belt was, and making her take shallow breaths when the effort of walking seemed to demand more. Using what movement she was allowed in her arms, she held the palms of her hands up and concentrated on making each step count while the nurse studied her first steps as a schoolgirl with professional detachment.

She approached the door, now feeling more at ease, as it magically swung open, and she passed through holding her head high and mustering all of her dignity as it closed with a thud of finality behind her. Standing to catch her breath, she found herself in an octagonal room, doors on every side. Beside each of four doors stood a woman dressed in the same way as Carria was, and looking as uncomfortable. Carria recognised one of them as Ula. The others she did not know, but they were all beautiful women, and she could not help casting her mind back to her nights with the mystery woman who had brought her here, or at least had allowed her to find a way in the palace.

There was a sudden swishing noise and one of the doors on the other side opened. Four guards entered, dressed with the black and purple plumes from their black uniforms, except all of these guards were female, and even they wore chains to their wrists. They stood in a perfect symmetrical arc, and then a figure came marching through them, standing with authority at the room's centre.

Carria felt like a soldier at inspection, and without thinking she stood to attention, and noticed that the other new recruits had done the same.

The woman in front studied them in turn and Carria took the time to return the compliment to her. She was not tall, something made more apparent by

68

the relatively low shoes, but she was certainly well built, muscles bungled, and she had a fighter's stance. All of which was offset by a flame red spray of wild hair and a freckled face. But the eyes were hard, and they scanned each of them without mercy. The woman stepped back, satisfied that the intake was good.

'Hello girls, I am Helena, the headmistress of the Companions' school for Girls. Whatever you have been, you start fresh from here, from those who have been here but failed before –' she looked at one of the girls '– to those of you that have come to us recently. In my eyes you are all fresh, and must learn obedience, elegance and discipline. All these things must be learned as second nature, and all privileges must be earned. Right now you are disobedient, lazy and lacking in all civilising factors. You will be treated as such until you can prove to me that you are worthy of anything more. You will earn your physical freedom only by submitting to mental discipline. Welcome to the Palace of Pleasures.'

Part Two
Schooling

6

The First Chamber

Helena stood on a raised platform, a stark metal frame of steel arcs behind her. In front of her the four girls, kneeling and, behind them, the guards. Helena addressed them, her strong legs now towering over them, and her voice powerful and zealous.

'At the school we are here to help you. We want you to succeed. But there can be no sliding; the programme you are on has provided the highest quality of Companions for a hundred generations. Only I want every one of you to pass. Each year two graduates should join me with the guards, and two should be selected for the Sultan's pleasure rooms. There is no compromise. If any of you are not deemed worthy, then those appointments are not made, and I will have the Sultan's Mistress asking me why. I do not intend that to happen.

'You will pass the first grade of training, and get to wear the blue skirts of undergraduates, giving you the modesty that you will have earned. Before that you are not allowed to cover any part of your body. Then you will graduate. Failure at any time of any task is punished as laid down in the Code.' Helena held up a thick and old volume. 'If you do not wish this then you may leave, but you may never return.

'Now, is that understood? Good. As I call out your name you will come up to me for your first beating. This is so you know what pain awaits digression, and this is the mildest punishment. Yvonne, you are first.'

The guards pulled Yvonne to her feet roughly, as Helena prepared a metal ring under the frame. Yvonne's collar chain was attached, so that she had to stoop under the metal cage. Then Helena pressed a switch and the whole apparatus rose steadily until Yvonne was balancing on the tips of her boots and swaying a little, her face grimacing as the chain tensed and pulled her nipples.

Helena selected a long whip from the rack and made a few practise strokes before bringing the full force of her athletic arms down on the tottering Yvonne. She tried to swing forward from the blow, but this only tightened the chain more and she rasped a noise that signalled pain from her gagged lips before arching back in time to receive a second stroke across her buttocks. Another swift blow followed with a distinct crack, and then the guards were on her, unhooking her and pushing her back to the kneeling position at the front. Carria glanced over to see the girl quietly sobbing, and steeled herself for her turn.

Zena was called next, her waiflike frame a contrast to the rigid steel, and she too returned whimpering, but Ula, she noted, didn't blink; in fact, the woman seemed to return to her place with a look of contentment, as if she had just been pleasured. Carria felt like she could not show herself to be weak, and she held her composure as the steel frame rose, keeping her feet as far apart as her ankle chains would allow to keep her balance and being sure to stand straight. The whip landed with a searing pain on her, and she felt like every fibre in her had tightened, but she stayed still and as the next landed she kept repeating to herself that she was two-thirds of the way through the ordeal.

The final stroke was the hardest, but she swallowed the scream and allowed herself only a deep breath, then it was over and she felt her body finding the ground again and the arms of the guards pushing her down to the ground.

Helena replaced the whip and, looking at them in turn, resumed her lecture.

'That was the training whip. It is the lowest numbered whip in the rack. It is a "one" while the highest is a "twelve". Tonight, imagine what an experienced woman could do to you with a "twelve" and think about the fact that your arse isn't the only sensitive area that can be whipped.

'But whipping is only one lesson. Other measures are less painful but last longer; some are both long and painful. You must remember that you will not know how you will be punished in advance, so be wise and follow the rules. Each time you are bad you will also lose a link from your arm chains: there are seven links in all. Lose them all and you start training from the start, after waiting until the new term in the school maid service. If you want to know what that's like, ask Yvonne. Now the guards will take you to your dormitory. School starts at the sound of the whistle; assemble here – fully dressed for deportment.'

And with a wave of her hand, the guards pulled the women to their feet and led them off to a corridor at the side, to what Carria hoped would be a rest, but which was to be another ordeal.

The dormitory had four beds, arranged in a circle, with the entrance, the bathing room and toilet, a dinning room and, across from the door, a series of lockers, each named for the four girls.

As they entered, the guards closed the door and made sure that it was locked. Above her, Carria could see a large glass dome, with mirrors and tubes that sent light out in all directions. She was distracted by another girl who had arrived from the dining area, wearing a short dress which puffed at the sleeves and came high up to her neck, concealing what was a familiar collar. This, Carria was sure, was the maid, who started to remove their gags one by one and placed them carefully in the lockers.

Still unsure as to whether they could talk, Carria gestured to the maid who nodded, but indicated that she could not. Carria broke the silence by asking the maid for water, which she brought. That made her realise that she needed to relieve herself, and she asked the maid how to undo the chain that was now beginning to press into her pussy, but the maid shook her head and indicated that the chain was there to stay for now. Embarrassed, Carria took as much dignity as she could to the bathroom and, with the complication of her wrist chains as well as having to pee through her pussy chain, managed to spray her legs with her own pee. Helpless, she wondered what to do until the maid reappeared and dutifully wiped her. Carria remembered what Helena had said about the life of a maid and the thought sobered her.

When she found the others they were seated in the dining room, and some form of normal conversation was taking place, and what had happened had clearly not gone without notice. Yvonne was explaining her brief period of waiting until the new term.

'I was only a maid for a week, but I'll never go through that again, or the other punishments. Believe me, I know about them all. I lost every link, and then –' Yvonne shivered. '– the beating, the humiliation and then being a maid to my former colleagues. Well, just don't.'

Zena looked worried, and in a voice that was soft asked about the training.

'Nearly a year; four months until you have a skirt,' Yvonne explained. 'And it covers everything. By the end you are both a lady and an experienced courtesan. Well experienced in theory, you must wait to the second grade until you can begin to sample sexual delights.'

Ula spoke for the first time, her head lifted up as if making a speech rather than a point. 'Isn't that only fair? After all, we are here to serve the Sultan, not our own pleasures.'

'I'd say that is the best attitude,' Yvonne confirmed. 'I still carry the scars for thinking otherwise.'

'Then why are you here?' Carria asked.

'Because there is nowhere in this world, or any other, where you can sample every carnal delight; nowhere that puts pleasure above any other pursuit. This is truly a paradise, but now I understand that paradise must be guarded.'

'Hence this thing biting into me,' Zena noted glancing down at her chains.

'Yes, to protect you from yourself . . . or from others.' Yvonne looked around the pretty faces of the other three. 'We are about to undergo training that will make us all sexual creatures first and foremost, and here there are no boundaries. But the fear of punishment will help us all get through this.'

A lull settled over the table and the rest of the meal was conducted in silence. Then the maid reappeared and signalled them one by one out. Carria found herself being undressed, her wrists chained to the bed and her other clothes removed, being carefully placed in her locker, before she feel asleep and dreamed about other nights far away.

* * *

There was no natural light, but the luminous bars on the ceiling began to glow brighter, and Carria started to wake. The maid secured a loose hoop around her and chained her wrists to it before shaving her and showering her, then diligently fitted her corset belt and collar to her. The boots seemed to fit better today, and the bit for her mouth seemed less awkward as she waited for the other girls to be fitted.

They were marched by the maid along a long corridor, without any natural light, the floor stone, but the sides and ceiling of a dark soft material that shimmered in the flickering light of the torches that clung to the walls at intervals. For the first time, actually leaving the dormitory in the training harness, Carria experienced how the uniform was changing her sensations. The tight corset and collar denied any tactile involvement with the surroundings, but the exposed flesh of her thighs, back and breast compensated, becoming more acutely aware of each and every minute change in temperature. Everything she did now forced her to think in a sexual way. Even just standing pulled at her chains and caressed her.

The maid stopped and pointed them to a opening in the wall with the number one printed in large script on the side. Inside a very tall and imposing woman stood. She wore boots as high as they did but her whole uniform was dark blue and she seemed to float on her heels as she approached them, pacing each immaculate step with a long ebony cane.

'This is the first room of training,' she said. 'You must pass through here before you can go to the next class, and you will pass. Failure will be rewarded harshly.

'You are new –' she looked at Yvonne with an icy stare '– and you have no beauty. All this welcome, but first you must learn to walk before you may run.

To carry yourself as a queen is the first and most important stage to being a woman.'

This was the deportment class, taught, as they discovered, by a perfectionist called Mistress Kay. Her sharp eyes focused upon the new recruits from behind a perfect make up, and her voice had a highly trained accent to it, as if she was a noblewoman. She clearly held herself to be superior to anyone else and her well-pronounced voice sarcastically rolled off commands: 'walk, sit – no not like that, like a lady, hips, more sway, less sway, be delicate.'

Yvonne, as expected, did well. For Zena, Carria and Ula it was hard work as they followed each other around in a circle day after day with Mistress Kay shouting to them that they walked like pigs and prodding them with her long stick. She took great delight in reminding her pupils that they would each be examined that failure was a disciplinary matter, worthy of losing a link and some cruel punishment that she kept as a surprise.

As the weeks passed, Carria grew used to the routine: the maid silently helping her, the classes, a break for their hapless maid to refresh them and help them with their toilet, more classes, another break, classes then a long, tired sleep. Mentally she left her previous life behind. At night she missed the feel of the bit in her mouth, and regarded herself as clumsy when not laced into her high heels, her body now feeling secure in the restrictive clothes.

But the routine was not to last long. As this first course came to an end Mistress Kay beckoned them into the classroom for the examination. Now walking with ease and fully aware of exactly how far the chains on her feet would allow her to walk, J'nie carefully walked the circuit that her teacher had laid out. This time it was different: there were obstacles and benches to cross, that had to be completed with elegant manoeuvres, by seating herself and swinging around with her legs kept closed. She was nearly there when somehow her chain became caught under her heels, and she fell over, her hands trying to save her although their chains kept them constrained.

Carria recovered as she had been taught to at the end of the cane, and nothing more was said until all four had finished the course. Mistress Kay applauded them as they stood straight and to attention at the end.

'Very good. You have all passed. You may have the rest of the day off. The maid will bring you food and water pipes. However, you –' she turned to Carria '– you may have passed, but you blemished the record of the group.'

Carria tried to apologise, making slurred noises through her bit, but the woman was not so easily appeased.

'Sorry, I don't want to hear "sorry". There is no such thing. You did wrong, you messed up, therefore you must be responsible for your actions and be punished, and you must take your punishment as a fair exchange for failure. Maid!' she called to the waiting and silent maid, who came rushing in, her short dress rustling.

'Take the others back to the dormitory and attend to them. This one –' she pointed straight at Carria with a steady finger '– must stand here until I return, as a punishment, and I want her standing straight, no slouching, to teach her a little bit more about having dignity.'

The maid nodded and led the others from the chamber. Carria stood staring ahead of her, trying very hard not to let the others see her shame in failing, but she couldn't help catch a long, hard stare of pure disgust from Ula. A month ago this was a means to an end, but here she was feeling like she had let the side down and, in a way, she felt that it was right that she should be punished.

Mistress Kay stood watching Carria until the maid rustled back. Carria saw the mistress point to a spot behind her and the next sensation she had was of her pussy chain being dragged back. Carria gave a little involuntary whimper as the metal dug into her soft flesh and she closed her legs tightly. Then she felt a final tug and the maid's hands work, as a cord was passed through the top of the chain, and she could feel the cord go taut. Mistress Kay nodded to the maid and left.

Only when it had been quiet for some time did Carria dare to look about her. She tried to step forward, but could not. She twisted around, but there was nothing there, and the movement pulled her chain tighter. Finally Carria looked up to see she had been tied by a cord to the low rafters of the chamber. She tried to move her hands around to relieve the tension in the cord, but the chains prevented her from doing anything but touching the rope with her fingers. This was what the mistress had meant by 'standing straight' then. Hours must have passed, but still no one came. Carria began to wonder if they had forgotten her. Her feet hurt and, worse, she needed to pee. She attempted to shift weight onto one foot but the relief was only temporary, as it soon became tired, then she tried to sit on the chain as if it were a swing, but the chain bit deep into her and she found she could only hold the position for a matter of minutes until a stinging pain swelled up from her crotch.

Standing straight was the best solution, but even this was hard and she started to experiment, attempting to find some position that would give her some comfort. She tried two legs, then the left leg only, then the right, then letting her body relax and sitting on the chain, and swapped positions until she had developed a routine, but as time went on she found that she had to shift these positions more frequently and that each time it was more and more painful.

The effort was now becoming difficult. She began to perspire and could only hold a position for seconds before the pain grew too much. Moaning and wincing at the continued torture, she realised that she was dancing in time to her muffled yelps like a puppet wildly being thrown around. There was no escape, however, in writhing on the rope, and now she really had to pee very badly. Biting down on her bit she concentrated on other thoughts, of the town and nights in satin, but the memories only made her swell and the chain bit sharper into her. The efforts of keeping herself moving and trying to hold onto her bladder etched themselves on her face as sweat dripped from every part of her exposed body. She tried to call out, but the bit made every attempt seem like a sexual moan, which merely merged with the frustrated cries she let out from the pain.

Carria cursed the tight corset. It allowed her little ability to breath and she took many short breaths as she struggled against her captivity. It also kept pressure on her abdomen and this made it harder to control her bladder. She felt a warm drop of liquid race down her inside thigh and hoped it was sweat, but it was followed by another, and then she could control herself no longer and, with a sense of shame and relief, she let herself piss, letting the warm juice trickle over her thighs and speed down the polished surface of her boots and down to the polished stone floor, where it stayed as damning evidence of her guilt.

Still, it was done, and there was a sense of a crushing pressure being relieved, almost like a climax. Somehow it eased the discomfort of her predicament, or maybe the shame blocked out other feeling as she hung, her head bowed, but her feet together neatly in the middle of a golden lake.

Numb, she didn't know how long it was before she was aware of other people in the room. Carria raised her head and saw Mistress Kay considering her, the headmistress, Helena, to her side. Neither woman looked to be happy.

'See,' Mistress Kay announced in her clear tone. 'The girl is no more than an animal. It has no self control; no discipline.' The last word was said with emphasis.

Carria looked up to the hard eyes of the mistress and started to cry softly. She felt as if she had no right to be in the same room as these elegant and severe women.

'I think she should be dismissed. She has fouled my studio and her colleagues must be shown how serious a digress like this is.'

Helena spoke and, through her tears, Carria thought she sensed a little pity. 'You know that this is in no way a matter of dismissal. She passed the class. How can you consider throwing her out? On the other hand, you are right – she must be made an example of. First, her colleagues must know what a dirty girl they have amongst them, then I think we need to get the nurse to teach her more control. Maid!' Carria was aware of some barked commands, then when she looked up again Yvonne, Zena and Ula were standing in front of her.

'I think, one minute of quiet contemplation to consider how this girl has let the school down,' Helena commanded, and the three girls let their eyes wander over the scene.

They all stood looking at her, and the shame that Carria felt welled up inside her, bringing a deep red flush to her face and making her tremble a little. She tried to look each girl in the eyes, but couldn't bring herself to meet them. She hung her head as the minutes ticked painfully by, then a noise made her glance up. It was Ula, who had started making little choking noises – she was laughing! Carria flamed, but Ula's behaviour did not go without notice and Helena rounded on her at once.

'You think this is funny, do you? You think this miserable scene is for your entertainment? Do you? Then you will help clear up this mess.' Helena walked up to Ula and, taking hold of her chained vagina, dragged her over to the puddle that Carria stood in. The headmistress placed herself inches away from Ula's ear as she stood looking ahead as the woman shouted a stream of obscenities close and loud, and the girl, now with a look of fear on her, stood still as the headmistress unlocked her bit. 'I want her clean: her boots, her legs and her pussy, and you will not leave until I am satisfied that you have done a good job. Maid, untie the other one.'

Finally Carria felt the tight pressure on her pussy released, and she let out a sigh, causing a reproachful glance form Mistress Kay, so Carria resumes a rigid position, even though her legs were now numbed. Below her she heard the scraping of Ula lowering herself onto the cold stone floor. Ula swallowed hard, then got down on her hands and knees and started licking the wet drips from Carria's boots, starting at their point and moving with a methodical care up the long shiny leather boots until she ran onto Carria's exposed thighs, then with a quick shove from Helena onto the other leg. Then she was made to follow each inside thigh, where she sucked until the skin was clean, and Carria, despite her exhaustion, began to feel a sensual pleasure sweep up over her.

'Open your legs wide girl' Helena barked, and Carria spread them until the chain was straining. Ula whispered, 'Bitch,' under her breath. 'You'd better not enjoy this,' and sank her face into Carria's shaven pussy, licking it with firm and regular strokes, her tongue catching her clitoris in a clumsy way and forcing Carria to bite down again on her bit.

'Enough,' Helena commanded, and Ula gingerly rose to her feet. The maid replaced the bit and escorted the girls from the room. On the way out Ula gave Carria a look of total disgust.

Helena now turned to face Carria, still unsteady on her feet from the punishment, and the sensation of being licked.

'You need to be trained in self discipline, young lady, so while your fellow students take a rest you will go to the Defaulters' Room, where the Nurse will show you how to behave. Also, I am taking one link from each chain.' And she unlocked Carria's arm chains, then reattached them with a link missing. Carrai was escorted from the room and led away, swaying and finding it difficult to gain her balance now that she could move her arms even less.

7

Default and Correction

The white ceramic tiles reflected the harsh overhead light, and created a room without shadow. No place to hide, Carria thought to herself, as the nurse who had examined her walked into the room, her uniform covered with a heavy rubber apron.

'Ah yes, you again. Already lost a link, have we? Well, let's see what I can do to help you correct your faults. The headmistress tells me that you need to learn self-discipline. Well, we have devices for that. Young woman, I would like to introduce you to the Glove.'

A high beam on legs, like a hurdle, was positioned in front of her, and she was forced to bend over, until she could bend no more, and her collar was tied to the ground. Taking her time to check that Carria was exactly the way she wanted, the nurse undid the chain between Carria's legs and placed it in a bottle of fluid. Next she eased her boots off and tied her legs so wide apart that Carria wondered if she would be able to walk afterwards. This position and the missing boots made her stand on tiptoe to remain balanced, and she experienced a jet of cold water up her arse and the powerful water jets push deep inside her pussy.

After a pause for her to dry, the nurse took a small transparent plug, the shape of small lozenge, with a tube hanging from it and without a word pushed it roughly up Carria's pee hole. The nurse attached the clear tubes to a bulbous penis shaped object with more tubes hanging from it, but this time longer, and eased it into the mouth of Carria's vagina, then pushed it home. A large object then slipped forcefully into her anus, turning and screwing its way up her until it was seated firmly in her.

Carria could not see any of this, and the sensations she was getting made her wide eyed with worry. Already today she had experienced pain beyond her imagining, but what was the woman going to do to her?

Untied and pulled up, Carria was made to walk as best she could, tubes trailing on the floor, to stand directly under the harsh light. She saw the nurse delve into a glass draw and hold up a very wide beltlike object made of polished rubber, with six straps running around it, and many small plastic tubes dangling from it. She felt the stickly fabric touch her nipples as it was draped over her and secured to her collar. Then it was wrapped around her, covering her from the neck to just below her feet. The tubes, which hung like a tail from her, were passed through special holes and then one by one the belts were threaded through their buckles, then pulled, each notch fastened, then the whole process started again from the top. Her arms were pushed into her sides, and she nearly fell as her legs were forced together. The rubber was adjusted tight and high around her neck. Looking down Carria saw her body encased like a long triangle of shiny black, her pert breasts sticking out in front of her, with the pressure of the rubber pushing down around her nipples and causing a dull throb as they were pushed against her ringed clamps. Two threaded holes allowed the very tip of her nipples to poke out into the light, but the nurse quickly attached two long hoses and screwed them down with a savage jerk.

Unable to do anything, she considered what might happen to her, but she did not have to wait long. Wheeling a low hammock into position the nurse took her weight and laid her down with consideration, then attended to wrapping her feet in the rubber. The already constricting shroud was then laced into the hammock, wide thick laces threaded through eyelets on either side and tugged until the sides met. Carria looked down at her cocooned body and thought that she had been powerless before, but this was different: there was absolutely nothing she could do. She could not flex a single muscle. Whatever happened to her now was beyond her control.

Carria could just turn her head enough to see the tubes running from her being adjusted and plugged into a machine with glass gauges with measurements on their side and copper pipes. Admiring her work, the nurse stood back and read Carria's thoughts.

'Oh yes, there really is no escape from me. But don't be afraid. I'm here to help you get better. It is just the bitter taste of the medicine that will help you learn.' The nurse crouched down beside the horizontal and motionless body, and started to gently trace her latex gloved fingers up the length of the outline.

'Soon you will be fully enclosed, and you will be taught to discipline your body. If you are good and learn well then you will be rewarded.' She touched one of the tubes and a warm feeling spread through Carria from her pussy. 'But if you are bad . . .' She pressed another and a sharp pain went through her, causing her to shake and whimper.

'I have other ways of teaching your body. Your body is now, literally, my plaything. I touch this and you may pee; if I do not you must wait – and that is the first thing to learn, that your functions are not yours anymore, they are the school's.

'Even your right to breathe, and what you smell are mine. Time is mine, and only if I am sure that you can take your place with the rest of the class shall I release you. Now we don't want you being distracted by any noise or light, do we?'

Content with her body, the nurse turned her attention to Carria's head. The bit was removed, but instantly a ball gag was forced into her mouth, but this had a hole drilled through it, from which the back of Carria's tongue was touched by a well oiled tube. She stopped breathing through it, but darkness followed, as a hood was placed on her, and she knew her face was encased in thick rubber. No eyeholes, just the faintest of light from holes below her for her nostrils, then that too went as tubes were screwed up her nose, and she had to smell the chemical odour of rubber.

There was no light, no sound except for her own fearful gulps for air, and no sensations of any kind. A whirr, and Carria felt the air being sucked from her sheath, pulling it even tighter over her. Carria wondered what was going on outside. Was the nurse still there? She panicked. Had she been left? For how long? What was to happen to her. She tried to keep calm. After all, there was nothing to be done, so she settled down to wait, to try and forget, but the strong bonds constantly reminded her of where she was, and the rubberised scent kept bringing her back to her predicament.

Hours must have passed, she really didn't know. Maybe they had forgotten her, or the nurse had been called away. The panic gripped her and this time there was no way to lay it to rest. Carria started to struggle, rocking the hammock from side to side, but getting no nearer freedom. A pain throbbed up from her pussy, making her stop. This was her punishment for moving.

There was nothing to do but feel the pressure on every part of her body, endure the total imprisonment and her weakness. Letting go and relaxing she was aware that she was unconsciously starting to wet herself, but something prevented her expelling anything from her body, then a sharp pain like the one she had felt for moving shot up her, and as she gasped for air her gag hole closed, leaving her to breathe from her nose only. Then the reason for this was apparent: a joltingly sharp and acrid smell was pumped into her air supply and her body tensed with disgust. Just as she felt she would faint between the smell, the pain and the tight constrictions on her it stopped. A long period of nothingness started, during which she had much time to contemplate her situation. Don't move, don't pee: endure.

There was a hiss. She couldn't breathe through her nose. She automatically tried to breathe through her gag, but instead a distasteful fluid filled her mouth. Trying to breathe through her nostrils she met resistance. Swallowing, she discovered that once the foul liquid was gone she could get a breath, then the fluid returned, then air. The nurse, or her machine, was forcing her to drink!

Eventually the tube was clear again, and she could breathe freely, but there was something about the bitter fluid: it seemed to pass through her, and she needed to pee. Cowed by the last time, Carria decided to lie still for however much longer she could. Trapped and restless, the hours passed slowly with agonising cramps in her insides as she fought to hold herself. She attempted to slightly shift her position, careful not no trigger any more painful retribution, but each movement just made the straps sink into her and she lay still again. Did she sleep? She couldn't be sure, waking and sleeping seemed the same in this prison, but she knew she was awake as an urgent pressure built in her, and now she needed to pee again. Remembering how she had been punished, she waited until she really could hold on no more and she could feel the warm water seep around the tubes in her. But there was no reprimand this time, only a gentle sucking from the tube, carrying her waste away and leaving her with the feeling of a thousand soft kisses on her wet pussy. Carria relaxed, and a gentle soft pleasure was released over her from inside her cunt as the large plug started to throb and squeeze against the inside of her. A reward for waiting.

Time passed, another forced drink, and this time she took the fluid without resistance, getting used to the way the tubes worked, and submitting to their regime, happy too in having something to break the long silence after such a long wait. She tried to urinate again, but this time she found that she could not, and a deep shock was sent up her. Confused and hurt – yes, hurt by the unfairness – she tried to think about why this had happened. She waited until she could not hold it any longer and she was allowed to relieve herself. The difference was time. She now knew she had to wait until a set time after her drink. Carria counted to ten thousand before she next dared to try, but this was fine, and she received the pleasurable sensation for her vigil.

She realised that the drinking times were becoming more infrequent but that she was being given more to drink each time, making her work harder to control herself. However, she remained determined not to try any other pattern and wait until she was sure she would not be punished before relieving herself. How many times it happened, she lost count but, as the nurse had predicted, she really had learnt to control herself.

Waiting for the next drink seemed much longer, and she was feeling a growing effort to hold on to herself as she found her mask being taken off. The nurse looked down at her patient and smiled.

'You have been a good girl, and I think I will pass you for the next class. Now I'm going to release your gag so you can thank me.' And she bent down and slowly took the ball from Carria's mouth, and planted a kiss on Carria's lips, and at the same time flicked a switch which made Carria pee with all her might down the tube, giving her a feeling of warm gratification. Carria felt an overwheling gratitude and kissed the nurse back, pushing her tongue deep, and surrendered herself.

'You see,' the nurse noted. 'The school really does control you and your feelings. Remember that, for always.'

Carria used all her energy keeping her walk elegant as she made her way back to the dormitory, the silent maid by her side. Her pussy stung, and it was difficult to walk with her legs together, but she knew that a thrill had run through her; something she had not thought posssible. She was happy that she had been punished, she accepted the pain and loved – no, needed – the pleasure she had been given while helpless. This was not what she had expected when she had embarked on this journey, but it was a bonus and a smile formed at the edges of her bit.

She returned to find the other girls sleeping, and she made for the bed exhausted, in part from her ordeals, but also from the excitement she had experienced, for in the night she couldn't help but reflect on the pleasure of being helpless and controlled by someone or something she could not see or hear. During the night, when she was sure the other girls were in a deep sleep, she pressed herself deep into the bed so that her chain rubbed over her clitoris in minute waves, one link shifting from side to side.

Morning came too early and Carria rose tired from her night. The other girls gave her questioning looks but, until the evening and the bit gags being removed, there was nothing she could tell, and she wasn't sure how much to tell anyway.

They filed through the corridor that had become familiar during the first month of deportment class, and were led past that classroom, Carria giving it a lingering glance, and deeper into the palace to another room. This was very different. The walls were made of crystal that softly shone light, there were five shiny mats and a woman who stood apart, and nothing else.

'Welcome to the second class,' she intoned in a sing song voice. 'I am Pertruvia, and I am going to teach you about sexual gratification of your body. If you succeed here you will earn the right to learn about more, er, advanced things.'

Pertruvia unwrapped her robe to reveal her body. Except for her wrists chains and collar, she wore no skirt, no panties and no chain.

'You may have noticed that I am free of any of the baggage of the graduates or the students. You, too, will be free here, but I warn you any misconduct will be punished in a most severe way. Now who wants to be first to feel free?'

Zena pushed herself forward and had her pussy chain and boot chains removed and placed to one side, carefully labelled for reuse at the end of the class.

The other followed suit and by end of the morning each girl was lying on a mat, her legs bent before her and her fingers probing each soft area that their instructor told them.

'Only if you can be hungry and happy can you fulfil your purpose of entertaining the Sultan. He is very demanding,' Perturvia reminded them as she walked about them, dismissing clumsy attempts and re-positioning the girls' fingers. 'A girl must know where she feels pleasure, she must know what gives her sexual lust, she must be able to provide herself with satisfaction, before she can hope to provide others.

'Once you leave this grade you will be taught the use of implements of pleasure. You will be expected to give any man or woman the greatest ever experience. This is the purpose of the Companions. Now try again, and Zena –' she turned sharply to the girl '– this is a lesson in knowing your body, not a lesson in trying to achieve orgasm; that must wait, or . . .' She dangled a pussy chain in front of her.

'Patience, my dear, or there are punishments. The whole purpose of this is to make you understand how to give pleasure. You are not here to receive it. Hungry is good, spoilt is bad, and I will tell the headmistress of anyone who fails me.'

Zena gave the new mistress a guilty look, then let her eyes fall to the ground, but Carria was sure that she detected a small but wicked smile on her delicate face.

The new classes allowed Carria to explore her body through touch and smell. She learnt which armours gave out what sexual signals, how to massage and how to please a woman. They played with models of penises that rose as they sucked and licked them and that spurted into their mouths so that they could swallow with grace.

94

Days were spent trying different sized penis shafts and toning their muscles to give as much pleasure as possible. Strange guages measured the girl's efforts with the probes, and the mistress swiftly withdrew the devices the moment any of them appeared to be enjoying the experience too much. As she repeatedly pointed out, it was for them to please, not be pleased.

Carria seemed to be the head of the class, even better than Yvonne who had been through this class before. She wondered if those days she had spent in her room by the harbour had pushed her on to new heights. It was a fact that seemed to register with Ula who now glowered at her, and avoided her in the evenings. Carria was glad of the bit gag. It made sure they couldn't speak during the day.

But each day also brought a growing sense of frustration: all this theory, but no one to actually make love to. Carria realised that she spent more and more of each night thinking about the strange woman who had brought her here and about the time in the Glove. She re-imagined the events, but as she was released, in her dreams she kissed the woman from the brothel. Then sometimes she reversed the scene and had her tied into the device and made her suffer for leaving her. And then she woke to find a wet area in her bed.

She knew the other girls were feeling the same frustrations too – the strange lustful looks and little sighs. Ula's square form was the only one that seemed immune, but Zena's slim frame dreamily wafted about the dormitory and Yvonne, who should have known better, started to sit with her legs crossed, then recross them frequently. Discipline, Carria thought, and in a way she understood the need for her chain. Would it be worth Helena's whips for a moment of climax? She wondered.

Zena hid it well, but as she bent over to get into her bunk Carria saw clearly that somehow Zena's pussy chain was loose. The teacher or the maid must have locked it wrongly. Carria lay awake that night thinking of her woman when the unmistakeable noises of ecstasy came from Zena's bed. By the half light she raised her head and saw Zena rubbing her exposed cunt against the corner of the bed, while she held her left breast in her right hand, pawing and grasping it.

The doors swung open and two guards pulled Zena down as she fought with a wild passion to press herself once more on the bed edge. How could they know? Carria looked up and knew, the mirrors in ceiling, they showed everything to the guards, they must be above and looking down at them at all times. Carrria suddenly released that she had had no privacy at all, her most intimate moments had been observed.

Zena was now screaming and the other girls woke. The guards quickly covered her mouth and inserted her gag then, roughly securing her chains and pulling the pussy chain up as tight as they could, frog-marched her from the room. Carria did not see her again for a day, during which time they were told to rest. The following day they were all called to the podium room to watch Zena get her instruction on how to 'behave' as Helena put it.

The pale figure of Zena leant her back against the whipping frame, her legs spread wide apart and tied to a steel rod, her hands bound to her sides. Helena stood in front of them and beckoned them to be seated. Addressing them, she outlined again that discipline was the foundation of the school, and that a person could fall from grace, but redemption could be earned through pain, and that the punishment must always fit the crime.

Helena took a pair of long gloves and stretched them over her strong hands, then gently started to stroke Zena's labia. When it was engorged with blood and swollen, she casually opened a small black bag. Zena must have seen it before the others, because her face dropped, and a pleading voice came from her. This time, Carria realised, she had not been gagged so that the class could hear her pain.

Helena presented a set of large silver clamps, each attached to long silken ropes. With the delicacy of a watchmaker she pulled at Zena's folds of skin before settling on exactly the right spot to release her tool, and suddenly the room was filled with a sobbing. Helena, though, was not being sidetracked, and clamped her on the other lip. Tugging the ropes to be sure that they were attached securely she passed the ropes under the steel rod, and then pressed her foot down onto the floor. There was a whirring as the rod began to rise. Zena was now screaming, unsure what was happening, her pain nothing to the fear of what might happen.

Helena's muscular body held Zena's weight as her feet rose, then her legs followed, and finally Helena let go as the girl dangled by her feet inches above the ground, the ends of her long blonde hair lying unkempt below her.

Helena slowly started to pull the silken ropes down, causing Zena's labia to stretch upward, then she carefully clipped two spheres to the ends of the ropes. Then Helena produced a small silver funnel and inserted it into Zena's gaping hole. She placed a third, larger sphere in the funnel and stepped back to explain to the now terrified Zena, and her audience, the fittingness of the punishment.

'As you know, and some of you have experienced –' Helena shot Carria a very dark look '– the school motto is Freedom through discipline. Yes, that word discipline again, something that this class has yet to comprehend. So your unfortunate colleague there will be used to demonstrate why you must endure for the good of the future.

'She has a choice. The spheres will slowly drain, lightening the pain to her cunt – the author of her downfall – which she might endure. But the cunt has been so bad that it deserves a little punishment of its own, and as the load lightens more fluid will fill her cunt, and in that sphere there is liquid that will sting with a vengeance, quite apt. Now the decision: should she wait until the weights have gone and endure the stinging, or should she yell for mercy? Ah, but if she yells, each graduation on the spheres will be a dozen strokes with the whip. Logically she should endure, and maintain her discipline in which case she has learned. But if she is weak she will learn she should have been stronger when the whips strike her.'

Helena brushed her skirts under her and seated herself next to Carria as Zena jerked with the pain that Carria could only imagine. With aching slowness the spheres emptied and her swollen lips regained their shape, but her face twisted in agony as the other fluid stung her in the sensitive place. The fluid gurgled down, occasionally popping up from the funnel as air was expelled from inside Zena.

But she held on, and when the maid had washed her down and refitted her pussy chain and Helena had ceremoniously removed two links from her wrist chains, she motioned her to sit with the others, which she did, taking great care of how she sat down and allowing herself a gulp as her weight was transferred to the bench.

Helena made sure she had the attention of them all, then made her speech: 'Perturvia has told me that you have done well in the last two months, and that you are ready to move onto the next class. So tomorrow you will start the use of the Sultan's pleasure machines, then you will have earned your modesty.'

8

An End and a Beginning

Helena herself instructed them in the use of the Sultan's machines of pleasure. They were led to the furthest room along the right hand corridor so far, so a long walk from their beds, and sloping down into the depths of the palace. It was in an oak-panelled room that was filled with strange looking apparatus, the walls hanging with all sorts of straps, chains and spheres. The room smelt of oil and leather and, one by one, the basic tools of their trade were explained to them.

There were lessons on fitting women with the metal device that Carria guiltily recognised as having already used, and the best way to climax a lady after she had worn it. There controls to learn on the long, fluted, flower-shaped objects that held a man's erection and sent shivers down him as it brought him to the highest level of orgasm.

There were dull lectures on the cleaning of mechanical sex dolls, and lessons on attaching harnesses with metal ridged phalluses to each other, which caused them to laugh until a very unamused Helena told them off. In the evening, Yvonne told them of the how in the second grade these harnesses that faced both ways, amongst giggles from Zena and a frown from Ula.

They were taught the differences in penetrating another woman or a man, and how to tie ropes that caused pleasure, and those that caused pain for men and women.

At the end of each day they returned tired to the dormitory. Carria found that she was beginning to form a friendship with Zena and Yvonne, but Ula always kept her distance from them. She seemed aloft from the goings on, and reserved a special look of distaste for Carria.

Still, Helena seemed pleased with their progress, and even started praising Carria, never making any reference to her previous embarrassment. Time slipped, and suddenly the girls found themselves on the final day of the course, and assembled again in the podium room, kneeling before the frame.

Helena appeared with a pile of large blue boxes in her arms, and two of the black-and-purple plumed guards behind her. In the corner the nurse stood to attention, and the seriousness of the day dawned on the girls.

Helena displayed the name on each box to the girl it was named after, then placed them in front of the girl. Opening them one by one she held up the light blue harness, panties and short pleated skirts of the second grade. Then they were repacked and stacked with ceremony in a small room off to the left of the podium room; a place where the girls had never been led before.

'The left is for the second grade. You are nearly there. Once you finish this class you may change a cross to the next level, actually under the Companions' chambers, in the inner sanctum of the palace. You will not be full Companions, but you will help them. You will be allowed solo pleasure and you will be allowed to put your theory to use. However, I remind you, any sexual intercourse with another person and you will be thrown back to start the training, after a most severe punishment. If you have the urge you must inform me or a class mistress who will grant you time in a playroom or your room.' Helena grinned. 'But first there is a final test. You have received pain here when you first joined, but now you must learn to give it too, from the gentle brush of the whip that makes the nerves receptive to the harsher taste of the whip that you may be asked to give clients with special requirements. For as you have learned pleasure and pain are not opposites, but one in the same here.'

Helena motioned to the guards. 'Take Zena – she hasn't been a good girl – and tie her to the frame.'

Zena approached, a mixture of fierce pride that she was to pass the first grade and resignation to the pain on her lightly coloured face. With no prompting, she held her hands ready to be unchained, and lifted them into position on the frame, now raised and standing like a cage on the podium.

The guards strapped her tight and Zena automatically placed her heels as far apart as their chain allowed. Helena motioned to Carria and she rose, taking a set of thin leather straps bound to a handle from Helena. She was told to give six strokes: two from the left, two from the right, across Zena's buttocks, then two strong upswings to catch her cunt.

Carrai started the first swing softly, but Helena told her to start again, this time with force, and she responded. By the third stroke she was accurate and, although Zena kept her mouth shut, Carria could tell that she was hurting. Carria began to enjoy it. She swung again with a vicious energy and then put as much force as she could with the limited swing her arm shortened chains allowed in punishing Zena.

Then it was over, but Carria remained full of energy, and she felt powerful.

The other girls were paired, and Yvonne even squealed in delight as she made a final thrust to Ula. Zena was studied but very precise as she whipped Yvonne, then Carria was called. She felt the cold metal of the frame, then a stinging that took her by surprise. She cried out. There was no leniency from Ula who now struck again with a force that made her first whipping seem like playing. Ula, who had not lost a single link on her arm chains, was using the extra reach to power the strokes across her arse so strongly that some of the strands strayed into Carria's pussy. Carria knew that this was a personal matter, but she was determined not to give Ula the satisfaction of seeing her cry. She swallowed hard and gritted her teeth as the last two strokes jerked up on her, as if they were going to split her in two.

When they released her, Carria turned about to see Ula covered in the sweat of hard labour, but her green eyes grimly smiling as her long blonde hair fell back over her wet shoulders.

'Good girls,' Helena noted, as she approached Carria and unlocked her chains and gag. 'Now, Carria, you first. Go to the changing room and put on your skirt.'

Carria found the nurse waiting for her, who gently extracted her pussy chain and unbuckled the corset and collar, then beckoned her to shower. Naked, Carria noticed for the first time that her body was changing. The tight corset was making her waist thinner, and she found it hard to walk barefoot, without her heels, so it came as a relief to find the nurse unpacking her new uniform.

The wrist bands and the boots were similar, but in light blue leather and without any chain, but the belt was replaced by an even tighter corset, laced at the back and shaped to cup the bottom of her breasts and raise them. The nurse fussed with the lacings, pulling them tight, then starting again from the bottom, as if playing a musical instrument, and only stopping when Carria was unable to take anything more than shallow gulps for air. Assured that she would get used to it, Carria wondered how they could have made this much smaller costume for her. It confused her for she had only just discovered that her body had changed, so they must have expected that, she thought.

The collar was now a separate item, high on her slender neck with three gold hoops around it. There were, to her joy, no nipple rings, and the sensation of the blood returning to her made her sigh. Her arm chains were of gold too, but one single chain secured both arms through a hoop in her collar, allowing her to extend one arm as long as the other was pulled up to her neck.

A then she was fitted with a pair of light-blue panties with a high waist, which hugged her skin and squeezed every part of her. Made of thin rubber, they showed every line and valley of her intimate self, until they tapered to a narrow band at the back which pressed into her crack. The nurse had to roll them onto Carraia and, with a tug, she fastened them to the inside of the corset with a metallic snap. It was only then that Carria looked down to notice that the front of her corset contained a small brass plate with a strange, but unmistakable, keyhole.

'Same job as the chain,' the nurse commented. 'But more comfortable, more modest, and more becoming of a lady. Chains are for animals to stop them, panties are for ladies to keep them from dirtying the silk sheets you have earned.'

Carria murmured a 'thank you' but the nurse was already slipping her skirt around her, telling Carria about how to work its tiny catches, and checking that it rode exactly the right height, so that it hung level with the bottom of her panties.

Dressed, Carria held her mouth open ready for the gag, but the nurse just shook her head. 'Not now. You have made the first grade. You are halfway to being a Companion and, as long as you remember to speak only when spoken to, there be no need of a gag.'

Carria closed her mouth and checked her clothes and, finding herself very pleased with the new and shiny uniform, marched through the door to the right, and into a whole new world.

9

Temptation

One by one, the others joined her in the antechamber. Carria could not believe how they had changed. From a group of diverse women, they now all carried themselves with regal bearing. The skirts registered identical little flicks as each walked and they all now had the wasp waist that was the preserve of the palace. They were, she thought with pride, no longer girls: they had become ladies.

Carria mulled over the transformation. This was, she must remind herself, only a way to get close to the Sultan as she had vowed, but she could not but help feel pride in herself, and feel it was a pity the woman from the inn could not be there to see her. This had been easier physically than emotionally. She had not prepared for the emotional dangers, she had not been ready for the thrill of sexual fulfilment. She realised that she must concentrate.

A door creaked its way open, and a gaunt woman in full Companion's uniform, like Helena's but dark red, stood in the doorway. Her gaze moved over them one at a time, measuring them. Then she turned and walked back out.

'Passport control,' Yvonne whispered.

'What's that?' Zena asked.

'I don't know, I never got this far,' Yvonne admitted.

'Carria,' a voice called from the other room, and Carria walked through.

She was in a huge cavern, with a lake that seemed to go on forever, stretching out to infinity. Stalactites dropped down from the high ceiling, some right down to water, while others dripped with a sorrowful echo and caused ripples to speed across the surface of the water until they were out of sight. The clammy air held an icy edge, and only a radiation of heat from a fire kept Carria from shivering.

She found herself on a wooden quay that reached out into the lake, but it was not the cavern, the quay or the lake that held her, but the boat. A low carved boat of crystal that seemed to float on the water and, at its helm, in defiance of the magical scene, an old and wizened man dressed in filthy rags, who leaned on a stick and gazed with unreserved lust at her body.

There was a cough, and Carria turned to see the red woman sat behind a high desk, a brazier heating the scene to one side with all its might, throwing occasional sparks into the air.

The woman asked if she wanted admittance to the palace sanctum, and Carria nodded. The woman informed her that she needed her passport stamped. Bewildered, Carria agreed, and nodded again.

The woman instructed her to lie over the desk, and stood up. She told Carria to grasp the legs with all her might. Carria did as she was told, then felt her skirt being flipped up and her panties being smoothed into her crack. Then the instruction to hold tight and not move at all, whatever happened, because it would only be more painful.

Carria felt nothing for a while, and she wondered if she was alone and this was a joke to humiliate her. Then her nostrils were filled with the stink of burning flesh. Where was it from? Then the pain came and she knew it was her. She fought the urge to get up and run, repeating the words of the woman over and over as if it would make the pain go away.

Nails dug into the desk legs, teeth clamped together, she held on and rode the pain. Something cool eased the pain and, prising herself up, she made her way as directed to the boat, as Zena's name was called behind, echoing in the enormous cavern.

'Arse hurt, does it? Well, more than that'll get sore.' The man chortled, until it turned to a thick cough. Carria said nothing, but drew her legs together defensively and kept her eyes on the lake. 'I like a good stamping do I, always turn up for it. Sometimes I think it was worth sacrificing my balls to be here just to see you pretty fine girls get burned. It'd you secret now see, what you think they gave you the skirt for eh? Only Companions get that mark, and it's only you and me that'll see it. I'm probably the only man other than the Sultan and his high and mighty guests what gets to see your pretty branded arses.'

'That's enough, Retainer,' Helena's voice came clear and loud from the dock. 'Keep your eyes to yourself and off my girls. And make sure you get us over the Alpha without sinking.'

'Go fuck a guard,' the man growled under his breath.

The girls sat, two on each side of the crystal boat. The Retainer stood in the bow, chuckling to himself and staring out over the lake, giving the girls lecherous glance from time to time, or passing a dirty look back to Helena, who sat in the stern, calling out time to the girls as they each handled glass oars and rowed the boat steadily across the lake. Carria sat taking in the natural wonders of this subterranean kingdom, trying to avoid the dull pain from her seat, and turning over the fact that whoever she had met at the inn has passed through here before her, and must have been a Companion.

Every once in a while the Retainer would consult a strange brass circle with routes like maps on moving wheels, and then shout new directions to Helena, who relayed them by shouting for the port or starboard oars to stop until a new direction was gained. Flying fish skimmed the surface, and darker bigger creatures poked hideous heads above the waterline to try and catch them.

They slowed and gradually the boat drifted into another dock, a mirror of the previous one, where the boat was tied up. After they disembarked another red dressed woman lined them up, told them to touch their toes and pulled up their skirts to check the whip mark, then, content opened a gate to allow them through into what she called the 'Junior Companions' chambers.

Helena led them off to a small circular hall, around which four doors were arranged. In the middle a fountain gushed scented water and lilies floated at its base. Helena pointed to a dining hall along the corridor where food would be prepared by the automated chefs as they required. For each girl she allocated a room, with its own shower and toilet that allowed the girls to call for their new maid to help them in private. Zena gave a smile, and was faster than the other girls to realise the significance of this arrangement, and it didn't take long for her to petition Helena and ask if she could use the services of the maid that evening. Carria was glad the doors to the rooms looked thick and well soundproofed.

Tomorrow, Carria reminded herself, they would use the real toys of the palace: they would be allowed to pleasure the Sultan's guests, or at least assist real Companions in doing so. Excited, she spent as little time as she could in preparing for bed, and called the maid who obediently helped change her and only locked her wrist bands together for the night, slipped a loose but short powder-blue nightdress on her and expertly locked pair of panties in place, this time to a wide metal belt, which was locked too.

Carria wondered if she could now touch herself a little, through the tight rubber of the panties, and give herself some relief but, once her room door was closed and locked, she tried every position to thwart her constriction, with no result. The chains held her agonisingly just too far. Exhausted, she quickly slipped into a long deep sleep on the blue silk sheets and dreamed of allowing herself fulfilment the next day.

The light was still dim, the steel cock that called the morning – was it really morning? She had lost all sense of day or night underground – had not crowed. Yet she was awake, and there was someone in her room, she could sense it. She'd been lying on her front, and she turned her head to glance backward with a quick movement. Struggling to find wakefulness, she tried to make out the outline. It must be the maid – how had she found out about her attempts last night to play with herself? What would the punishment be? Guilt rushed over her. Maybe she had been bad, she should be punished, a sound whipping on her pussy would be required, or even what Zena had gone through.

Thoughts tumbled through her as her eyes gradually accustomed themselves to the half light, then a doubt. The still outline didn't look like the maid. It was too tall and the clothes weren't like the maid's uniform. Helena? No, the figure wasn't built as strongly. Carria puzzled as the figure stood by the door, clearly studying Carria's prone form.

Caria's heart beat fast, but her mind was sharpening. The figure approached, and Carria studied it carefully. Short dark skirt, tall elegant heels, wrist chains and collar, so it was a Companion, but there were other things, a mane of red hair and the collar and corset sparkled with points of light. The figure neared and her face came into the shaft of red light that shone from the night lantern.

'It's you!' Carria shouted in disbelief as her lover from the inn strode forward.

'Yes, I wanted to see you. I've been thinking about you a lot, and when I heard you had made it to second grade I couldn't resist seeing you. I knew you'd make it though, I'm very proud, and only one little slip,' J'nie smiled indulgently. 'The Glove can be quite an experience, for pleasure or pain.'

J'nie folded her skirt under her with one hand and sat at the edge of the bed. She spent some time just gazing down in the low red light then, extending one arm and pulling the chain tight, causing her other hand to be drawn to her collar, she leaned over and kissed Carria on the cheek.

'You really have grown. You aren't the curious and eager girl who came from nowhere, are you? And I would think that you might be getting very hungry by now,' J'nie whispered as she began to draw her fingers across Carria's shoulders.

'Who are you?' Carria rolled over and throw the sheets aside with her two chained hands.

'Me? I'm our secret. I'm something that you can never tell, for both our sakes. If you feel for me as I feel for you; if you need my body as much as my body needs you, I will care for you and love you in ways that you have not even started to experience, but –' she paused to press her long fingers to her mouth '– you will never tell a living soul. These walls contain

111

devices that make the Glove seem trivial, and Helena is an expert in using them to maximum efficiency.'

And with she passed her finger from her mouth to Carria's then traced it over the lean shoulders, then down her breasts in a slow, meandering way, down her lithe body, and then over her hips, until at last she came to the top of Carria's thigh. Pausing to fondle the hem of the garment, she swiftly threw the dress up.

'It's locked,' Carria protested, with equal measures of fear and anguished frustration. But there was a grin and before her there was a tiny round key of gold. She was motioned to turn over, and she could detect the key slipping into place, a well oiled sliding of minute metal bar, and then a release as the metal sprang apart. Instantly she leaped from the bed, allowing the belt to fall and clang to the floor, then her wrists were freed and she rolled the tight panties down in one motion, stepping out them. The dress slid off her, and she stood there, naked except for her collar, and free for the first time in nearly half a year.

'This is my second present to you,' J'nie said, as she unlocked her own clothes. 'But now I think for giving you such delights I am owed a present in return.'

J'nie fell back on the bed, her long legs spread wide, showing her swelled orifice clearly in the red light. Carria needed no further prompting and, getting up onto the bed on all fours, gazed for a second, before dipping her head down and starting to work the soft flesh with regular thrusts from her tongue.

Carria tasted a strange scent, like strawberries, and pushed deeper into her. She knew no constraint. Months of lectures and diagrams, of animated dolls and models, but now, for the first time, she could put it to use. The eager student becoming the teacher, teasing and coaxing, bringing her partner near to the abyss, but then pulling her back to safer ground, only to rise again and let her topple on the brink, where only a slight pressure would cause her to plunge recklessly down.

With a stifled cry J'nie climaxed. Too long, she thought, too long since I had this passion. From this girl, from the Sultan, from anyone. She felt a need to return the gift, and threw Carria down on to the sheets, then started to lick her clean, unscented pussy with vigour, devouring its taste, sucking its plentiful juices and massaging every part of it with her lips.

They lay awake, Carria idly tracing the brand on J'nie's cheek, and contemplating whether this was another test. If it was she had failed, but regretted nothing. J'nie looking peaceful, as if the world could collapse and she wouldn't care. Then a wicked glint entered her eyes.

'Do you think I ought to punish you? I really think I should,' J'nie proclaimed as she recovered from another surge of satisfaction. 'You shouldn't be doing this, and that's very naughty.'

Carria responded automatically, knowing that she really shouldn't have done this, she wasn't allowed, and that she needed to be corrected. But this woman's punishment was pleasure to her. It would make her feel worse, dirtier, and now she felt like she had betrayed her uniform. No, she must be probably punished for this, for the guilty secret she had.

'Yes, I must be punished, but later, mistress.' Carria noticed that at the last word the woman straightened herself and gave Carria a very strange look.

Suddenly the steel cock crowed, and they both jumped. The night has sped past them and the others would be rising soon. Carria helped the woman back into her costume, clicking the locks back into place and noticing now that the sparkles of light she had noticed the previous night were diamonds. But there was no point in thinking about that, and knowing that they had precious time before the cock crowed again, the woman kissed Carria once more before making for the doorway.

Carria suddenly noticed that the woman had left her golden key and, throwing on her dress, she ran after her, catching her by the fountain, now showering the room with the scent of jasmin.

'Your key, you forgot, now I have to go, my panties, my wrists! I need to lock them,' Carria begged.

'Thank you.' J'nie took the key in her hand and kissed Carria quickly, then ran away, her heels making delicate ticking noises around the hall as the steel cock popped up from its column, its breast inflating with a hiss, then the deafening crow.

Carria swung back, but something caught her eye. Standing in the doorway of the dining area was Ula.

'When I was a younger woman, I worked in the diamond mines. They always rise early there, or your nipples get diamond weights on them. It's sort of become a force of habit,' Ula rasped as she moved forward to the fountain.

'I wonder what our spoilt little Far Islander has been up to? No wrist chains and –' Ula grabbed the edge of the dress and flipped it up exposing Carria's naked cunt '– no panties. Tut, tut, what would Helena say? If it was the maid, well, she might just keep quiet if you are good to her, but me? I'm not so sure I can keep quiet about you spending the night with a Companion.

'You are a disgrace to this school,' Ula hissed, and Carria felt that it was true. She really had been bad, but Ula hadn't finished yet. 'The only reason I won't tell the headmistress right away is that, unlike you, I have pride in my uniform and I wouldn't see some greedy little slut like you fuck it up. I'm warning you, Far Island girl, if you do one more thing I swear I'll see you back on the first grade whipping frame, and this time I'm going to personally get to whip you so hard you'll never want to sit down on your disgusting little arse ever again.'

Carria stood stunned for a while, then ran back to her room, making sure she snapped every item of her night costume tightly shut.

Emotionally, Carria felt torn. The school that she had come to love, although she had never wanted to, the woman who wouldn't tell her her name, the mission, that waited like a thief to slip into the light when the time was right. And then there was guilt, guilt about her night of illegal passion, guilt about getting caught by Ula, guilt that she had let her focus on the mission go.

Carria decided that she needed to be punished. It was the only way to put things right, but there was no way she could tell Helena about what had gone on, and no possible way to get punished without Ula telling on her. It was the third day of training that provided her with an answer.

The girls had each been assigned a full Companion to assist, and Carria had been assigned to Meve, a friendly dark skinned girl from the far side of Estra who had a speciality in serving the Sultan's guests who had particular tastes.

The shuffling and coughing Retainer had collected them from the school and taken them through a dark winding passage, and then up a long spiral of stairs to an old metal door that seemed to know they were coming and slid open without a human hand. Then on, through metal boxes of tunnels, and finally to the creaking and complaining mechanical corridors that shifted as they walked and made the girls wobble on their heels as the Retainer laughed and called them 'my pretties'. As the old man stared at their legs and arses, Meve attempted to explain the way the rooms worked, starting at the first level for visitors and going up to the Sultan's own rooms for the most perverse experiences.

After much grunting from the Retainer as he consulted his mechanical brass map, checking the alignment of the wheels and letting it click and settle before following a route with his fingers and pointing them forward, the girls eventually stepped off into their allocated chamber to prepare for their guest.

'He's a special guest of the Sultan, a trader from the East. They say he commands a harem of a hundred girls in his land, but quantity is no subsitute for quality. So he comes, stays in one of the other houses for the less important guests, and the Sultan has prepared some extra delights for him to seal a trade deal. He doesn't know it but his drink has a small dose of sleeping draft in it. About now he's fast asleep and being bought here, where we shall entertain him.

'For this –' Meve laughed '– the Sultan's Mistress, J'nie, has made me ready.' And Meve removed her skirt and showed Carria that she was naked from her corset down.

They worked on the machines, checking the long pendulum and ropes of one, the connections to another, the gas and water pressures, the steam lines and oiling every joint to be sure that no power was lost with unwanted friction.

As they finished a knock came on the door and the Retainer waved in the nurse who pushed a trolley. On this there was a clean-shaven young man, clearly from the eastern lands, and he was in a deep sleep.

'He's out all right,' the nurse explained. 'If you aren't ready there's more sleeping potion here.' She pointed to a large glass vial held by a metal hoop which contained a bright green powder. 'Just mix it with this fluid –' she took another vial and held it up to them – 'and pour a little in his mouth. No more than a measure mind, three can be fatal.' And with a little goodbye, she followed the Retainer out.

Meve and Carria set to work. First taking the sleeping form and washing him, then gently raising him into the padded ropes that formed a giant swing. Meve checked that the angles were right, checked the steam gauges for the powerful mechanism that drove the cams, then made a final check that the machine swung level with just the right distances.

Then she set up a high beam, supported on four tall wooden legs and directed Carria to tie her to the beam. Carria dutifully made sure that Meve was positioned correctly, then tightened the old and worn straps over Meve's legs, arms, neck and waist, pulling on them until Meve gave her permission to stop.

Carria walked around so that she could see Meve's brown eyes look up at her, and asked if she had done well.

'Yes, you have aided as you should.' She paused then chuckled. 'I've always liked this room. I love the feeling of captivity, knowing you can't escape the pleasure, denied the chance to feel guilty about being fucked and doing nothing. Ah, but you know that feeling too, don't you? Now remember this is a surprise for him, so use the full ball gag so I can't make a noise and make him worry how I am. Make sure you use the oils, then wake him gently as you have been trained and, as he gets hard, help him enter, then walk away until he has emptied himself into me. Then you help him to the rest place, before you untie me.'

Carria did as she was told. She selected the large red ball gag and placed it with care into Meve's open mouth, working around to the strap with her wrist chains tensed by the effort. This was a new idea to Carria. She had been tied up before, and enjoyed it, but now her superior was asking to be tied up, by her! And be gagged. And she wanted to be. She did not regard this as a duty, but a pleasure, and she was doing it to be considerate of the guest. The life of a Companion was more that Carria had ever dreamed.

She took the special oils from the rack and, pouring a good quantity on her hands, she worked the thick, scented fluids all around and into Meve's wide open slit, massaging them until she was sure Meve was sufficiently lubricated for the task and Carria could feel her fingers slip easily into the warm caverns of her prone body.

Then she turned her attention to the slumbering figure, laying very slightly on the harness that held him, and very lightly kissed his penis, pecking the limp form with the most delicate of kisses. Carria realised this was the first time she had ever touched a man's penis, and the warm sleeping thing she looked at was nothing like the tall erect models that she had trained on.

But while its owner continued to slumber, his sleeping manhood was beginning to awake. Carria found that before her eyes the form was growing, and hardening. Everything she had been taught did not prepare her for the fully erect monster in front of her. She gave a long lick down its veined side, and licked the balls. The sleeping man stirred, and she knew it was time. Cupping her hand she guided the hard fleshy tube into Meve's waiting pussy, until she was sure that it was in correctly, then she pulled the lever to the side and walked quickly away as the steam pressure rose and steam pipes started to play a resonant march.

The machine groaned, then trembled, then started to rock back and forth with decisive movement. Each arc took a slow, leisurely path, then suddenly gave a forceful snap at the end. Carria walked to the farthest corner so as not to divert attention, but watched fascinated as Meve's body began to syncopate, and the sleeping man shook himself awake with a shout of joy, which he repeated as each stroke drove home.

Carria looked on, feeling like she shouldn't watch and glancing away, then being drawn back as she had to see, and knowing that at the moment she wanted to be Meve.

Glancing about she saw a large upright casket with a figure of a woman on it. Intrigued, she distracted herself from the swing and looked at it in detail. Around the painted head the name 'Maiden's Delight' was inscribed. Where the left breast should have been there was a knob with degrees of sensation marked out from 'mild thrill' to 'orgasm' and on to 'pain, second grade punishment'. Beside it the second breast area had an arrow that marked out minutes, from green to red and was marked 'timed lock'.

From the wing there was a long wild animal cry of abandon, and Carria hurried back to the swing. She pulled the lever back and lowered the harness, allowing the man to stand on his shaking feet. Politely he thanked her and promptly fell down in exhaustion. Carria hurried over to Meve and released her. Although her face was dripping with sweat she beamed at Carria.

They called for the Retainer, who came, grumbling, and Meve told Carria to clean the instruments. She'd send the Retainer back for her in an hour sharp, and left Carria helping the man to gain his balance.

Carria got to work. It didn't take long to wipe the mess from the floor and refold the ropes back. Then she wheeled the trolley to the side, checked no one else was in the room or was spying on her, then took one of the empty oil vials and poured as much of the sleeping draft as she could into it. Carefully, she put everything right, then slipped the vial under her breast, where it sat uncomfortably, but secret.

Then she sat down to think. This wasn't how it was meant to be. She was guilty about the previous night, ashamed that Ula had seen her, and now she had stolen. She longed for someone to punish her, but if she did anything her lover would get hurt too. She was sure of that. The woman had seemed very certain that everything they did was a secret. She started to cry. She really wanted to feel pain: not just the gentle beatings, but the same pain as she had experienced when Ula had whipped her cunt.

Without thinking she found herself at the 'Maiden's Delight' and calculating the time she had left. She didn't think. Something else drove her on and, as if she was watching someone else's fingers, the timer switch was set and the knob turned to full. Then she opened the front and, holding it with one hand and hitching her skirt up with the other, she stepped back into the dark casket.

At first nothing, and Carria wondered if the machine was still functioning, then an orange light swept over her, and then the walls seemed to move in on her, soft rubber walls pressing against her, holding her, making sure she couldn't move.

Then she felt them. A thousand needles shooting into her breasts, her buttocks and thighs. Trying to scream, she found a bar roll over her tongue, reducing any attempt of a noise to a low grunt.

Then the needles started to vibrate and grow hot at their tips. Carria so wanted to scream, but she couldn't, and some part of her took satisfaction that this was hurting, that she was finally being punished for her crimes. Her body convulsed, she shook, she even, despite all her training, wet herself. As a white agony engulfed her it stopped. The needles withdrew and the walls relaxed. The door opened, and she shakily walked out, expecting her body to be covered in pinpricks, but to her surprise there was nothing, not a sign of her ordeal.

Carria quickly tidied up, resorting to sitting in a cleaning bucket to wash off her dirty panties, and then wriggling on the rugs to help dry herself. She got up the instant she heard the door creak open, and there was the Retainer, now with a wide toothy smile on his face.

'Ready to go with the Retainer, are we? I'll take great pleasure in escorting you, I will. You are my favourite. You know that? Thought there was something about you from the first. Saw you at the boat, I did, and I says, that girl, she's got class, she'd be good to poke into.'

Carria was too shaken to think. She said it was nice of him to notice, and now she'd better be getting back to her room. But the Retainer hadn't finished.

'Nicest arse I've seen since the Sultan's hussey, but I bet you'd do more than she would for me, eh?'

'No, yes, just let me past, will you? I need to go.' Carria protested, and made for the open door, but when she looked all she could see was a sheer drop.

'Won't get far without a map, will you,' the Retainer sneered as he waved a flimsy peice of paper about. 'Only one what knows the routes. Now follow your superior, my pretty,' he wheezed as he walked out of the door, which to Carria's amazement was now a corridor.

10

Plans

Carria hid the vial in her shower room, taking care to place it amongst the cosmetics and shampoos that the maid never used. The pain of her ordeal was subsiding, and somehow she felt like she had been set free by it. Carria started to think again about the mission, about what she would need, and how to get it, and about the best time to strike. For the first time in a long time she began to regard herself as the royal heir she was, the daughter of a warrior king. A tool with which to avenge him.

The Retainer was a revolting man, dirty and obscene, but he had the map; he was the key to finding her way around the maze of changing routes, and the only way to ever get to the Sultan. So she steeled herself. The Retainer it would have to be. And her lover – the woman with the diamonds? If she made it from the palace, she'd come back for her.

Meve had asked Carria to assist on two more guests. One wanted Meve to fuck him while wearing a mask that allowed Carria to feed him special vapours, and another woman guest wanted to be lightly whipped as Meve licked her from head to toe. As the experienced Meve pointed out, this was all rather beneath her training and station as a Companion.

But after the second guest was escorted out, Carria was again left alone to tidy and wash the room and, as she had planned, the Retainer lurked around, attempting to talk to her when her time had come to be escorted back to her room. But this time she knew what she wanted to say, and was determined.

'Master Retainer, I was wondering if there was something you might do for me?' Carria started off, in a faltering and soft voice. 'My Companion has told me about a room where guests are immersed in a forest of delicate tentacles. She says it is the greatest of pleasures. I know I am not allowed to sample its delights, but I would dearly love to see it.'

'Ah, the Groping Room – a favourite of mine. Particularly fond of seeing the Sultan's lady guests enter it, I am. Even made a little hole so I can see for myself the fun. Yes, I can take you there, indeed.' The Retainer inspected Carria's body with lingering looks, moving his rheumy eyes from the top of her short red hair, over her pert breasts, down to her pointed boots and back up with a greedy expression. 'Yes indeed, but what can my pretty do for me in return? Would you come and play with me?'

Carria was ready for this, and nodded, not too eagerly, in part because too much haste might seem suspicious, and in part because the filthy specimen before her genuinely revolted her, and she mentally prepared herself for what might happen.

'Tonight then, there's a groping being prepared. Tell the maid you need to see me to tidy a room for tomorrow. I'll meet you at the stairwell at fifteen crows of the cock. Then we will see about payment.' The Retainer breathed heavily and left with an unsightly spring to his step.

Carria did as instructed. She waited in her room until the steel cock crowed fourteen, then rang for the maid, explained to the maid that she had to go, who seemed unconcerned, and, making sure that her uniform was all correct, Carria walked through the long passage to the stairs. With effort – the stairs did not make for easy climbing in her heels and the effort made her hot – she made it to the top, just as the cock crowed fifteen in the distance.

The cold air and her exertion made her shiver. Somehow see suddenly realised how little she was wearing, and felt naked and vunerable, but the thoughts she had could not last for long as the metal door slid open again and on the other side the Retainer stood, his few strands of hair swept over his head and a clean set of robes on him that somehow managed only to highlight his sickly flesh.

'My dear, how good of you to come. Now lead on,' he wheezed, and they made progress through the clanking and moving corridors, as occasionally Carria was directed left or right with a pinch on her behind.

The room was very dark, and the only light came from the open doorway, but it was enough to show the forms of the Groping Room: the twisting rubber walls, floors and ceilings covered with the limp forms of highly polished rubber tentacles of every size and shape. Some were plain, some ribbed, each with different endings of soft spikes, bubbles or suckers. Carria went in and touched one. It moved towards her automatically with a snaking motion and she stepped back with an involuntary shriek.

'Hah hah, ah my pretty one, they want to grope you. But such things are for you, you are to serve first, enjoy only through pleasuring other. This is the special reserve of guests of the Sultan, and very special guests too.' He pointed to another door to the left. 'Our guest waits in there for the signal, then enters. We should hurry.

'As a junior you shouldn't be here, but come with me and I'll show you something you'd never see, something of my own.' And he pulled her by her collar through the corridor, then a second later back through the same door.

But it wasn't the same room at all. This one was undecorated, with rusting metal panels. The only furnishing was a stool set by one wall and, on the wall in front of it, a porthole. The Retainer closed the door and it was dark, except for a dim green glow from the porthole. He returned to sit down on the stool and stared intently through the glass. Carria bent down to look too, and to her amazement she could see into the Groping Room. Although everything had a green cast it was clear and sharp, and the Retainer congratulated himself on his inventiveness in installing the window.

'Always pitch black in there. They'll never know this is here. When the guests go in they think they are alone, no one watching, but I see!' He sighed and his face took on a dreamy expression. 'And here comes our guest.'

He lifted Carria's skirt and pulled her down so that she was sitting on his lap. But Carria was already distracted as a female figure was briefly silhouetted in the doorway, then dark until her eyes adjusted to the dim green light.

The woman was noble, that was clear from the way she stood, and even naked the regal bearing was clear to Carria, and she sported the single thin line of pubic hair favoured by the Southerners. But the thing that riveted Carria was that she seemed to shine, until she realised that the woman had been oiled head to foot. She made her way uncertainly to the middle of the room, feeling her way in her darkness until she met an outstretched tentacle and stopped.

Things happened quickly from this moment. There was a rustling, like leaves on an autumn day, and then her body was entwined with tentacles, squeezing her breasts, probing into her mouth, slinking themselves between her toes and pushing themselves between her legs. They gripped her and eased her legs apart, then lifted her from her feet, carrying her and holding her.

The tentacles reached down inside her. Every part of her was explored and covered. She screamed in delight, but the room absorbed all noise, and the tentacles kept moving, finding new areas and new ways to bring the silent cry to the woman's lips. Carria meanwhile became aware of the Retainer's penis becoming stiff under his robes and pressing against the thin rubber of her panties.

Hours passed, and still the tentacles played, until they lifted the exhausted form of the woman back to the door, where she staggered back to the antechamber for what the Retainer noted would be a long rest, before grumbling that he would have to collect her in the middle of the night. Still, he gleefully pointed out, that gave Carria several hours in which to entertain him and, with his erect penis making a bulge in his robes, he led Carria back through the shifting corridors to his own private chambers, where he promised her they would not be disturbed.

Carria scanned the quarters with sharp eyes as the Retainer readied himself. It was better than she could have hoped for: there was a pile of the strange brass maps strewn about. She wouldn't even have to make a copy. As long as she could steal one she was one more giant leap forward. But the Retainer needed to be distracted, and with a shudder of revulsion she noticed he was naked in his full paunchy manhood before her, his small but hard penis sticking up almost vertically.

'Ah, my pretty, what shall I have you do? Little pretty can't be fucked, can she, but there are plenty of things she can do for me.' He approached her and pressed his drooling lips onto hers. Carria held down the nausea she felt, and let him slip his rough tongue deep into her, as his arm moved around her waist, pulling her close and making her sample the sensation of his short thin penis against her abdomen.

The hands moved down, stroking her skirt, and then to the tops of her boots, slowly finding their way up and under her skirt, and massaging her inner thighs. She gasped for air. Even in this dirty little man there was something that was exciting her, and to her horror she found her body responding. Her pulse quickened and there was a hot flush running over her. Her fingers could just reach down to touch the top of this foreskin, which she pushed back, and she imagined that her rubber panties had been soaked with her own hot, messy juice.

It was suffocating, but she didn't want to move, and she got to her knees and started to give him a long suck, but he lifted her to her feet and reached behind him. It took her a while to understand what was happening as he fiddled with belts and buckles, but then he pulled her skirt up and she saw the harness fastened to her and, coming from the front, a thin shaft of ribbed amber.

He oiled it well, and with mounting anticipation Carria grabbed the folds in her skirt, bunching it high on her waist, then as he bent over the table she slid the amber dildo into him, working it slowly at first, then with more vigour until she was pushing with all her might. The Retainer shouted encouragement in an increasingly high-pitched cry until his body went still and Carria felt a wave of relief herself.

127

He managed to bring himself to unbuckle her before making for his washing room. Carria thought fast and, with a fumbling move managed to pick up one of the brass maps, and with extreme difficulty hooked one of its ornate edge swirls over her panty lock, throwing her skirt down over it, where its very edge just made itself visible. She cursed, and with an effort pulled her corset down, which just allowed the edge to disappear.

The Retainer returned, looking much calmer, and selected a map. Carria looked on in fear, but he seemed to see nothing wrong and walked her out, his hand now continually feeling her arse.

She returned to her room and studied the map until she was certain she could use it. It was a very strange thing, a map and a timetable at the same time. A clock ticked very quietly away, moving the brass wheels in the centre so that the routes marked on the other wheels changed minute to minute. Each wheel marked a level, and it was clear that getting from level to level would be difficult. But there at the top was one wheel within a wheel that did not move, and was marked 'Sultan's Chambers'.

Once studied, Carria quickly hid the map. All she had to do now was wait until she was sure she could slip away undetected and she was sure that no one would see. She slept uneasily that night, knowing that she could be discovered, and yet she was so close. Tomorrow, she vowed. Tomorrow would be the day the Far Islands would be avenged.

But it was not to be. Helena called them together to congratulate them on their first two months of second grade; halfway, she reminded them, to being a full dark blue Companion. And to mark the occasion she was pleased to inform them that the Sultan's Mistress, J'nie, herself would address them and present them with new gold edged panties, to signify their success.

Whatever Carria had expected, she was shocked as J'nie entered the compound. It took all her strength to stay still. The tall, fair skinned woman was her woman her lover. And there she was in her diamond studded collar and corset pecking Zena on the cheek and handing her the folded bundles of panties. Carria did her best to stay calm, and took the bundle with a nod, but as J'nie kissed her on the cheek the Sultan's Mistress whispered, 'I miss you,' in her ear.

Carria's mind turned. No wonder she had wanted to keep this secret. It would spell disaster for both of them. She had to keep calm, and somehow she did until Helena instructed them to kneel before the mistress and thank her, then from the corner of her eye she caught a dark look from Ula.

When the ceremony was over Carria tried to avoid the blonde girl, but Ula cornered her at the dining table and whispered to her.

'Now you really are mine. When I graduate you are going to be my slave forever, and don't think your precious mistress will help. She's mine too. One word from me and you are finished,' she said in a low tone. 'But I like you suffering. I can wait. Watching you squirm, it makes me hot.'

Carria said nothing. She knew that she just had to keep Ula happy a little bit longer, and if she had to play along for a few days, well what could do?

That night, the maid came to Carria's door carrying a small bundle and offered it to Carria with a small note. Carria closed the door tight and opened the document. It was in Ula's illiterate scrawl, and a pair of her panties.

'Dirty girls get dirty work. I want these licked clean', the note read, and Carria thought that the next few days might be the longest so far as she gingerly started to lick the rim of the clothing, then forced herself to run over the distinctively smelling lower parts.

The worst thing that could possibly happen, Carria mused, was for Ula and her to have to work together: the exact thing they were instructed to do. Meve had another special guest who wanted to suck, be sucked and be penetrated at the same time – something that required three girls – and, as Zena was helping her mistress and Yvonne was being taught how to use the swing, it fell to them. Neither girl looked happy at the prospect, but there really was no option. However, the bad omens continued to get worse. The client was late, and then even the charms of Meve took time to get him fully erect.

Lying on his side, Meve, who was the only Companion, and thus had an open cunt, held his face firmly between her thighs. Carria attended to his anal needs with a carved amber piece that the guest had brought especially, and Ula took him fully in her mouth.

After much confusion, they finally developed a rhythm that kept their guest well satisfied, and he jerked forward with Carria following as he came. Meve took a sharp intake of breath that resulted not from pleasure but a hard bite to her pussy, and Ula choked, spitting out the white seamen with a retch. The guest went away satisfied, but the pain to her cunt had made Meve no less professional, and she made the girls stand together as she berated Ula for spitting out the guest's juice.

'How long have you been here? You never, never let a guest's fluids spill onto the floor. This isn't a small matter, and I will not let it pass. You will report to the headmistress tomorrow and you will tell her what you did. She will not be pleased. I'd think you'd be lucky to get away with six lashes,' Meve fumed as she paced.

Ula grew red, then shouted, 'It wasn't me, mistress, it was Carria. She pushed him and made me do it. She's evil. She shouldn't be here at all. The other night I saw her . . .'

'Shut up,' Meve snapped as Carria went cold. 'You can tell the headmistress about it tomorrow. I'll collect you myself. Both of you.'

'I will,' Ula vowed in a low whisper that Carria was meant to hear, and could not avoid understanding.

The Retainer collected them, and they walked in front of him in silence, ignoring each other. It seemed like the longest walk ever, and Carria knew that right now she stood on the brink of letting years of work fall into nothingness, and her heart felt constricted and her throat dry.

When they returned to the rooms, Carria told the maid she felt ill and that she would go to bed immediately, waving the offer of changing her. She only asked the maid to leave, locking the door until the cock had crowed for the last time, in case she wanted to get up and go to the dining area. The maid, grateful to have one less toilet to attend to, cheerfully agreed.

Carria lay still on the silk, listening and waiting. There was no time left. She had no doubt that Ula would tell the headmistress everything, and then? She was done for, doubly so if they found the map and poisonous sleeping draft, or if they found out who she really was. What of J'nie? Her embarrassment would be complete, and years in the Sultan's penal colonies, farming rubber plants, extracting the precious substance from the imported plants in their sweltering glasshouses on some remote island didn't seem a fitting end to a woman that she loved, and yes she did love her. She knew that now, the moment she could lose her forever.

She came to a decision. There was only one course of action that she could take, one way to put everything right, and as the cock crowed its penultimate cry of the day, she collected the vial and map and opened the door just enough to see that nobody was in the fountain yard, and ran as quietly as she could down the long dark passage.

11

The Rope Room

Instinct drove her on, through the dark passage and up onto the stairs, where she tripped several times, but made it to the door faster than she had hoped. She checked the brass map in her hands: one unit of time until the first steam corridor would be there. She caught her breath, then stepped forward and the door dutifully slid open. Yes, it was there. The corridor opened up in front of her. She calculated that it would take two units until the third door would be in alignment. She jumped through and made it through to the next wheezing and clanking room.

Consulting the map again she made another change, then she knew she was right, the corridor she was in was dark blue. She timed the next move very carefully, entering a small hall, and narrowly missing getting her arse pinched in the closing door.

Knocking hard, she waited a while then jerked the high handle open and walked in. J'nie was halfway to the door, her sleeping harness on.

'Carria, what in the Sultan's name are you doing here?' J'nie exclaimed. Carria knew she was in for a long explanation.

Carria described what had happened, as J'nie's face became a white mask of horror. Sobbing and damning her own stupidity, Carria took her back to the bed and held her. She cried then, with clarity, she understood that she had to honest. Totally and completely honest.

'That's not everything. Please call me Carria – I love they way you say it – but –' she swallowed '– it is not my real name. I come from the Far Islands, and my name is Carriana Oman.'

J'nie stopped sobbing, and stuttered, 'Oman Khan's daughter? They said you killed yourself when he disappeared.'

'Well I'm here, although my father is dead I am sure. All he ever wanted was for our two kingdoms to live in peace, but his ship sailed for Estra and never returned, killed I'm sure by one of your precious Sultan's warships. The Council was then powerless, they tried to fight, but divided and leaderless they fell. The Sultan was quick to take advantage, ready as he was to invade – convenient that was. My father was a proud warrior and statesman. It would never have happened if he was alive. The Sultan should have shown less mercy to me, too. I will avenge that death.'

'Come with me J'nie. When I return the Islands will be united and independent again and, without the Sultan, this –' she swept her manacled hand around '– will fall. Rule with me, at my side.'

J'nie tried to absorb each shock and think them out clearly, but her mind could not function and she let her emotions decide. Kissing Carria in a long deep kiss, she reached under her skirt and withdrew the golden key, releasing both of them from their bonds and irrevocably changing their future.

J'nie found her old uniform and made Carria change into the dark blue uniform of a full Companion so that she could move about more easily, then she sent a message bird down the coloured pipes, instructing the Retainer to fetch Ula, give her a sealed message, and take her to the fifth level room for a special client. She signed both notes with a passable forgery of Helena's hand.

Ula was just about exhausted. Already washed for bed, she just waited for the maid to lock her door. She had stood in front of her dressing mirror rehearsing her speech to Helena, presenting her evidence with dramatic timing and damning that bitch Carria to a life of maiding, if she was that lucky. As for her friend, the Sultan's Mistress, well if she was out of the way maybe the Sultan would be looking for new mate, someone who knew how to use power.

There was a knock, and the Retainer walked in offering a note. The headmistress wanted to see her now! Away from the other, where they could talk undisturbed, due to the unsettling rumours she had heard. The instructions were clear: follow the Retainer, wait for three units in the room he showed her to then cross the corridor that would be there to the Rope Room, where Helena would greet her.

Ula watched as the note thinned to nothing in her hands the moment she had finished reading, but the Retainer explained that this was normal for a message in the palace, and started to guide her through the passages, her nightdress fluttering in the slightly salted breeze.

She did exactly what she was told, and crossed the corridor that awaited her. Then she stood in the torch lit room, anticipating Helena's arrival. She felt her wrist chains unlock, but then her arms were thrust behind her back and wrapped in something unyielding and cold.

She tried to turn around and shout, but there was something on her head now, and she felt the old sensation of a gag: this time a hard, rough metal circle forced her tongue down and hurt her if she tried even the most pitiful of noises. They strapped it fast, over her head and below the chin so that she smelt its leather, and the collar forced her to keep her head high.

Staggering, she was released and saw J'nie and Carria laughing at her. Then they marched her to an old oak frame and, with her eyes fully open in terror and disbelief, they made her kneel. J'nie fitted the spider web of straps onto the compliant and docile form of Ula.

Pushing her forward, they tied her feet up behind her and secured an oak plank behind her arms and, when sure that everything was tight, fed an old frayed rope around her corset, under her pussy, where J'nie added a couple of knots in particular spots, and back up over the frame to the plank, where it was looped once before being twisted under her pussy again and secured with an elaborate bow.

Ula tried to look down to see the state of her captivity, but the wide strap around her neck prevented her from seeing anything but her breasts, however hard she tried to stare down.

J'nie took more rope and wound it around Ula's shoulders, under her breasts, and in ever smaller figures of eights, until her already large breasts swelled into globes.

Carria leaned down and swiftly pulled her old pale-blue and gold panties over Ula, so that the leg holes allowed her to see and her nose and mouth were buried deep into the gusset.

'Lick these clean,' Carria instructed as she got up. Ula moaned and started to thrash with what little movement she had available to her, whimpering as the ropes dug into her.

'I'd move as little as you can, and don't wear yourself out trying. You are very well bound, and every muscle you flex drives the ropes deeper,' J'nie advised. 'Now goodbye.'

J'nie and Carria walked out, extinguishing the torches in succession, until it was black.

Outside, Carria consulted the map, and its moving dials. The cock on level five crowed fourteen times, and Carria looked up.

'Fourteen. We have ten segments until the maid notices Ula's gone. Then maybe a couple of crows until they get the Retainer and look for her here,' she noted. 'We'd better get started. Maybe it will be easier this late.'

'Not on the upper levels, Carria. The night is only just beginning up there.' J'nie pointed up to their destination.

Part Three
The Palace of Pleasures

Part Three
The Palace of Pleasure

12

Humiliation

The corridor hissed and rumbled up through the levels, as Carria consulted the map, then consulted it again, this time cursing and frantically adjusting the outer dials. Finally she looked up at J'nie, who was now shaking, the initial rush of adrenaline having faded; she looked scared and unsure. Carria pulled her close and put her arms around her, gently kissing her on the forehead.

'There's a room where we can wait for the next corridor to take us up to the top level, but we've just missed the last one, and there are only two a day up and down. So,' she paused, and smiled encouragement at J'nie, 'We can wait overnight, but that means they will probably have found Ula by the time we get going, or we can take the one other route through the top level's pleasure rooms. Are you okay? You can do that, can't you?'

J'nie nodded and gave Carria a weak smile, acknowledging that their roles had reversed, and it was she, the previous mistress of the Companions, who was submitting to this young and determined woman.

Carria fiddled with the map again, and pointed to the third door, waiting for exactly the right moment before flinging the iron door open and walking into the first room.

She stood still, waiting for the shock to subside, for everything here was different.

The walls were of fine tiles, each decorated with a sexual position. Water ran down one wall and collected in a trough from whence it ran down into a marble slit set into the floor, making sighing noises and filling the room with a heavy scent. Six large exotic birds with long plumes gazed at her imperiously from gold cages and clucked to each other. But the thing that made her stop was the light. Instead of the dim torch light and glow strips that had been her only light for deci-seasons, here blue light poured down from above. Whatever cycle of day and night they had become used to in the school was different to the outside world. It had to be hours out, but then that made sense if the Companions' duties were likely to be serving the guest until the early hours. Carria looked up in wonder to see that the ceiling was made of blue tinted glass and, above, she found herself looking directly up another Companion's skirt at her bare flesh. Above that again there seemed to be another transparent floor and, above that, she could see clouds!

She was so taken in by the scene that she jumped when the voice called out to her, and she just blinked for a few sands before registering what had been said.

'You're late! The banquet has almost started. And who removed your wrist chains? Where are the long chains? Didn't the headmistress prepare you? And why aren't your pussies cuffed for the journey? You're very lucky I have spare chains. This is very bad. She says she can't spare anyone at all today, then you come here late. The Retainer's run off too, has he?' Snapping out of her shock, Carria turned to see a dark skinned woman in what looked like a maid's uniform, but this time it was gold, and she certainly did not act in the demure manner of any of the maids she had met.

But it was J'nie that responded. 'It's quite all right Stewardess. I told the Retainer to leave. As for the chains, I am sorry. We had to unlock them, then he had to go quickly at the Sultan's request. We will have to borrow some of yours.'

The Stewardess turned her attention to J'nie, and then curtsied, with a look that said she was pleased to see her and that somehow all these mysteries had been explained.

'Ah, mistress J'nie. I'm sorry, I did not see you there.' Then a puzzled look crossed her eyes. 'But surely, mistress, you are not going into the Banqueting Room?'

'Yes.' J'nie spoke calmly and, regaining her the voice that was used to being obeyed, snapped, 'I am first and foremost a Companion, and I choose to inspect all of the Sultan's pleasure room personally, to ensure his guests are satisfied. Otherwise standards might slip. Now fit us with the long chains, Stewardess. I wish to spend a long time in the room.'

The Stewardess did as commanded, and J'nie strode forward, Carria following behind her and moving carefully as to not reveal the map that she had hidden under her skirt. They were now both with chains that allowed them to hold their arms out, but that were fixed to their nipples to prevent any sudden movement. In addition, a long gold chain was attached to their collars.

The three women crossed the floor to the waterfall and following the Steward they ran under the cold scented water into a passage with doors along each wall.

At the last door the Stewardess knocked, and a slot opened: 'Women aren't allowed to walk upright here.

143

Get down on all fours and behave. Stewardess, you know that. Take their skirts.'

J'nie and Carria glanced at each other then slipped their skirts off, revealing their clean shaven pussies to view. Carria took care to fold the map carefully into her skirt to hide it. From this room on she knew the way to the Sultan, but she'd need it if they were ever to get out again and back to the passage to the harbour that J'nie had described. J'nie was thinking the same, and instructed the Stewardess to store their skirts on the shelves that lined the passage.

Carria and J'nie both dropped to all fours and the door swung open, and they padded forward to the Banqueting Room.

Carria looked up and scanned the room before the voice hissed at her to keep her eyes down at all times. Around her there were Companions on all fours, being lead by their chains over to a long table where each had a large gold tray rested on their back, heaped with the finest cuts of meat and fruits from all over the known world.

Around them men and women lay on soft divans, raised from the ground and making small talk, or in passionate embraces. Carria felt the weight of a tray on her, and the man who had told her to look down picked up her chain and pulled her to a position.

'You are the sweet truffle tray. If anyone asks, you go over to them. But you do not look up. You do not speak. When the second bell sounds make your way to the kitchen with grace. OK, go.'

Carria did as she was told. This was not the time to draw attention to oneself. She knew J'nie must be there too, but she couldn't see her. She kept her eyes to the ground so that all she could see were the guests' feet and the patent leather of the man's boots and strapped heels of the women.

A bell tolled and music started to pump from somewhere. The party began, and Carria sensed that the couples were drinking heavily. The talk became less orderly and louder, then came the first squeals of delight as the men started to make lewd sexual suggestions. There was a call for the sweet truffles and Carria crawled over to a table, being very conscious of her exposed arse but unable to do anything about it.

The other girls were moving too, with calls for everything from the fine Quafy wine to the delicate, sweet oils of the Barka Valley to aid their sexual arousal. The talking was intermittent now, and most of it whispered as couples paired off and grouped together in orgies, with sprawling legs and wild groans of passion.

To her left there was high, raucous laughter, and a voice commanded sweet truffles and the fruit tray. Carria dutifully made her way over, dragging her boots over the smooth floor. A man's hand pulled her collar and made her stay in one position alongside one of the divans.

There was more laughter, and this time Carria was aware of two men and a woman. She caught part of a good natured debate about whether it was better to use the short and wide pomine fruit or the long ribbed and slightly curved gehsme fruit. That conversation seemed to last a long time, but the participants were in no hurry, and laughed at each new suggestion.

'But pomines are too squishy. They might break.'

'Then Evealine here would suck the juice out.' More laughter.

'Not me. Even a split pomine is longer than what you could offer!'

'Ah well, the geshme then. Not too soft and I always liked their bright green colour: very fresh.

145

Nice and bouncy in the middle – and wide. Like it might still grow given the right climate.' An uproar this time.

Carria knew someone was behind her, and delicate feminine fingers were peeling her lips apart. A wince of pain, then the oil released its vapours into her and she relaxed, the long fruit sliding into her, widening her and filling her until her lips stopped on the wide middle part of the fruit, soft and spongy as a rubber ball. There was a pause and she felt the fruit being wiggled, a pressure on her and the unmistakeable touch of another woman's buttocks pressing into her, the fruit inserted into both of them. With a command to the woman to make sure everything stayed where it should, Carria found herself with her mouth filled with a large, erect penis, and felt a light stroke of a cane over her arse.

'Slow now,' the voice commanded and pulled her collar a few times to demonstrate the speed with which she should move. Carria responded, taking the man in her mouth and sucking hard, rocking on all fours, forwards and back, and feeling the hard fruit rub her inside. Each backwards movement ended with her arse hitting the other girls, and a final extra drive deep into her.

Carria couldn't help but get excited by the sensation. The oils kept her wet and sensitive, the regular motion became hypnotic, and she wondered with a thrill whether the girl behind her was J'nie, or Meve, or maybe a Companion she had never met. The idea that she was having sex with two strangers at the same time made her flush hotly, and she started to put more effort into her pushes, driving the fruit deep and wriggling a little.

The woman poured more oil onto the fruit as the girls rocked forward, dripping it all over them and letting it mingle with their natural wetness and sweat before running down their thighs to the floor and making the floor so slippery that their knees skipped and their heels locked into each other.

Carria could feel the other woman push hard as well, and heard a low moan come from behind her. Her man was now yelling in impatient yelps, and started to cane her, urging her to move faster. Both girls needed little encouragement and pushed against each other, the pressure splashing the oil, sweat and juice mixture in a fine spray over their now wet arses, but the men continued to cane them, spurring them onto greater efforts. Carria lost herself, forgetting everything about her mission or where she was. Her only concern was getting herself satisfied.

Something happened. The pace became manic. Carria couldn't bear it. Everything was wild. Her sweat-dampened hair fell over her eyes, her muscles ached, but the need to keep going was stronger; stronger than she could control. She couldn't stop, but she had no control. The thick stiff member in her exploded. Hot, sticky semen shot to the back of her throat and she instinctively swallowed as all her muscles tightened and then she too came with a low moan.

Acutely aware of herself again, Carria brought herself back to the room, to her position on all fours, and her now sweating and wet body. The man slouched back in the divan, and Carria, scared to move, stayed attached to her unknown accomplice as her body shook from exhaustion and relief.

She didn't know how long she waited, but around her the noises of the party were changing. There was the smell of water pipes being smoked and the rattle of tray girls being led away. Eventually someone came to her and patted her so she moved forward, the geshme coming out of her with a faint hiss of air escaping.

Still with her eyes down she was led to the kitchens, where her tray was removed. Finally she was allowed to stand up, given skirts and directed to the wash rooms and instructed to clean herself before waiting for the morning and the Retainer, and the corridor back down.

Carria followed a line of girls, keeping just a little further behind them than needed. An arm came out of a doorway and she turned to find J'nie.

'Come this way. The Stewardess will be busy. We can use her rooms,' J'nie whispered.

'Which way? Good, that's the right way to go forward. There should be a passage over to the left that leads to the gardens, then only two more until we get to the grand staircase, and the Sultan.'

They hurried on, J'nie not forgetting to correct the wrist chain lengths this time. They quickly cleaned themselves, Carria giving herself a little more attention, particularly to her pussy, washing it with jets of water from the special fountain the Stewardess had, and shaving it cleanly, causing J'nie to comment.

'What happened to you?' J'nie demanded.

'They made me fuck another girl. I guess that's what a full Companion gets to do. It's not so bad, is it?'

But J'nie frowned and led them to the exit. Carria took the lead from this point, using her memory of the routes and bringing them through more passages to a door engraved with leaves and fruits. Becoming more cautious, they opened the doors, stepping through while glancing about them for danger, into what Carria had noticed the map had called 'The Garden of Earthly Delights'.

13

The Hunt

The light was now intense. Three stories above her Carria saw a transparent roof, and in front of her exotic trees from the hottest climates reached upwards, while tall ground plants attempted to steal the light from above and creepers hung from branches as thick as arms. The whole glasshouse was hot and a fine spray of water from came from brass nozzles on tall spikes around the floor that maintained a humid atmosphere. The room spread out in every way as far as she could see, the bulky forms of the trees and bushes disappearing into the misty distance, the leaves unclear in the haze, but creating areas of deep shadow.

Carria pointed to the middle of the room. 'Under the main roof beam, on the other side; it's the next door. We have to make it quick. On the map, this room is big!'

J'nie nodded. The moment the two girls entered the room they had started to sweat, and there was a temptation to rest, but time was not in their favour and, looking at each other in silent agreement, they pushed on, picking their way through the thick, lush undergrowth, staggering from time to time as their heels dug into the soft earth.

The more they went forward, the more disorientated they became, and they followed the line of the roof, high and indistinct above them, in order to be sure that they were on the correct path.

Carria followed J'nie, allowing her to bend and clear the path before them. Not for the first time, J'nie had dirty thoughts as she saw the well toned arse in front of her. She was lost in thought when J'nie suddenly stopped and stood quite still. Unsure as to why, Carria stopped too. Out of one of the trees a long green snake uncurled itself and dropped slowly onto J'nie's bare shoulders. It coiled itself about her neck, and then began a long descent down her quivering breast, now shiny from the sweat of heat and fear. J'nie drew sharp breaths as its undulating form rode over her nipple and slithered around her waist, its forked tongue sensing the air at all times.

It unwrapped its long body from her neck and wrapped itself fully about her waist. J'nie struggled to breathe, but whether this was fear or the snake beginning to constrict, Carria could not tell. With a sudden burst of speed the animal reared up, its head now level with J'nie's, eye to eye as if in conversation, then darted down, pulling itself through her legs and tightening its grip.

J'nie started to cry, wet tears falling from her face, more from stress than emotion, for she stayed still, and the snake, sensing something – whether danger, or the fultility of trying to capture such a large creature, or pity – allowed its body to relax and slid around her legs and off into the thick jungle.

J'nie stood in shock, and Carria, not much better herself, embraced her, kissing the wet tears from her face and then moving to her lips until the fear, the shame and the adrenalin mixed together as a sexual cocktail. The two women kissed deeply, running their chained hands over each other, Carria stretching her chain and allowing the tip of her index finger to just touch J'nie.

Time – the precious commodity that they feared wasting – stopped, and they were lost, J'nie jealous but forgiving of Carria's actions in the Banqueting Rooms, driving her to hold the girl closer. Then she knew that whatever happened she wanted to be with this person forever; whatever she was planning for the Sultan – whatever. And she knew that Carria felt the same too.

The horn sounded, its long mournful call repeating twice, rudely interrupting the moment and forcing the lovers to return to the reality of the glasshouse, and the fact that they were not alone. Listening closely, they heard the unmistakeable bark of dogs and shouts of people.

'The Hunt!' J'nie cried. 'Run.'

'The what?' Carria questioned, as she too started to run through the swishing leaves and dark shadowed patched of the man-made jungle.

'The Hunt. One of the special treats. We're really unlucky they're holding one now. The huntsmen and women release girls into the jungle, then track them down. When they capture a girl they spank her hard, so the girls will try harder to avoid capture. But, of course, with the dogs it's not easy to avoid them. After, they choose which ones to fuck.'

'Can we escape?' Carria wanted reassurance as much as odds.

'Maybe. They release a lot of girls, and eventually they get tired. When the deep horn sounds, its over. I think we'd do better if we split up. We'll be faster and more likely to go undetected. I'll go left, you right. When the deep horn sounds make your way to the far side in the middle. I'll join you. Give me five segments after that. If I'm not there go on. If you don't I'll try to get out of the palace.'

She meant that she might get out and, somehow, if Carria's plan wasn't discovered, she might make it out after whatever punishments were inflicted and they could at least be together, but the odds were so against it she dare not say it aloud.

J'nie ran, crashing through the dense jungle without regard to the noise now, just trying to keep a distance between her and the barks and voices behind. Stumbling, she cut her thighs in the sharp edges of the leaves, and swore at the chains that stopped her getting balance. She remembered – she had a key! Why hadn't she thought of that before? Running and trying to unlock the chains at the same time, she cursed her stupidity. And she could have unlocked Carria. She was a fool.

Something tripped her. It was a root she saw as she flew head over heels, then, clutching the key, tumbled down a gentle bank into a pool of wet mud. Covered completely in the foul smelling, slippery mud, she attempted to get up, but kept slipping, until a final effort made her lose all grip and she fell into a fast-flowing stream.

Oddly it wasn't the danger of being swept by the currents, or the Hunt, or the fact that she was bruised that first went through her mind; it was the fact the she had expected the water to be cold, but in the atmosphere of the hothouse it was warm. She realised that she had stopped. How long had she been in the water? She couldn't tell, but a fallen tree had held her from being swept down the rapids. She looked down. The key was still there. She used it, and got up. Apart from the cuts and a bruise on her arse she was safe, if wet.

Stumbling through the water, J'nie found a firm bank and walked out. There was no evidence of being pursued and the roof was a clear indicator of direction.

* * *

Carria tried to move carefully, but the jungle was against her. Every step echoed about her, every leaf broke giving away her position, and the dogs barked louder and louder. It was no use: her wrist chains held her arms too close to her and she couldn't get balance. Maybe they shouldn't have put them back on, but then if she was caught without them she'd be sent back to the school immediately. As it was, there might be a chance to get out before they found Ula, but the mission would be over. She gritted her teeth and ran faster. She just couldn't be caught.

The dogs. Where were they? She couldn't hear them as clearly. Perhaps she had escaped them, or they were following another scent. Carria allowed herself to stop and rest, and listen. It was true, they had gone. She waited for a few segments, then collected herself and, making out the main roof beam, walked forward into a small clearing. It was at that moment that the nets got her.

She struggled, turning left and right and trying to pull them off her, but all her actions only made the nets become more effective. Her wide, panic-filled eyes scanned the clearing, and slowly they came out of the shadows: men and women in green clothes and wide hats, that blended into the jungle and kept their faces hidden in shadow.

There were four of them, and another further back in the mist holding the dogs, that were now yapping in excitement at the capture. Carria wanted to scream, or something, but no words came to her and before she could collect her thoughts a hand was pushing something into her mouth. With a hiss it inflated, filling her and holding her tongue down.

They tied her wrist cuffs together, then threw her to the ground and tied her legs together at the knees and the feet with rough rope. Only when they were sure that she could not walk or talk or bite or scratch did they pull the net off her, and rolled her over so that she could see two men and two women staring at her with a look of contentment.

One of the men spoke. He was the oldest of the group and had a small, well trimmed beard with streaks of silver, and seemed to be in charge.

'A good catch. We've done well today. This one takes the tally to six. Shall we call it a day?'

'I think so. We should give ourselves time to enjoy the spoils.' A woman spoke, she also older and, Carria thought, probably a long time mistress of the Hunt leader.

'How did you like it?' The man turned to a young woman, who seemed to be flushed with the excitement.

'My brother told me how much fun a Hunt is, but I never thought it was this thrilling. It's really the best thing.' She acknowledged the second man.

'Well, my dear,' the woman said. 'Hunts have traditions. As this is the last catch of the day, and your first Hunt, you must do a Scenting.'

The girl laughed in pleasure, and started unbuckling her belt, then slipping her green dress off her, but leaving her boots and hat on, she squatted down over Carria's face. To Carria's horror she pushed her now wet pussy down so that Carria had no choice but to breathe the thick aroma of the girl's wetness. And then she felt a little dampness spread over her as the girl urinated.

As Carria struggled to wipe the scent from her by rubbing her face in the grass, the girl casually dressed, carrying with her an air of bliss at having finally become a Huntswoman.

Carria was left on the ground, now ignored, her purpose over for now. After they had finished with the ceremony, and toasted it with liquor from their flasks, the older woman commanded the fifth man, still standing with the dogs, to sound the deep horn, and a low, rumbling growl shook the now quiet jungle. Carria was again paid attention to. They rolled her over onto her front and onto the net, squashing her breasts under her bound hands, and tied her to a long pole. Before she realised what had happened Carria was lifted up and being carried as if she was meat across the jungle floor.

She could look up, but not for long periods, and became aware of the camp from the smell and noise first. When she did look she saw a clearing, and five other women, like herself bound in nets to poles, slung between two long benches in a row. The camp had a small fire, where food was being prepared, and cages in which the dogs were placed. Along the back of the clearing, large fabric sheets were hung from ropes attached to the trees to keep the sun out, and tables and benches were set out, each with well used iron rings screwed into them at different points.

'We'll spank two before the meal, and the other four after. You –' the man indicated the youngest woman '– can spank the last one we caught. She seems fit and was the last to be caught, so she should take a little more beating.'

They took the first girl down, cutting the ropes around the net, and letting her fall to the ground, where she tried to kick. But it was pointless and soon she was tied across a bench, in a position of prayer – and indeed, she may have been asking the gods for mercy.

The beatings were quick and savage. They had none of the ceremony of the school, and were clearly intended to hurt rather than excite. They had arranged the benches so that the remaining victims could see clearly what was going to happen to them.

When the first two were finished with they retied them to the poles, but this time without the nets, so that the weight was held by rope. Carria glanced over to see that the girl next to her was crying. Her rope had been wound around her breasts and thighs, so that it would be painful to stay still, but more painful to struggle or move; something that amused the Hunt as it sat down to eat the roast delicacies that were being served.

Carria couldn't do anything. In the background she heard the voices of the Hunt as they swapped stories and ate. The gentle sobs of the two beaten girls beside her and the bark of the dogs completed the only sounds in the jungle – and a soft welcome voice telling her to stay still. She thought she must be dreaming, then felt her ropes being cut.

J'nie crouched down behind the poles, keeping her head down and patiently working the ropes with the Hunt's knife. Carria felt blood flowing back into her hands and ankles, and a dull throb as the nerves realised that they could tell her brain about the discomfort.

J'nie moved along the line, whispering reassurances, and loosened the other girls' bonds, but kept enough rope on them to keep them suspended from the poles. Then she was gone. More time passed, then there was a huge rustling sound and the cloth that was above the tables fell, enveloping the Hunt like one of its own nets. Next to it another sheet was falling into the fire and quickly catching fire. Muffled shouts came from the strange bumps under the fabric as J'nie shimmied down the tree, running back and slashing the remaining bonds on the girls. The two who had already been spanked stood in amazement, wondering if they had anything to gain from running now; the others were less unsure and ran into the jungle, disappearing like ghosts into the mist.

J'nie ran over to the dog cage. The dogs, now in a state of excitement, barked furiously at her, and the cage even rattled, but the firm iron bars did not yield. J'nie spat at them and jammed the knife into the lock, twisting it so it broke inside.

'Let's get out of here!' she yelled at Carria. 'The doorway isn't far.'

Carria obeyed, following her lover through the patches of light and dark as behind them there were cries of: 'It's not fair!' in a young woman's voice and more commandingly, 'Sound the horn again: time to hunt.'

But the dogs were locked in, and with so many girls to try and recapture Carria knew they'd make it this time.

J'nie and Carria stopped near the doorway. They were both sweating and Carria still had the faint trace of urine in her nose. J'nie slit the inflated gag and it fell out of Carria as a limp shrivelled mess. When finished, they walked carefully to the door and, as J'nie prepared to open it, Carria held her by the arm.

'Why did you come back? It was dangerous, and we agreed if I wasn't there . . .'

Carria shook her head, her golden mane catching the light.

'I had to, Carria. I couldn't leave you. Not you.' She let the last word hang, and Carria kissed her, whispering 'I love you' so quietly she never knew if J'nie had heard, as J'nie pushed the doorway open a crack and peered into the next room.

It took a while for their eyes to adjust back to the dimmer light. This room was only a storey high, and the glass was tinted more deeply, making it impossible to see the floor above.

'The map calls this the Toll Room. Beyond it there's the Preparation Suite, then the stairs to the Sultan's rooms themselves,' Carria explained.

'Yes, the Preparation Suite is where the Retainer brings me. You'll enjoy that bit.' J'nie grinned.

As they became more accustomed to the gloom, they could make out a sparsely furnished room, the walls, floor and ceiling all of the dark glass, and two high-backed armchairs facing each other across a small table, also made of glass with little bumps on every surface. A cold waft of scented air blew across them and somewhere out of sight there was the sound of water rushing and splashing. Directly opposite, a doorway loomed out of the half light, it too of dark glass, but this time red, and designed so that light came from it, bathing them in its glow as they approached.

Carria moved forward, attempting to touch the smooth glass door but, as she approached, one of the glass tiles she was stood on lit up. A fanfare played from long horns that grew up from the floor and, to her amazement, the door lit up brighter, revealing some signs. Undaunted, she strode forward, J'nie holding her hand as they made out the forms of the symbols.

'What are they?' Carria asked.

J'nie moved forward, Carria noticing the scars to her legs from the jungle for the first time, and wondering how dirty the two of them must look. Hardly the regal uniforms that they had started with.

'Its high Estrian,' J'nie noted. 'The old language of the Sultans. This must be something from the first Sultan's time. I can translate. I was taught it as a High Companion, when the Sultan chose me.'

J'nie studied the symbols hard, while Carria thanked the gods that she had J'nie with her.

'It says,' J'nie relayed, 'Give, Receive and Enter.'

'What does that mean?' Carria asked as she attempted to push the doors. They did not move.

J'nie went back to one of the glass chairs and settled herself slowly onto the cold surface to try and think on the riddle. The arms were high and allowed her chained forearms to rest at shoulder height. She shifted until she found there was only one comfortable position. This was very relaxing, her arms on the rests and her feet apart. Despite trying everything, Carria eventually gave up attempting to push the door and, exhausted, she settled in the other chair, also discovering its unforgiving demands on posture. With a final sigh, Carria sank back and there was a metallic scrape – the sound that a bolt makes – and a sudden increase in the water noise.

J'nie saw it first, but was too slow to react. Some of the glass bumps snapped forward, turning into tubes that held her at the wrists and ankles. In terror she forced herself to look over at Carria to see that she too was trapped. A final glass tube snaked its way to a spot just under her left breast. J'nie couldn't see it well, but it seemed hollow.

The horns started to play a fast, regular beat, as the table in front of her was lit up from above. Squinting, she saw a clear glass panel open in the ceiling, then the table opened up, like a flower, to show a mass of whirling cogs and water wheels furiously rotating.

'What's that?' J'nie yelled as she felt something cold between her legs. She looked down to see a tube taking shape from what had been a glass bump on the chair. She noticed that there was one on Carria's side too, and each tube had a shiny end that was starting to push its way inside her.

There was a change in the sound of the water, a gear shifting and things turning faster. Out of the table two slender brass arrows appeared, swinging downwards. J'nie's heart beat faster, and she realised the horns were following her heartbeat. The arrows too began to twitch and move upwards, and inside her the glass probe pushed deeper and started to vibrate. She thought back to the present she had given Carria, and held the thought as she allowed herself to start enjoying the sensation of the twisting and shaking thing in her. The arrow moved upwards sharply. Then she knew what was needed to do; she understood the words on the door.

'Relax,' She commanded Carria. 'If we let ourselves go it'll let us into the next room. This is the toll – we have to give ourselves to the machine, then we'll receive the reward.'

Carria nodded back, her body already responding to the orders of its carnal needs. J'nie pushed herself back into the chair and let her mind wander to her dirtiest thoughts – the thoughts of being a young girl chosen by the Sultan and seduced by him, before he became obsessed with power; of dreams she had never shared such as Helena's powerful body stripping her and beating her until she cried; of Carria in the jungle, their hot, sweating bodies holding each other.

Her body tried to turn, but the chair held her. Only her head moved, rocking back and forth as she gritted her teeth in frustration and cried. Drops of sweat rolled off her furrowed and taut face. She opened her mouth wide to scream, but no sound came. She tried to catch gulps of air, but there was such a strong feeling of constriction. She wanted to stop, but she wanted it to never stop, the jerking movements of her body throwing small droplets of sweat about her.

Briefly she slipped away from her thoughts. The horns were blowing fast now. Carria was moaning loudly across from her, the arrow on her side almost vertical. Below her the probe was very rapid, making little greedy noises of moisture in her. She let out a cry and and she was back in the school as a young woman, being trained for the first time, experiencing her first … her first … her … J'nie's mind went blank. The thoughts just slipped away from her she couldn't think. There was only the name Carria and the sensation of falling. Moments later she was sure she heard her name shouted too.

She was aware of her damp hair, plastered over her face, and then bit by bit the situation came back to her. She was still in the chair, but there were no bonds now. Carria peered over at her in a dreamy way. But most of all she was aware that the door was open.

She got up, shaking from the exertion. When she got to Carria she put her arms around her and kissed her.

'We must go on. The cocks will be crowing soon, then they'll start searching for us,' J'nie stated as she helped a weak Carria up. Together they had passed the test the first Sultan had set his mistresses, and now they were close to the Sultan.

'The next room is good,' J'nie assured Carria as she regained her ability to walk in a straight line. 'The Preparation Suite is just a chamber to get ready for the Sultan in. After what we've been through we'll need it.'

Carria smiled weakly and nodded. Yes, she needed to change. One look at either of then now and the Sultan would scream for his guards. But if she could look well presented, and with J'nie there too, she could make up an excuse.

This chamber was unlike any of the others. It was, Carria mused, close to the brothel in the harbour. Where everything before had been cold and clean, this was hung with the richest of fabrics. The most exotic rugs were laid onto the ground, and incense burned from golden containers that hung from the ceiling. Plush seating and desks with fine face powders and mirrors were placed to one end, near the doors.

J'nie checked that there was no one to question them, then unlocked her chains, and those of Carria. In silence they took their boots and collars off until they stood tired and dirty together. Carria very carefully removed the vial of powder she had kept in her corset.

Mirrors in the walls allowed then to see themselves for the first time, the dirt marks streaking down their legs, the occasional scar, their hair matted together and stuck to their smudged faces. J'nie busied herself tidying away the clothes as Carria looked on, beginning to feel aroused by their mutual ravaged appearance.

'There will be a new set of clothes in boxes.' J'nie pointed to an ornate wooden box on the floor, placed on a rug that had clearly been made for it. 'The Sultan used to like me to dress up in different things, but there are spare uniforms too.' She paused, thinking that she had used the word 'used' as if it was a different part of her life.

'First, though,' J'nie motioned, 'the showers. Then we'll get dressed.'

Carria wondered what she meant, but just nodded and followed J'nie to one glass door. They were in a tiled circular room with tiny brass tubes around them. J'nie pressed something and they were suddenly being hit by strong jets of water from all sides. The dirt was blasted off them with such force that they held onto each other, then began to gently massage them with warm jets of scented water. Carria couldn't help but start to feel aroused again, and she knew that J'nie was feeling the same way as she held her.

Then the water became a fine spray. Carria noticed that bubbles were forming in the air, and the room was full of multi-coloured floating spheres.

The water stopped, and steam piped into the room keeping it warm, as J'nie started to soap herself, rubbing the slippery fluid over her body. She turned around and asked Carria to soap her back, and diligently she responded, making small circular motions, then longer stroking gestures. J'nie's breathing started to quicken, and Carria slid her hands around to the woman's breasts, cupping them in her hands and gently squeezing, letting the nipples run through her fingers.

J'nie, turned around and planted her lips full onto Carria's, letting their slippery bodies slide over each other, their breasts and stomachs touching, their legs intertwined. Carria felt wet, soapy fingers massage her buttocks, then start probing down further. She held J'nie really tightly, pushing herself against the firm body with all her passion. The chair had been nothing to this, and they both knew it. The water sprayed onto them again and they separated before climax, but were left with a sense of oneness.

Water turned to hot air and they dried themselves, returning to the main room to brush their hair. J'nie helping Carria, brushing the short hair in sweeping movements and setting it with small wooden sticks into curls, and using a fine brush to apply the rare powders that only the highest of society's ladies wore. Finally J'nie took a silver razor and, oiling Carria's pussy, shaved it clean. She then attended to herself, keeping her hair straight and applying colours with more fire in them to match her hair.

Lying on one of the plush seats, she stretched her legs out and worked the oil into the stubble that denoted where her pubic hair should be. She took the razor, but before she could cut Carria stayed her hand, took the blade away from her, and started to shave J'nie. As J'nie made sighing noises Carria finished her work, and with the lightest of touches kissed J'nie, who spent several segments lying on the couch before raising herself and without a word taking clothes from the box on the rug. Item at a time, J'nie sorted through the contents: skirts, one piece suits; lace, velvets and silks that imitated guards' uniforms, nurses uniforms and cheap women from the town's brothels. There were ropes and bars, wooden paddles and metal poles; ornate sets of silver plugs and chains; vials of oils and soft rubber clothes folded carefully away, tubes and masks, from the beautiful to the practical.

J'nie explained: 'The Sultan has lived here all his life. There is no perversion that he hasn't seen. His room is full of his personal favourites, and as his mistress I have to serve his needs. Sometimes he prefers that I dress for him in advance.' She caught a look of jealously in Carria. 'It's not something I dislike. In fact, I don't dislike anything and some are just wonderful experiences. My problem is that he hasn't wanted me to entertain him.'

She found what she was looking for and placed the folded clothes back into the box, leaving two new shiny uniforms and chains. When they had finished ensuring that their hair and powder had dried correctly, they helped each other back into uniform, taking pride in how they would appear to the Sultan. Carria handed the vial over to J'nie, and explained how to use it. Confiding her plans to J'nie they helped each other pull the straps on the corsets tight, fasten the skirts and attach the fine gold chains.

Feeling tall and important in the dark blue leather, they walked with graceful stride, to the outer door and up onto the oval stairway that connected them to the highest levels of the palace. They fell into step and did not talk as they climbed the glass stairs, making echoing ticking sounds as their heels hit the wide treads. Both were lost in thoughts of what they were going to do next, and avoided each other's gaze.

The climb was quite short, but somehow took an unbearable time. Although they had long since gone past the point from which there was any return, each step made the decision more apparent. It was almost a relief to reach the top. The door was glass, as were the walls, floor and ceiling. For the first time in a long while Carria felt suddenly aware of herself; that her most intimate parts were visible from below, her breast were on show for anyone, and that apart from the corset and boots she was naked. She shook the feeling, because here was the moment at which reflection was no longer possible, and action could fill the void.

14

The Sultan's Room

J'nie took one last look back at her lover, then marched forward through the glass door, with Carria following. As she closed the door on them the ~~temperature~~ dropped rapidly, until they started to shiver, then the outer door opened and they could walk on.

'The Ice Room: it makes your nipples pert. The Sultan had it installed seasons ago, and it amused him greatly for a while,' J'nie explained.

As they walked into the first chamber of the Sultan's room a bell sounded. J'nie explained it was connected to the floor, and that they should wait. Soon a peacock appeared and led them from the chamber. Passing through corridors with rich fabrics and strange devices that shook with steam pressure or whistled with air, they arrived at the very centre of the Sultan's domain; his inner study.

The peacock announced their arrival with its high, yelping cry and the girls stood in the doorway, surveying the room and waiting for acknowledgement.

The Sultan's study was covered on all sides with white silk, as if it were a tent, and the sun shone brightly through its silken roof. Around the edges there were cushions and couches, also of fine silk, and incense burners that gave the air a hint of spice. In the centre there was a low table piled high with books and maps, brass instruments and parchments. At the table a man sat crossed legged, his back to the girls, and drawing on a waterpipe which gurgled with regular plumes of smoke. He made no motion or sound, just keeping his silk robed back to them and concentrating on some papers.

They must have waited for a whole segment, shifting a little as the tall heels began to upset their balance. Finally he spoke.

'J'nie, I did not expect you, nor did I send for you. Why do you disturb me?'

Carria noticed the voice was tired, its owner absorbed in other thoughts, and not really wanting to divert too much attention to his mistress.

'I have brought you a surprise.' J'nie spoke with a strength that surprised even her. 'She is in a way an ambassador.'

The Sultan slowly raised himself from the table with reluctance.

'Ambassadors! I've had enough of that. Can you not see I have other, real politics to attend to? Trade agreements and treaties, not formal banquets and flattery. I spend every moment in negotiation with someone. What need have I of more ambassadors from areas I have never heard of?' He spoke bitterly, the table bearing witness to his efforts.

As he turned he glanced at J'nie, and on to Carria, pausing to glance over her body. Carria was more subtle, but she too was noting the Sultan. It was funny: all this time and she have never really thought of him as a person – merely a thing – and had never actually asked J'nie what he looked like. She had expected an old and fat man, corpulent and bloated with the wealth of Estra, his face ravaged by the depravity and debauchery of excess. Instead he was young, slender and athletic, with fine white skin, blond hair that fell over his eyes, a thin and fashionable moustache, and the deepest blue eyes she had ever seen. He was attractive and somehow that made her hate him more.

'Who is this?' the Sultan impatiently asked, ready to get back to the table.

'This . . .' J'nie paused for emphasis. 'Is Princess Carriana Oman. Daughter and heir to Oman Khan, ruler and king of the Far Islands. I have bought her to you, trained as a Companion, to cement the alliance of the Far Islands. The uniform of the Companion shows she will serve you, her chains that she is your slave. I bring her to you to do with as you see fit.'

Carria glanced fiercely over to J'nie, then shouted, 'Bitch.' The Sultan was still, but to J'nie it was clear that his mind was thinking very fast indeed. His face twisted into a grin and he moved over to Carria, holding her head in his strong hands, and twisting it up to look at him.

'J'nie, why did you not tell me that you had such a prize?' The Sultan kept a firm hold of Carria as she struggled to pull his hands away with her chained hands, but without success.

'I only found out a few segments ago, then I brought her to you, Lord.' J'nie curtsied.

'J'nie, please bring me some wine, then retire to the maiding room. I'll send a peacock when you are needed. She is safely in chains. Oman Khan's daughter and I have much to discuss.' His grin broke into a smile.

J'nie went over to a table of amber and selected a tall bottle from the variously shaped containers, pouring two glasses of rich green wine and then setting them by the low table. Then the Sultan's

Mistress left the room, going to the maid's room where she could wait in comfort. Carria looked up at the Sultan's blue eyes, feeling his breath on her, and sensing his strong masculine scent.

'Well, well, back from the dead to spy on me, are you? To see how the Sultan plans to keep your precious Far Islands away from the Council? The Council must have a lot of power over you. You might be pretty but that won't save you from a life in the rubber plantations.'

Carria swallowed, then spit her words out. 'I'm not here for that weak Council. They can't get drunk. I'm here for me. Your bitch mistress might have let my secret out, but I'm determined to negotiate with you.'

'Yes?' The Sultan raised an eyebrow. 'And exactly what would you want to negotiate?'

'A way to unite the Far Islands again, as my father did, in peace.' Carria gently laid her lips upon his and kissed.

'I am a man of politics, not lust. That side has long gone.' The Sultan broke away, and held Carria at arms' length.

'But I am a woman, and I want to talk politics on your bed.' Carria pushed herself closer to him. She placed her hand on his chest and pushed him back, until he was close to a couch, then she leaped forward, throwing him backwards into a seated position.

Carria reached over and carefully gave him a glass of the wine, filled to the brim, before taking one herself and sipping a little of the thick, heavy fluid. The Sultan followed suit, drowning the liquor in one quick tilt of his head. Carria put her glass down then seated herself beside him.

Carria slipped her hands inside his robe and opened it, massaging his upper body, then kissing him with passionate lips, working her tongue into his mouth. She pushed him flat onto his back, keeping her mouth to his all the time. At first he resisted, but then became calm. Carria's belly could feel his manhood thicken and grow and now nature commanded his actions. She worked his silken pants down and pressed her hot, wet pussy down onto him.

Suddenly he came alive. His arms joined around her neck and she felt his lips pressed onto hers. Moments later his tongue was in her mouth. She threw herself down, pulling the Sultan on top of her, crouched on all fours. He started to stroke her hair and whisper to her. Carria responded by sliding down the couch and stretching one chained hand down so that she could reach, then running her fingers around his hairless scrotum, squeezing it and stroking. The Sultan let out a cry, and she moved a little further down, taking him in her mouth and sucking. She placed him so that she could peel back his foreskin and lick the very top of his penis, while one hand stoked his toned buttocks and the other, held close to her collar by the chain, gently pumped his testicles.

The Sultan moaned louder and Carria started to probe his anus, pressing the point of her well shaped finger into the soft skin. Above her a voiced cried in pleasure demanding her to make him come, but Carria ignored it. She waited until she was sure he was nearly at climax, his body damp with exertion and impatient, then she stopped and, taking his penis firmly but carefully between her teeth, pulled him to the edge of the couch. She released him and stood up, then pushed him on his back again, this time savagely driving him into herself as she sat astride him, ignoring his pleas for speed and very slowly rose and fell on his wet body, her own wetness mixing with sweat to make a powerful perfume. By degrees she started to lift and fall more quickly, making sure that he followed her lead, until she too was sweating, her skin shiny with the effort. Only when she could no longer hold her need did she start to let herself become wild and erratic, letting him slip out of her once, and she dismounted to lick him clean before remounting and thrusting with renewed vigour.

With a spasm of delight; he came, and Carria worked herself a final few strokes against his still hard member before screaming her submission to her body's needs. Then she rolled off him, to lie at his side.

The Sultan praised her, and she was genuinely flattered, but most of all she now knew what it was to be a woman. She had made love to a man, had let his penis enter her body for the first time, and she felt strange, emotional and unbalanced. This was not the physical form of the monster she had expected. In fact, she felt affection for this man who had taken her girlhood away.

'You really liked me?' she asked innocently.

'Yes. Maybe I have spent too much time with the papers.' He waved his hand in the direction of the table. 'I have neglected the pleasures of life. I think I'm bored of everything. Of the palace and all the Companions; of the politics; the constant signing of papers. I'm bored of it all. I should have spent more time with my Companions. I am a fool. What's the use of more money if you cannot have pleasure?'

Carria stroked his hair casually, but inside she felt as if everything was unravelling. She needed to get herself back into the right state of mind. There was no time to waste. She needed answers. She needed them quickly.

'What happened to my father?' J'nie asked in a shaking voice.

'Ah, politics again.' The Sultan sighed. 'Your father was a wise and good man. I liked him a lot, but he wouldn't see the danger the Council presented, both to the peace and to him. He came to me on a ship and made reassurances but, even as he spoke, news of the Council calling for war came. I never wanted a war. If nothing else, the Far Islands are a long way to have to go to fight. I would have asked your father to take a treaty back to the Council, but by then I was worried that the last thing they would want was peace – or your father back as ruler to broker one and take their power away.

'To stop the dreadful madness of war, I tried everything. I even imprisoned your father, stopping him from trying to go back and causing another faction, but he escaped. The Council sailed out to his vessel and sank it. Of course, the council blamed Estra and, despite the distance, I had to take revenge. I never looked for you though, thinking you were dead.' The Sultan paused. 'I was wrong to imprison him, but I never wanted to harm him. I was foolish, and since then I have dedicated myself to peace.'

His eyes fell to the table and its papers cluttered on top. Then his eyes closed and his breathing became shallower.

Carria yelled for J'nie, who came running in to see Carria kneeled down beside the Sultan, holding one of his limp hands, tears running down her face.

'What have I done?' she cried out.

'What we planned. I thought I was rather convincing, and I liked your 'bitch' remark,' J'nie calmly answered. 'He couldn't resist talking to the rightful heir of the Far Islands. While you occupied him I slipped the potion in the wine. I thought fucking him for revenge was a nice touch – but he is good in bed, isn't he?'

'But that's the point,' Carria sobbed. 'I was wrong. I've avenged myself on the wrong person. He was a good man like my father. He did wrong, but he didn't really kill my father. He doesn't deserve to die!'

'He did me wrong too – I have spent years training; years being a Companion before being his mistress. He was cruel to me. He would have me beaten with his devices if I complained, but hardly ever took me to his bed.'

'But does he deserve to die for that either?' Carria stood up and faced J'nie, her face screwed up in pain, the tears now running down in rivulets from her face to her breasts.

'No,' J'nie glumly stated. 'No. Punished for failing to protect your father; punished for failing to be my master – yes. But to die? No. In fact, until you knew what had happened you should never have sought to kill him. So I didn't put the full dose into his wine.'

Carria stopped crying and looked up at J'nie, who gave her a weak smile. 'I could never have killed him – he is my master, even if a bad one. I have other ideas.'

J'nie strode over to the low table and after a moment pulled out the familiar form of the brass map machine. Then she wrapped the sleeping Sultan in his own silk robes. Taking the key she unlocked her chains, and then Carria's.

Pulling the unconscious form of the Sultan, the women consulted the map and made for the door. This time they could take a different route, the corridors having changed again, J'nie was more familiar with the rooms, being mainly the ones she had to come through to visit the Sultan. She pulled the limp form with a determination that Carria had not seen before. After the hunting and this she could only love her more.

J'nie stopped and opened a door into a light, clinical chamber, and the two women rapidly pulled their load in, closing the door as in the distance the mechanical cocks crowed. The room was tiled and plain cabinets lined one wall. On the other, a water fountain made a low babbling sound. There were doors on each wall and in the centre of the room a large device of white painted and metal stood, dominating the space with an air of menace.

'Where are we?' Carria asked, panting from the effort of pulling the Sultan.

'A special room. One I have visited a few times. I am, after all, the Sultan's Mistress. I cannot be punished like the rest of the school. This is where I am "corrected". And it is where I think we should place the Sultan.' She laughed with a vicious tone that scared Carria a little.

They unwrapped the Sultan's sleeping body and laid him out on the floor. Carria checked that he was all right from the journey while J'nie started to open the cabinets and rifle through their contents.

'I think,' J'nie announced in a loud voice, which Carria could not be sure was intended for her or the world, 'that our great Sultan needs a taste of his own medicine.'

She threw a round rubber gag at Carria, who took care to insert it carefully. The Sultan spluttered but did not wake. When Carria looked up J'nie was carrying an armful of things. First, J'nie took a small bottle of oil and spread it over his bare body, then she took a small razor and shaved every hair from his face and body, going over areas again and again until she was satisfied that he was smooth.

When that was done she took a collar of fine, dark blue leather and locked it around his neck, threading fine gold chains through its hoop and securing them to two wrist straps. With Carria's help she found a pair of boots that could just about be squeezed over his athletic legs. The corset was the difficult thing, but with much pulling on the straps they managed to fit his masculine body into one and then tighten it until there was a distinct wasp shape to the waist.

Carria completed the transformation with a skilful application of women' powders she found in one of the cabinets while J'nie attended to the Sultan's genitals, binding his testicles inside him with tape and pulling his limp penis under him with cloth secured to the corset and fastening a short skirt onto the prone body.

The sleeping potion was starting to wear off, and they struggled to get the body to the machine. J'nie attached extra chains to the wrist cuffs, holding the hands in a surrendering position, then attached similar chains to hold the legs apart. A waist chain completed the imprisonment, but J'nie made sure by braiding the long hair back to the machine's central post with fine rope. She checked the dials and levers at the back of the machine one last time, then taking a cup of water from a drinking fountain she threw cold water into her captive's face.

There was a pause, then a shake of the head, then eyes that registered fear and incomprehension. The chains tensed but held tight. J'nie picked up the polished brass map and held up the flat back so that it gave her prisoner a clear view of the restraints and clothing.

'Hello. I don't think you expected this, did you? You went to sleep a boy and woke up a girl. But for playing politics with Oman's daughter and for failing to treat me with respect, we have arranged for you to be punished; punished as you punish your mistress. Now you can feel what it's like to be a lady; to feel the pain of beauty.'

'And what a pretty girl. Such a shame she's been bad,' Carria added.

The captive woke fully and glanced at the reflection and then down to the smooth line of the corset and skirt, across to the chains and back to the captors. As if wanting to confirm the futility of the situation, he struggled more violently, but J'nie ignored the muffled cries and taut chains.

Putting the mirrored surface down, she approached the frustrated figure and pulled the short skirt, letting the terrified eyes in front of her gaze down to see the absence of manhood. There was a horrified sob.

'Not very ladylike,' J'nie noted. 'You have been very naughty, and what better way to teach you to respect us than be like us? And you are a girl now. You look like a girl, you pee like a girl, you are dressed like one in a pretty corset and skirts, and you shall be punished like one. I think a big girl like you should be able to take twice my punishments. I'll set the machine to sixteen.'

She moved back behind the machine. A lever was pulled and a low creaking noise started to emanate from the back of the room. Slowly, the chains grew straight with tension. J'nie reached over and pulled the skirts high, clipping them to wires that hung down for the purpose. Next, the frame moved, making the figure bend at the waist, with hands still outstretched, and a noise of ratchet teeth being engaged filled the room. A long rod moved out of the machine and moved, with some help from J'nie, under the uplifted skirt and slid into the exposed anus. It started to spin and thrust slowly, then made a swish as a large circular paddle drove itself down the rod and hit flesh with a loud clap.

'I wonder what *she* will get first: an orgasm or a sore arse?' Carria mused.

'Ah, *she* will get both, once *she*'s learned to love the machine and accept the mercy of the spanking.' J'nie laughed. 'I know – this is the regal punishment for when I needed correction. It's both pleasure and pain, but in this case its mostly my pleasure.' Carria joined in laughing, less at the comment and more at the helpless and humiliated figure in front of them.

J'nie periodically went over and, with a nurse's care, adjusted the chains with dedication, making sure that the cuffs did not bite or leave welts while being sure that the mechanical paddle was inflicting pain. Carria found that the situation was making her very sexually excited, and started to lift J'nie's skirt, pressing herself against her skin. J'nie returned the gesture, finding her fingers already groping in soft, wet flesh, while she kept one eye on the spanking machine and felt each clap as a little burst of pleasure.

Before she knew it, they were both feeling inside each other and time had slipped away. She might have heard a cry of climax and pain from the machine. She felt warm and content herself, and J'nie had her eyes closed in a dreamy way. She looked back to the figure trembling in chains. There were all kinds of emotion there too, and unmistakeable tears on the rouged cheeks.

A crashing noise broke the euphoria. Together the women turned to see advancing figures led by a woman with a shock of red hair that could only be Helena and another who seemed to run in a slightly bow-legged and pained fashion. Behind Ula there was the old Retainer and four guards followed. J'nie and Carria ran to the door behind the machine, pulling cabinets over as they went and plunging themselves into darkness.

Helena stopped, wondering which poor girl they had this time. Only when she had switched the machine off and instructed the guards to untie her did she recognise the girl as the Sultan and involuntarily laughed. It proved to be catching and soon the whole room was filled with laughing, which only ended as the Sultan walked out silently and unsteadily on his heels.

None of them said a thing, and now began the pursuit in earnest, leaping over the spilled contents of the cabinets and rushing through the dark corridor.

For J'nie and Carria there was no time to do anything – even consult the map. They ran from room to room, hoping to find a steam corridor, but there were none. They moved from dark to light and back, crashing through rooms where men wore ornate masks and drank glowing wines as women in Companions' clothes gave them oral sex; rooms where drugged fumes made the men and women stroke each other and lick every part of each other's bodies; rooms of strange sucking machines that made the women in the room squeal with delight and rooms where their presence was noted with quizzical looks from skilled Companion Rope Mistresses, coiling the long silken cords from roof beams that could give any man or woman the greatest pleasure of feeling like flying or pain, depending on their whim.

As they ran, they knew they were getting tired, and it was no use – there were no corridors down. They were trapped on the upper levels.

'We have to find a way down!' Carria screamed. 'If they catch us . . .' She didn't need to finish the sentence.

'There might be a way.' J'nie left Carria standing and dashed back to the last room, returning with a silken rope coiled over her shoulders. She directed Carria to follow her and, with a combination of snatched glances at the map and luck, managed to bring them back to the Sultan's chambers. J'nie led the way, and from one of the rooms lined with books and magnifying tubes they were suddenly out on a wide walkway, the whole region laid out below them.

'It's the Sultans observation deck. We used to make love here. Nobody can see us up here, but we could use the magnifying tubes to see them – sometimes right into their bedrooms!' J'nie explained as she tied the rope to a rail. 'If we can climb down and find a room with a window we can get in. Either there'll be a corridor at some point, or we can keep doing this till we reach ground. Whatever, we should be down to the ground before the outer guards are aware of anything and be able to run into the town. I know a man who will help us.'

Kicking their boots off they kissed quickly, then Carria dangled her legs from the cantilevered platform, her breathing too fast, her body tense.

'What is it?' J'nie kneeled down beside her.

'I'm scared of heights,' Carria meekly stated, trembling now.

J'nie hadn't expected this of the strong Far Island girl. For so long they had been fearless women, using their wiles and wit to get them this far. Suddenly, Carria was a little girl. In a way, she loved her for this: knowing that she had weaknesses; that there was more to her than the strong, determined exterior.

'Come on, you can do it. Just don't look down. Look up; look at my arse as you go down,' J'nie reassured her, and gently pushed her so that she had no option but to hang onto the rope.

J'nie followed, allowing Carria to distract herself from the height by looking up at her partner's firm, round arse. J'nie looked down from above, and waited until Carria had found a window and swung in before starting the final descent herself. She leaned out, pushing her feet against the stone and glass of the palace wall, holding the rope with all her might and trying to stay calm as she heard the shouted voices of guards above her.

With a jump she swung herself through the window into a small dark chamber. Before she had time to adjust to the dim light she felt her arms being held behind her. Panicking, she tried to break free, but the guards were strong and well trained. As her eyes grew used to the conditions she saw the white impassive faces of her captors, defined by the shiny black hoods that covered their heads and necks. In the far corner of the room Carria was already gagged and tied hand and foot. Her eyes had pity for J'nie in them, then looked down in shame. Helena stood by the chamber's door, rope and a fresh gag in her hands.

'I think,' Helena said in a measured tone, 'that the Sultan has plans for you.'

J'nie tried to speak, to tell her old friend what had happened, but she had barely got two words out before the round ball of the gag was forced into her mouth. She tried to struggle but, exhausted and knowing that it was useless, she rapidly let her body relax, and allowed her hands and feet to be tied.

15

The Trial

The fear kept them from attempting to move. Occasionally Carria looked up and caught J'nie's eyes, seeking some form of hope, but even when their eyes met, J'nie just shook her head and looked away.

Helena left the room, and there was talking outside. Carria thought she heard Ula's voice, then she and Helena were back in the room. Ula had a hideous expression on her face. Carria would have described it as evil. She was still speaking to Helena, casting the occasional glance at Carria, in particular, that contained wild fury.

'They have to be punished. We should leave them tied up in the Rope Room forever!'

'They will be punished.' Helena used her strict, official voice – the one she used before beating a girl. 'But it will be by the law. This is a serious issue, make no mistake, and be assured, they will be suffering more than a mere whipping. There will be a trial. They will be exposed before the school. You will have a chance to testify, and then the Sultan will decide. They could be transported to the plantations and glasshouses, or made to row the galley ships. They could even be sold as slaves to the brothels in Koma.'

Ula seemed content to let her anger simmer, and marched stiffly out. Carria's only pleasure came in watching Ula leave. Her legs were kept wide apart and she waddled from the room, clearly in pain. Helena and two black clad guards remained to make sure that the women were secure and prepare them. Helena unstrapped the corsets, taking J'nie's key. She reduced the wrist chains to one link and tore their skirts off, then throwing them to one side she left the room.

Some time later there was the sound of clanking outside and one at a time they were led to two small cages. There was only room to crouch in them, but with some prodding from the guards they were made to sit in the steel barred cubes, their heads protruding from circular rings in the centre of each cage. The cages were locked shut, then long wooden poles were fitted down each side and, with a guard at each corner, they were lifted high onto the broad shoulders of the Sultan's guards.

Down through corridors, and through curious stares of their occupants that the two of them hardly were aware of, the cages descended the stairs and steam corridors until they returned to the depths of the school itself.

The metal bars of the cages floors were cold and uncomfortable. Carria tried to move as much as she could, but any relief was temporary. She tried putting more weigh on her arse, then shifting it from foot to foot, but any real way of making the cage more endurable was stopped by the inability to move from the crouched position that the way her head was held dictated.

They were held at the gates of the school, the whip emblem now a dire warning of their fate looming above their heads. Helena came out to check that the party was in order, scrutinising each of the guards, then marching them through the gateway. Around them the whole school was assembled Companions and undergraduates, lined against the corridor as they were slowly paraded through. For Carria this was the price of failure, and her annoyance at being wrong gave her the strength to endure the event. But even she wavered when she saw Ula giggling with Yvonne on the route. For J'nie it was the most terrible experience of her life. Along the walls, her past students were seeing her caged and bound, helpless; women that she had disciplined and seen on the Podium were there, laughing and grinning. More than this, she felt naked without her corset. There was not a single part of her that was not open to the gaze of anyone in the school. For the first time since becoming mistress her nakedness was on show. She would have hid her head, but the unyielding steel ring of the cage kept her head fully visible, and she only knew that she was crying when Helena shouted at her to stop.

She didn't remember the corridors being so long, or there being so many girls in the school, but the torment did come to an end as they entered a dark room deep underground. Helena attached three long chains to a hoop on their collars and to the wall so that each of the women had to stand in a particular spot and could not move. There was just enough slack to sit or stand, but no more. Helena ordered a guard to feed them and left.

Food had been the last thing on Carria's mind, but she gulped the morsels that the guard fed her and the sweet green wine before her gag was replaced and the door closed, leaving her and J'nie in total darkness. Eventually tiredness overcame her. She sat on the cold stone floor, now damp from her having to relieve herself and attempted to sleep.

Somehow the total lack of control over her situation, her failure to complete her mission, and her decision that it was wrong left her relaxed. She had decided to do something to the Sultan and she had – she had found the truth, and now she was powerless, having run her course. Others could now decide her fate. She chose not to fight it. She only hoped that J'nie felt the same, and that whatever happened she could be with her. Yes, there were only two things that troubled her: J'nie being caught and a strange feeling for the lonely man at the top of the palace. There was something in the man that made him attractive. This was not what she had expected, or wanted, but even seeing him vulnerable and tied to the spanking machine dressed in women's clothes had sent a small shiver of excitement down her.

Sleep began to eat away at her consciousness, and she drifted into sleep and dreams of the Sultan and J'nie.

She couldn't guess how long she had slept, and the strong bright light woke her so sharply that it took some moments to remember where she was. Collecting her thoughts she squirmed on the floor until she had a kneeling position, then she stood up. It was at that moment she realised quite how badly kept she was. Dirt from the cell had mingled with her own urine and sweat to form a dirty glue that had covered most of her body. Her legs and pussy had started to grow an unsightly stubble and her hair was matted. Most off all there was a stench that she knew she was the cause of, which made her choke, the gag stopping her from breathing through her mouth and avoiding the worst. A glance to her side showed her that J'nie had fared no better.

Guards entered and fed them, ignoring any attempt at conversation, then returned them to darkness. Sleep followed again, and the pattern was repeated more times that Carria could keep a mental count of.

The doorway framed Helena's form, holding a bright glow stick made of rare algae that cast a strong green light. She wore a black mask that covered her face completely, leaving only two large circles of glass from which she peered at the women. Helena inspected them both, then disappeared. The door closed again and then rain seemed to fall from above. It grew fiercer and Carria wondered if they were to be drowned, but after a while it stopped and the water was drained away. Shivering, they waited again until two guards entered and, unlocking two chains, pulled the third between Carria and J'nie's legs and marched them across the passage.

Carria recognised the surroundings at once. They were back in the Inspection Room, and the nurse stood awaiting them with Helena at her side. The nurse pointed to two identical wooden frames and the guards tied the women's legs wide apart to the corners of each. The nurse then instructed the guards to hold their arms and Helena unlocked the collar and wrist cuffs.

'You are now officially outside the school and in custody. Therefore, chains of rank are an honour you have forfeited. You are common criminals, and it is only at the Sultan's request that you will be tried in the school as an example to the others,' Helena explained. 'Nurse, see that they are prepared for he trial by thirteen cock crows.'

J'nie did not feel that she could be any more naked. Ever since she had entered the school she had worn a collar. Now, completely naked, she shivered and hoped her ordeal would be over quickly.

The nurse worked on them one at a time, cleaning them with soaps, shaving all of their hair off, and even attending to their nails to ensure they were correct. The guards stood at the end of the room, watching with a mixture of amusement and boredom. Using the same tubes and nozzles as Carria had experienced, every possible part of them was cleaned with powerful jets of cold water.

The nurse dried them, combing their hair and changing their old gags for delicate silver metal contraptions that ran up from a wide and heavy collar then over the backs of their heads and split either side of their noses before joining the collar again at the sides of their necks. The nurse took time to lock an oval metal loop into place onto fasteners on either side of the collar, then wound a mechanism with a key at the back of the collar. When she shouted, 'Silence,' the ovals sprang back pushing the women's tongues down. Then she shouted, 'Speak,' and it leaped forward allowing them to talk, which they did not dare to do.

Pleased with her work, the nurse fitted a tight black leather belt about each of the women's hips, which had straps on each side that she then pulled up and around the inside of each leg and buckled at the side so that it was firmly held in place and pushed the women's soft outer labia out, leaving their buttocks lifted and free. With the help of the guards she placed their arms in leather cuffs attached to the side of each these straps so that their arms were pulled down straight.

The nurse secured a chain from the front of the belt that ran through their now well defined pussies and threaded it through a loop at the back, leaving a long, trailing length. As a final restraint the nurse looped silk rope around each ankle, then pushed this through a shiny metal tube and, securing the ends of the rope together around the other leg, pulled the rope so that the knot was hidden. She then wetted the rope so that it shrank, holding the women's feet slightly wide apart.

When satisfied that the prisoners were suitably dressed for trial, she ordered the guards to watch over them and left. The guards, already bored, commanded them to come over to them. With difficulty, J'nie and Carria tried to walk with lurching movements that made the guards burst out in laughter – even more so when Carria stumbled and fell, her hands waving frantically but uselessly by her side as she toppled forward onto the suction table she had endured during her first visit to the nurse.

The women were pushed in front, the guards following with their leader holding the two long chains, which were cracked like whips to make them shuffle faster, or pulled hard, hurting their pussies, to stop them. Progress through the dark corridors was slow, and the women had to be very careful not to trip on the sloping floors as they descended into the deepest parts of the palace. J'nie was unfamiliar with these parts, and even the guards did not seem to know the way. After countless turnings they arrived at a set of imposing doors, the whip emblem stamped across one of them and a set of scales on the other.

The leading guard went forward and knocked and, despite her predicament, Carria could not help but admire the well trained profile of the guard, her glistening black pleated skirt and corset encasing a powerful body, the plumed headdress giving her an illusion of height even greater than her already dominating stature.

Smoothly and without a sound the well oiled doors swung open and the group marched onto a platform. Below them the whole school was assembled: all the Companions and undergraduates, the maids and trainers, and the complete complement of plumed guards. She saw Meve and Yvonne sitting primly with their eyes ahead. To the right was a row of desks, at which Ula and the Retainer sat, his eyes darting this over the assembled girls with greed. Opposite them was a high raised table, at which the Sultan and Helena sat on high, ornate chairs.

Carria and J'nie were directed to two spots marked on the floor. The guard checked they were in the right spot then unwrapped a black velvet sheet. It was hard to make out the objects, but their purpose was clear from their form. The guard held them up to the audience, then kneeled down before Carria, telling her with hiss to keep still. Carria tried not to, but finally she could not resist trying to see what was happening. The guard held in her gloved hand four cylinders: two big and two small, each made of finely detailed metal and topped with a jewel, cut so that light reflected from it in every direction. The guard rubbed oil over them and then Carria could see no more, but felt an object being screwed into her cunt, then her anus.

The guard commanded, 'Speak,' and her mouth was freed. The guard asked some questions such as her real name, place of birth; very basic, easy questions. The guard fiddled with something and then told her gag to silence her and turned her attention to J'nie and repeated the process. Carria tried to reason what was going on as she listened to the clinking of their chains as they were passed through the back of her collar and attached to something. There was the sound of rope being pulled through a pulley, and Carria felt herself rise slightly and a burning below. She stared down, then up to see her chain being pulled up into the ceiling, then stop, leaving her on tiptoe and swaying minutely as she balanced herself. Looking over, she saw that J'nie had suffered the same fate. She tried to look around to see J'nie better, but the collar held her so that she could only move her eyes.

'The prisoners are secure.' The guard saluted to the Sultans and led the rest of her guards from the stage. Carria noticed that the room was silent, and every eye was looking at her and J'nie as they tried to balance. Carria tried very hard not to open her hands in what she thought was a ridiculous and purposeless gesture each time she had to balance herself, and told herself to hold them down flat by her sides, but her body would not follow her command as she rocked on her toes.

A harsh banging sound came from the left. Carria turned her eyes to just make out the form of Helena rise and, taking some papers in her chained hands, start to address the audience.

'Mistresses, Companions, Retainer,' she nodded to the man opposite, 'guards and Master Sultan. This courtroom has stood idle for generations. No member of our school has committed such a grave offence since our Sultan's ancestors introduced our chains of freedom.

'The system of guilt and loss of links, retraining or leaving this sacred school has been sufficient for all us. But the crime here – the wilful desire to kidnap the Sultan himself, our protector and lord – is the most terrible of crimes. For this, the Sultan has reopened this court, and has invited you, the entire school, to see the guilty parties.'

A shocked silence greeted the announcement and Helena, encouraged by the impact her speech was having, turned to face the women on the stage as both Carria and J'nie shifted uncomfortably.

'Prisoners, I will remind you of the law: the purpose of this trial is not to decide whether you are guilty or not – that is already decided. It is to ascertain the damage you have done so that we, the judges, can determine your punishment. To do this

there are the Ancient's Truth Sticks inside you. These
are from a different, older time, made before our
people forgot their science. Each bar has a crystal
that beats in unison with its mate. When you are
allowed to speak you will tell the truth or the bars will
detect the change in your bodies' heat and heartbeat.
You will not enjoy lying to this court. Now the trial
shall start.'

Helena sat down and asked the Retainer to stand.
He rose to his feet, hunched and coughing. Helena
asked about the way one of his maps had gone
missing. His story was the truth: in his version, Carria
had tricked him by saying that someone was ill then
stealing the map.

Helena thanked him and asked him to sit, then
freed Carria's tongue, asking her if she had stolen the
map. Carria was angry at the Retainer, and decided
to get him into trouble. She was going to say that he
gave it to her, but before she got halfway through the
sentence there was an intense pain inside her and she
jerked about on the chain.

Helena shouted for silence and the gag slid back
into Carria's mouth, a dull pain now throbbing in her
vagina. There was a call to ignore her words and, to
Carria's dismay, the trail moved on to the next
charge.

Ula couldn't conceal a grin as she told the court
how Carria had dishonoured the school and how she
had tied her up and left her to endure a night of pain
in the dark, until finally the guards had discovered
her, cried out and incoherent in the morning.

Helena seemed to take some pleasure in embarrass-
ing Ula by getting her to describe the intimate details
of how she was tied, and exactly the method used in
the knotted rope through her pussy. Ula turned a
visible red, but told the court about the nature of her

ordeal. Asked if they agreed with the account, both Carria and J'nie had to say that they did, the lasting pain inside Carria preventing her from adding anything this time.

They did not ask the Sultan to stand, but merely read a charge of conspiracy to endanger the royal Sultan of Estra and he affirmed that it was true. J'nie realised that they did not want to inform the whole school of what had happened and embarrass him in front of everyone.

Helena proclaimed the evidence complete and the court was dismissed. The women filed out, eventually leaving the Sultan and Helena alone with the prisoners.

'Your decision, headmistress?' The Sultan talked in a calm, low voice, cultured and sharp.

'Given the crimes, they must be made an example of. I suggest a public piercing, five years on a galley, another ten in the rubber plantations then exile to the farthest point of the world – somewhere that has no shipping; somewhere they will live out the rest of their lives away from any chance of contaminating civilised people!' Her voice was strong and underpinned with righteous anger.

'Hum.' The Sultan paused, a light tone of amusement in his voice. 'That may be for the best. Thank you, headmistress. Leave me alone with the prisoners now. I don't think they are a danger. Wait outside with the guards.'

Alone, the Sultan walked up onto the stage and circled his two captives. He stopped in front of J'nie and freed her gag, then put his finger to her lips to silence her.

'J'nie, you have been my Companion for a long time. I know that I have not treated you well recently, and I think your anger may be because you love me.

I am going to ask you a question – just one – but remember you have the Truth Sticks inside you.'

J'nie nodded that she understood, and tried very hard to stay balanced, even though her toes ached and her pussy felt pinched by the chain.

'J'nie,' the Sultan asked. 'Do you love me?'

J'nie thought hard, frowning as she concentrated on how she really felt, then she replied: 'Yes.'

'Only me?' the Sultan prompted.

'No, I love Carria too.'

'Ah, I see.' He laughed and stood back so he could see both women. 'Carria, who came to me with enough powder to kill me. And I can only assume you wanted to, but you didn't. I don't need to ask if you think you think you love me. Only that could have stayed your hand. Oh, don't worry, I haven't told anyone about that, Carria. They'd want to do more than send you off to my plantations if they knew.'

The Sultan sat himself down between the two of them, so that they had to bow their heads and look sideways to see him.

'You might wonder why I hid that information from the court. The answer is that I don't want to cause you more harm than you deserve. The wonderful thing about your escapades is that it took me away from all the papers and charts I've studied. It made me realise that it is the heart that makes pacts, not paper. I was dull, and no good could come of that – for me, for you, for Estra or the world.

'You made me defenceless, humiliated me and made love in front of me, excited by my situation, and I liked it. In one night you have made me more sexually alive than in years of being the master of the palace. For once I could be free; my bondage made me free.'

The Sultan grinned, lost for a moment in thought, then returned to his theme, casually brushing his loose pants to hide a growing erection.

'So I have decided to make you two – my chosen mistress and Oman Khan's daughter – an offer. A choice if you will. Kinder than the headmistress would have too. You can be sent to the galleys, then five years in my plantations and from there exile: you can have passage to any place you like, as long as it is outside my domain. Or you can stay here, with me at the palace as my mistresses, but you may never tell of what you do, or there are the Bora mines to the north that will make the plantation seem like an easy punishment. There is one condition to this offer, however, and that is if you are to stay you must prove your love for me. And if you fail: the mines.'

He clapped his hands and jumped up. 'And so the time is nigh to make your minds up. Remember you cannot lie. Speak!' He yelled and the gags opened.

'J'nie spoke first. 'Master, I was wrong, but I love you. I will submit to whatever you desire as long as I can be with you and Carria.'

The Sultan nodded and turned to Carria, who took the time to compose herself before replying.

'As the rightful heir to the Far Islands, I grant you the rights to the title of King. If I am to be your mistress, then you must be my master, and J'nie too my mistress. I accept, and I will succeed for you and for J'nie. This is an uncommon love, and one the gods will want to be.'

'Very well.' The Sultan went to each woman and kissed her, then called his guards, instructing them to unchain the women and ensure they were well.

'Where shall I take them?' the lead guard asked as her colleagues started to undo the ropes and let the chains go slack.

'Where?' The Sultan seemed surprised by the question. 'To the dungeon, and let the headmistress know that I have decided the punishment and that she should announce it. Then I will need her to assist me there. Tell her it will be a whole cycle, starting as the great sun rises and finishing when it next rises. By then we will see if we have two new miners, or two penitent girls ready to be readmitted to the palace.'

Part Four
Ordeals

16

The Monkey Room

There was relief for both of the women as they sat on the cold stone floor and Helena untied them, neatly cutting the bonds from their ankles and unlocking the silver gags. The walk from the trial had been long and tiring, and although their hands were still secured at their sides by the wide leather harness contraption, they could now at least move the chains and pull their legs together, preserving some modesty and giving their sore and tender areas some rest from the metal links that had been cutting into them.

Helena and her guards left them chained to a ring in a cell. When they were alone they relaxed. Neither woman bothered to attempt standing, but instead they propped each other up in a sitting position, back to back. It was a small cell made of coarsely tooled stone and illuminated only by a sliver of light coming from an iron grating in the thick wooden door. Inside there was a metal bowl bolted to the floor for their toilet and a device like a small fountain to clean themselves with. Otherwise the room was bare, with no seating or furnishings or even straw to lie on. J'nie mused that this was meant to be an uncomfortable place, and grimly wondered if the mines were similar.

Time passed – there was no way of telling how long – and they shifted positions constantly, the cold stone floor allowing them to relax but chilling them, standing making them tired. J'nie seemed oddly relaxed about their situation, and calmed a worried Carria, reminding her that they had elected this course of action, and whatever happened at least they would be together. Carria was not to be calmed easily, however, and the woman who had systematically planned an assassination was starting to panic. J'nie realised she had to take her mind from the situation quickly; she needed Carria to be calm for them both to get through whatever the Sultan was planning.

'Carria,' she ventured, 'does your cunt hurt from the chains?'

'What? Yes, it stings a little.' She shifted on the cold floor, acknowledging the discomfort.

'So does mine. I think they want them to. That's why they haven't untied our hands – so we can't rub them.' J'nie shifted herself a little closer to Carria, and leaned towards her as if she was about to whisper a secret. 'But that's not the only way to do it, is it?'

J'nie smiled and rocked forward on her haunches, then, keeping eye contact with Carria, lowered her head, nestling herself deep into the woman's lap. Carria responded by unsteadily working herself against the rough wall and rising into a standing position. J'nie craned her head up, and the legs around her opened wide, then, with forceful flicks from her tongue, she started to make long strokes across Carria's bare labia, slowing her stroke at the crucial moment.

From the moment they had left J'nie's chambers they had been running or hiding in fear, and the execrations had made Carria's scent strong and, as she became wet, the powerful and sensual smell made J'nie hungry and wild.

Carria swayed a little and softly called out for J'nie to stop, but there was no conviction in her voice and J'nie started to lick deeper, letting the now slippery folds of flesh lubricate her efforts. Above J'nie the other woman spread her legs wider, rocking forwards and backwards in time to J'nie's now insistent licks. There was a low moaning that seemed never to stop, then suddenly a cry. J'nie felt her head being grasped eagerly by Carria's hands, their bondage allowing them just enough movement, and her face being pressed hard into the soft, wet flesh. J'nie responded with fierce probed, dragging her tongue over Carria's swelled clitoris, drinking in the hot, perfumed smell of Carria's excitement.

J'nie worked her tongue deep, pushing, but always allowing Carria a flick over her clit, which brought a sobbing cry and a rapid spasm form her. J'nie let a pattern settle, then gradually speeded her motions. Carria's sobs were getting more frequent and now she could feel the wetness on her cheeks as Carria's trembling thigh muscles ached and sweated, the mixture of juices and fluids trickling down and mingling with J'nie's own perspiration as she drove herself faster.

There was an intense scream and Carria fell back against the cell wall, to a seated position, her legs wide and her head gazing into the distance. J'nie struggled over to her and kissed her on the lips once again, as a final gesture of care, before motioning Carria to place her head in her lap.

Exhausted, they lay together, and time resumed its slow progress, only broken much later by a guard bringing them food and laying bowls in front of them so they had to get onto their knees and snatch mouthfuls of food. Although they were both too hungry to do anything but eat, the whole thing was degrading and J'nie thought they were being treated like cattle.

Finally, Helena returned with four guards and stood them up. She checked that their chains were clean and sound before threading them again through the harness and under them so that it was clear who was under whose control. With a hard pull they were being marched through the corridors again, although this time they did not meet any of the other students or mistresses; something J'nie was very glad of, particularly as she felt dirtier than ever before, catching the scents of sex and sweat on herself and carrying shame with the knowledge. She knew that nobody could know what had happened to her, but she thought that they would somehow be able to tell, and view her with contempt, or pity, or both.

They walked for many segments deep below ground, where the air was humid and still. Only the acrid smell of the torches burning on the walls gave any idea that these passages had been used in generations. After a short distance the stone sides to the corridor became rougher, and Carria and J'nie could feel the ground becoming coarse under their bare feet. Finally they realised that they were now in a narrow tunnel carved out of the rock, and the occasional wall torches that had shone a dim, flickering light ran out. Stopping at a crossroads of tunnels, Helena pulled their chains up to the wall and locked them to a ring set into the stone wall, telling them to kneel and await her return. Unsteadily they both dropped to their knees, the coarse ground making their position uncomfortable, but they did not dare say anything.

They stayed side by side on the ground until they were sure that Helena and the guards were far away and the sound of the heels on the stone was very distant, then Carria's curiosity got the better of her.

'Where are we?' Carria whispered, unsure how far away Helena had gone.

'The lowest level of the school. We're near what used to be the dungeons from the ancient times. I seldom come down this far, but I have a feeling I know some of what will be in store for us.' J'nie sighed. 'Whatever happens, Carria, I don't regret anything.'

Carria was about to reply when the sound of many heels striking against the stone flooring echoed through the passage. Helena returned. She said nothing, but signalled for them to stand up. She checked their shins and, satisfied by the marks on them that the women had stayed kneeling, signalled for them to pay attention. Helena checked that her four guards were standing in order, their black uniforms shining in the flickering light of the torches they now carried.

'I have,' Helena started, 'very precise instructions from the Sultan. We are to take you to the dungeons where you will be prepared for your ordeals.

'It is the Sultan's wish that I shall not draw your blood or cause any physical harm that will not be fully healed by the next three cycles. The ordeals are to be carried out by these rules. However, I have a complete cycle in which to break you. I am the willing servant of the Sultan and I will. I consider the Sultan to have made a mistake in being so lenient with you, giving you this chance, and I intend to take this chance away. You will be going to the Bora diamond mines, and two pretty girls like you should give the miners of both sexes some cycles of pleasure between the long shifts of scraping diamonds from the rock.

'You –' she turned to Carria '– are no better than a spoilt girl, crying because she can't have what she wants, and you, J'nie – I served you, I . . .' She paused on the brink of saying something, and J'nie was sure she was about to say she had admired, liked, or maybe even had wanted her. 'I think that you have been blinded by passion, and here you should know better than anyone that discipline must be maintained.'

Helena began to stride backwards and forwards, her guards standing silent and still behind her, Carria and J'nie looking at the cold floor, as if this telling off was the worst thing that could happen, but knowing far worse things were to come. J'nie had to admit that she was getting aroused by Helena's anger and, while keeping her head down, glanced up to watch the strong, firm round buttocks of her headmistress as they opened the pleats her skirt in a hypnotic wave. She understood how the Sultan must have felt, to be relieved of all the pressures and have no choice but to enjoy a sexual situation. She was determined to get through this – whatever it would be, she belonged with Carria and the Sultan. They were all the same, having submerged their desires for power, but now knowing they could, together, enjoy both. She realised that Helena was speaking again, and resumed her penitent attitude.

'The Sultan and I have prepared a series of ordeals, you will each endure: temptation, degradation and terror to prove your love of the Sultan. Each is worse than the last, and in the final, third room you will meet pain so severe that it has driven men and women insane. In short, it is better to quit earlier rather than wait till you can endure no more. And you will fail. I have personally assured the Sultan and I will be whipped if I fail. This is your last chance: you can leave and take the Sultan's mercy of five years in the plantations or, if you go ahead, you will be going to the mines.'

She looked at each of her prisoners in turn, but met only a determined look. Turning away, she motioned for the guards to bring the prisoners and, with the group of five, moved off down the tunnel.

As soon as they had rounded the next corner there was a transformation in the surroundings. The tunnel opened out into a wide path sloping still further down. Above them the rock ceiling became a large cave, which arched over them and whose walls became distant. On either side of the path the floor fell away to deep ravines into which waterfalls incessantly poured water. As Carria looked down, soon there was nothing but a dark abyss and instinctively she pulled back from the edge. She knew that they had to be below the lake across which they had journeyed to arrive at the school.

In front the form of a stone building grew ever larger, carved out of the rock itself. Carria felt the surface below her change from cold stone, her bare feet finding the new surface warmer and easier to walk on. Carria was so stunned by her surroundings that she didn't take in at first what was happening, for as they neared the building the floor began to shake and shudder, then shift gently upwards. As the group moved closer to the building, back onto stone and in front of a now distinct iron door, Carria realised that they had been on a drawbridge, which was now raising itself into the cold, damp air and cutting off all hope of escape.

Helena opened the iron door and beckoned them all in, closing it with a dull clunk. She motioned them over to one wall of the five-sided room where she locked them to the wall with a savage tug that made them both stand on tiptoe to avoid the chains hurting them again. The room was large and inside the stone was black and smooth, reflecting little light. Around them four metal doors were set into opposing walls, each door with a different animal inlaid in brass on it: a monkey, a stallion, a butterfly. Then there was the imposing main door, polished on the inside, and they noticed it too had a character – a skull.

Taking stock of the room, Carria noticed the leering form of the Retainer, gazing with unrestrained glee at her naked body. The four guards stood by the door, their torches now secured by holders to the wall, and in the centre of the room Helena started pulling sheets off strange and ornate devices set symmetrically across the floor, checking them with care and adjusting intricate little screws and consulting strange symbols.

'Have you prepared the first chamber?' Helena addressed the Retainer, pointing to the monkey door.

'Ah yes, headmistress. All the guests from the village are here, chosen by me personally from the brothels of the town. They are, of course, unaware of where they are – or indeed, with the amount of poppy juice I have given them, I doubt they know who they are.' The Retainer laughed in his rough, coughing manner.

'Good. Then we will begin.' Helena walked up to J'nie and Carria, dragging a large and heavy object. She struggled to place it exactly where she wanted, then stood to its side, revealing a brass timeglass the same size as a man. With a crank of a lever Helena inverted the glass bulb at its top and a thick red fluid started to drip down, making splashing noises into the first of three smaller glass bulbs held by rods to a lever. As one bulb filled, it gently pulled the lever until it weighed enough to trigger a bell and move the next bulb into position.

'This,' she explained with a wicked grin, 'will take exactly one cycle to empty, divided neatly into three.

You will hear the bell at the end of each session, but it will seem a long time off. Anyway, I expect then that you are eager to get started. Guards! Get them ready.'

Carria felt herself grabbed by four strong hands. Helplessly, her own hands flapped at her sides as her chain was roughly pulled out and detached. She was hoisted onto a wide Y-shaped wooden table, hollowed out so that she fitted into its recesses and her arse was exposed through a large circular hole. There was no point in struggling, and she meekly allowed the guards to strap her legs into the table.

From the corner of her eyes she could she J'nie was in a similar predicament, until the guards strapped her head down, and a Y-shaped lid with brass fittings on the side lying next to her table.

Helena craned her head over Carria, carefully checking the straps with a delicacy that contrasted with the agony she was about to inflict.

'This is one of the oldest machines in the dungeon, coming from the reign of the first Sultan. It hasn't been used for a long time by anyone but me. For modern purposes there are easier ways to generate a similar effect – but none of the new ways are better. They don't have the same depth this old way does. True, it isn't used now because this way hurts at first, but I don't mind that though.' She laughed in a polite manner. 'I think it adds something a little extra to the experience, the agony and the ecstasy together. And you won't complain, will you? Good. Now be a good girl and don't cry.'

Carria tried to shake her head, but the straps over her forehead and chin held her, and she was aware that her eyes were the only things moving. She lay still looking up at Helena as she pulled on a pair of thick black rubber gloves. Carria caught a glimpse of her black clad hands holding what looked like a needle with a rubber bulb on its end. There was a moment of peace, then Carria felt the rubber gloves on her pubic region, fingers probing her cunt, it being gently prised opened, and her clitoris being fingered, then there was a sharp and intense flash of pain running up her. She knew Helena had stabbed that needle right into her most private of parts. There was something else too: a warm, then hot, then boiling feeling as something was being put in her clit. Carria made a wild animal noise, as it seemed as if her clit was expanding, growing large and painful. There was another jab deep into her, then two more into both of her inner lips. Her body seemed to shrink – or was it that her cunt was the only part of her that mattered; the centre of her existence? Carria tried to move, but the straps held her tight and she was left jerking in agony, her eyes wide open with tears streaking from them.

Nothing else happened for some time, then the pain started to subside a little. Helena returned holding something else: a wide strip of dark fabric. Carria's cunt was now throbbing, but not actually painful, just very sensitive, and she gasped for air as the strip was fed through the opening by her arse and secured over her pubis to the leather harness. She winced again as it was pulled very tight then, after some fumbling, she felt a dimple pressing into her clit as the strip was fastened.

The pain eased completely and a new warm sensation came over her. She felt calm and relaxed. She didn't even worry as Helena made her open her mouth and pushed a tube into her, then fastened a close-fitting mask over her head, leaving her in the dark and breathing through the tube. Somehow she knew the hole by her arse was being closed because there was no cooling breeze on it anymore and she started to sweat, and then she could feel the lid being placed over her container. There was a burbling, and then she felt a rush of exhilaration as ice-cold fluids were pumped all around and into her. She breathed deeply from the mask, and even this air seemed scented with something that made her feel more alive than ever before.

The strip of fabric seemed to cling to her too, making her gasp as it pressed into her, then become hard, as if it had set. In a daze, Carria suddenly found herself lying on the table. All the apparatus had been removed and she looked up to see Helena above her again. She must have passed out, or somehow managed to escape reality or a while, but now she was back, and being spoken to.

'The drugs will take a little while to work properly. You will have all your normal faculties, but feel aroused by everything you touch, smell or see.'

'Why are you doing this?' Carria asked, wondering if somehow there had been a mistake, and this was not an ordeal but a reward.

'Because –' Helena spoke softly as if encouraging a pupil '– you have sworn your love to the Sultan, and to J'nie, and he must see that even under the severest provocation you will not be tempted by another. If you fail this ordeal, then how can he be sure that you will be loyal?' She turned to the guards. 'Release them and take them to the first chamber.'

Carria was helped up, and she noticed that J'nie must have been similarly prepared. With J'nie she was made to walk across the room to the first door. Walking gave Carria an intense sensation between her legs. She bit her lip and concentrated on making it to the door, but every movement made her wetter and hotter. She could feel the little dimple massaging her clit and inside her she felt a void needing to be filled. She looked at J'nie, who was staring straight at Helena's legs. Her eyes finally met J'nie's and they looked at each other with pure lust.

'Guards!' Helena commanded, and before Carria and J'nie could get any closer the guards were attaching a long chain to each of their leather harnesses.

Carria and J'nie were led through the door, and found what looked like a party being held in the room. Masked men and women were drinking long glasses of wine, some dressed in tight and revealing clothes, others naked. Every mask was in the likeness of a monkey, but each was different too, some shiny and hard, some of soft silk or fur. Music played in the background as water fountains pumped scented plumes of mist into the air. The masked people were all young and intoxicated with something. Several couples were fondling each other, and in the middle of the room half a dozen men and women were having an orgy, each member of which was satisfying at least two others, forming one large mass of sexual pleasure. Above a woman dressed only with a feathered hat was swinging on beam, and masturbating herself as she swung in time to the music above a coloured lake of water, bubbles rising to its surface and bursting with more of the sexual scent.

The guards avoided looking at anyone in the room, and chained J'nie and Carria to rings in opposite walls. Carria looked across at J'nie, and then felt a rush of fresh excitement in her; she squealed as she looked about the room. She needed something sexual to happen; her wet, throbbing pussy was demanding it. She wanted fingers inside her, or a long, hard licking at her swollen clit, her breasts to be massaged and sucked. She wanted a long, hard penis pushing itself up her arse as she wanked. The thoughts went through her, making her wetter and hotter as her breath quickened.

Every part of her wanted fucking. The music made her muscles convulse in time to the beat. She breathed in deeply, allowing the strong sexual smell to work itself into her, but most of all she saw the masked men and women playing with each other and she had all these sensations work themselves into a primitive emotional need for physical contact. Her body became a rash of sexual need; her cunt felt like the centre of her whole being; and the thought of that made her even more excited.

Helena stood with her hands on her hips, flaring her pleated skirt out more and grasped Carria's face in her hand, tilting it up to look at her.

'Right now you want to get fucked more than you have ever wanted it, but your little cunt is locked away.' Helena drew a finger nail over the strip between Carria's legs, the tip hard against the texture of the material, the friction making it vibrate and giving Carria the conviction that her juices were flooding down and trickling out of her. She caught the smell of herself, and it made her hungrier for something to happen. Carria leaned forward, her mouth open to kiss Helena, but the headmistress pulled back.

'Did I say you could kiss me? That's not allowed. But soon you can fuck all you want. You have two segments of time here. All you need to do is call and you can fuck the whole room. Just shout out my name,' Helena explained, holding a pair of amber and gold scissors up, then turned on her heels, the guards following.

Carria couldn't see J'nie now: there were too many people in the way. A woman in a mask that covered her whole face had sat on the edge of the fountains with a man across her lap, playfully holding his hand behind his back as another woman in a maid's uniform spanked him. Then there was one man in particular, he had been kissing a woman in heels as high as they were long when he pushed her away and came striding towards her, a fur edged monkey mask concealing his features, his body oiled over its naked muscular frame. He stood in front of her for a whole quarter segment, then without a word put his arm around her waist and pulled her against himself. He kissed her, his tongue darting into her mouth long and deep. Carria submitted hungrily to his insistent probing, leaning back and touching her tongue to his. She pushed her crotch against his hard member, letting herself sigh as he started to brush his hand over her arse.

Suddenly Carria felt another set of hands on her thighs, and breaking away from the man's kisses she looked down to see the woman in the heels kneeling below her and licking the edges of the strip. She wanted the strip to loosen itself, but the hotter she became the tighter it seemed to get.

There was another sensation, and looking behind her a man in a full mask was kissing her buttocks. Then someone started to massage her breast from behind her. It seemed as if the whole room was converging on her, and every part of her body was getting attention. She couldn't control herself any-more, and let herself sink to her knees, and then be rolled over as dozens of mouths and hands worked over every part of her body. Every part except the area protected by the strip, the part of her that most wanted to be probed and worked. Carria tried spreading her legs as wide as she could, but the fabric stayed hard and in place. She turned over, but none of the furiously working fingers could move it. Carria could feel herself getting deeply aroused through the fabric, but it only made things worse because she knew she wouldn't be able to come with this barrier between her aching sex and the orgy outside.

Carria started to cry in frustration. It was the one thing she needed but she couldn't have, then she started to think about the mines. Would it be worth trading a life of hard labour to relieve this overpowering urge? She wanted to say no, but then why not? She was about to yell for Helena when there was clarity: if she could survive this, then she, J'nie and the Sultan could do this every night! She thought of the three of them in the Sultan's chambers, and let the image fill her mind. All she had to do was discipline herself. She dug her fingernails into her thighs, causing little red crescents to form as she allowed the pain to clear her mind, then with a determination to ignore her body's needs she got to her knees, then stood up. She moved away from the masked orgy, her chain links making a ringing sound as she walked back. The orgy did not follow her, but instead started to fuck each other as Carria kept moving away from anyone who looked at her.

In the distance she caught sight of J'nie, also moving back, and, catching her eye, knew at that moment that the danger had passed; that they were going to pass this first test.

17

The Prancing Horse

As they waited in the pentagonal room, Carria noted that the timeglass was now one third empty, and one bulb filled. A third of a cycle had already passed. The sun would now be at its height outside, J'nie noted, as once again they where roughly hoisted up by chains and stood tiptoe on the cold stone floor.

Helena and Ula where discussing something in the middle of the room, and then motioned to two of the guards, who opened the main door and went out. Shortly afterward, there was a loud noise as some heavy machinery was operated.

Helena entered the room, making Ula go into another room, then pushed the women up against the rough stone wall and made them stand with their legs apart. She was deliberately rough as she unfastened the pubic strips, tugging them from the women's swollen and sensitive cunts. Hot and beaded in sweat from her efforts, she had the guards wash them in stinging ice-cold water.

Ula came back carrying something and placed a black cloth hood over Carria's face, so that once again she could not see what was happening to J'nie as she was unfastened and led from the wall to the room with the prancing stallion.

There were more mechanical noises outside, and Carria guessed that the drawbridge was being lowered again. Then she felt the chains go slack and there was a rough prod on her arse, forcing her to move forward.

She couldn't tell who was in the room – the hood over her head kept her visually deprived – but she smelt leather and the oils that went with it. Rough hands forced her legs apart and she could feel herself being shaved, then long-high-heeled boots being laced onto her so that she had to stand with her hips pushed slightly forward to keep her balance.

Her harness was tightened too, and she felt things being attached to each side, but had no way of finding out what. Carria tried to turn, but there was a hard jerk from the side of her harness that stopped her. Whatever that been fitted to her was solid and heavy.

She felt fingers working under the fabric of the hood and felt the unyielding material of a leather collar pushing her head up and stopping any movement so that she could not turn her head or move it up or down.

When this was pulled tight by laces the hood was pulled off and a guard quickly placed a new close fitting helmet on her. Carria didn't have long to look at it, but it seemed to be similar to the guards' helmets with a set of three plumed red feathers on top of it. It was also of hard black leather and had long, high sides closed in and prevented her from being able to see anything except if it was directly in front of her.

Finally, a guard placed a wide rod over Carria's tongue and fastened it behind her, leaving strips of leather dangling in front of her. Carria was confused as to what was happening, and the impossibility of knowing what Helena had in store for her next made her feel vulnerable and frightened. She also realised that she hadn't had a pee for a long time, and that she would have to relieve herself soon.

The black hood was suddenly over her head again, and blackness was everywhere. There was a pause, the mumble of voices somewhere, then a tug on the gag and Carria stepped forward, following the insistent lead and getting used to wearing such high heels again.

She realised that they must have come out of the room and, as the noise her heels made changed, guessed they had even left the hallway. The sound changed again, and she was sure they were crossing the drawbridge. There was a pause, and when she resumed being lead forwards she felt she was pulling a load secured to the harness. She heard the rumble of wheels, and made out many more shoes now, most with the distinctive click of the guard's heels, but another one like hers, which she assumed must be J'nie.

The ground became stone, she was sure. The party continued to walk at a brisk pace for a while, then she was halted again and there were more murmurs and the sound of a door being opened. Moving again, Carria was sure she was out in the open now. There was a clear breeze with a sea salt tang, and distantly seagulls were crying. Even though the hood blocked out all vision, she was convinced that it was lighter too. Carria stood pondering where they could be when Helena's clear voice broke her thoughts.

'You have suffered temptation, and not been found wanting. For that I admire you, but you will not succeed. The first ordeal is one of mental strength, the second of slavery. You are both proud women; you had positions in the palace; you are respected by the courtiers and idolised by the townspeople. But in order for the Sultan to be sure that you will serve him you must be ready to abandon all of your pride; to have no desire other than to do whatever the Sultan wishes.

'He and I thought hard to find something that would degrade you, to the point where you would rather suffer transportation to the mines than continue to destroy your reputations here. We shall see.'

Helena must have given a signal, for the hoods were removed and, blinking in the light, J'nie and Carria looked out on the narrow road leading down to the harbour. Carria couldn't look around, but somehow knew that J'nie was beside her. She also noted, with relief, that the road was empty.

Helena spoke again. 'And for you two ladies I have a special treat. My new apprentice guard will be help you see experience failure.' Helena made a small bow towards the figure next to her, making her skirt rise and revealing the branded emblem on her cheek. J'nie and Carria blinked again, and found themselves looking directly at Ula.

The first thing Carria noticed was that Ula looked good in the smooth black uniform of the guards, illuminated by the daylight. The close fitting rubber followed her strong body in long flowing lines, and she had an imperious manner in her heels and plumed headdress. Her haughty look completed the stern look of a guard and for the first time Carria actually saw her as a sexual being. Black suited her and with the drugs still flowing through her Carria couldn't help but admit she found her nemesis attractive. Even the hard, hate filled eyes gave her something of a sexual quality.

Helena walked out of their vision, and her voice came from behind them as the guards took positions along the road. 'Normally she would have to wait before she could join the guards, but she showed such enthusiasm, and so wanted to help you, that I thought she should have a sample of the delights down here. I think she will take good care of you.'

Now both Ula and Helena were out of view. Carria felt a sudden weight added to her harness, then the bit gag being tensed by its straps. There was a sharp pain on her buttocks, followed by another and involuntarily she started to walk. There was now no question; she was pulling Ula, who continued to whip her until she was running as fast as she could.

Carria felt a tug to the left of her bit from the reins, and then she was turning left along a side road. J'nie must have made a better turn because she could now see her lover ahead of her.

She had felt a little foolish when she had realised she was being treated as an animal, but seeing J'nie made her heart sink. She too would look like this: the high plumed helmet and blinkers allowing her little vision, but also letting anyone they met recognise them, and with the unmistakeable brand on their cheeks, they would be easily identified as Companions. And Companions who were guilty of crimes worth punishing in such an extreme way outside the palace.

Everything was made to make them feel humiliated – they had their breasts and pubic regions open for the world to stare at, and they stumbled in their heels as they pulled the light carts behind them.

There was another sharp lash from Ula's crop and Carria attempted to run faster. She realised that Helena and Ula were racing to the town. Ula's command of 'faster' rang out and a fresh series of stinging blows landed on Carria's arse as she attempted to pull up to J'nie's cart.

Up ahead Carria noticed a line of Guildswomen making their way up to the palace for a meeting. The ordered and prim women stopped and stared as suddenly two women in harness and bits ran toward them, pulling two other women behind them in the carts, their hands held high and holding crops in them which they occasionally brought down with swift movements.

Carria recognised one of the wenches from the inn where she stayed, and tried to avoid her eyes, but it was no use, the woman saw her and started to gossip with other women. As Carria raced past she heard them shouting names at her, and although she was already running as fast as she could, and had now overtaken J'nie, she felt the sting of Ula's crop again.

As she passed the stone marker, which noted that they were about to enter the town, Carria was conscious that her bit was being pulled back hard on the reins. She gradually slowed, half fearful that she would receive another sharp rebuke from the crop, and in part because the momentum of Ula's weight made it impossible to stop dead.

Panting, she finally came to rest, J'nie pulling up beside her, so she assumed from the sound of deep, exhausted breathing. There was a lightening of her load and Ula was standing by her.

'How much lower can we go, princess? From royal blood to a dirty little animal, only good to whip. You might notice that we are about to go through the town. For the benefit of those who don't know you, I'm going to shout your name out, and Helena there –' she must have pointed, but with her restricted vision Carria could not see '– will do the same for your friend. We want everyone to know who you are, so when you go to the mines they'll all call you animals, and you will treated like that. Unless you show me a sign that you want to save some decency. If you do, blink for me.'

Carria kept her eyes wide open and staring ahead. And Ula reached down to her skirt and took out two metal clasps on fine wires. With skilled hands she closed the metal bars over her eyelashes, then pulled the wires taut and fastened them to points on the helmet. Carria tried to blink now, but she could not. Ula called over to Helena, but the answer from J'nie must have been the same, for soon Carria felt the weight on her cart increase and the familiar sound of the crop as it sped through the air and landed on her.

The road to the town became more crowded; soon they were getting strange looks from tradesmen on horseback and sailors walking up from the harbour. At every questioning glance Helena and Ula took delight in calling out Carria and J'nie's names and positions.

Eventually they entered the town, and in the central square their riders tied them to the central fountain, in the shape of a serpent coiled around a naked woman, and walked off, their wrist chains jangling, to a nearby inn leaving the women still harnessed to their carts to the public scrutiny of the townspeople.

The tall sided buildings around the square quickly filled with faces peering out at them, then people started to form a circle around them. At first they were quiet, and whispered to each other, but bit by bit, as the crowd grew, it also became bold. Soon Carria found her breasts being squeezed by a dirty harbour hand and her arse being poked by a rotund woman who speculated on how these 'filthy beasts' must have done something so very bad that they would be reduced to this, and it was a warning to others.

Someone made a joke about them being poor stock, and the crowd started to laugh. Other jokes came then, and Carria wanted to look away, or shut her eyes, or even just lower her head in shame, but she could do nothing, and had to silently watch the crowd as it laughed, each part of their bodies being commented on or laughed at as if they were cuts of meat in a butcher's window.

Carria felt that her pride had deserted her. She longed to see J'nie but, although she was only a pace way, it was impossible for her to turn about to see her. In a moment of despair she let herself lose all control, and to the huge amusement of the crowd she realised that she had wet herself, and she was now standing in a puddle of her own making.

Carria thought back to the training she had been through in the school, and she managed to find a way of controlling herself, but for the jeering crowd it was too late; she had become 'the second fountain' and a round of laughter went about them.

Helena and Ula came back, their little metal heels making the unmistakeable sound of the school echo across the square. Carria felt the bit being removed, and a bowl being offered up to her to drink. She drank with a thirst, and even looked at Ula with gratitude.

'Last chance, princess fountain,' Ula whispered. 'After this we tour the harbour and maybe we'll pay a visit to our friend, GaJa. I'm sure he'd like to see what has become of us. Or shall I unhitch you and find you some warm clothes?'

'No,' Carria stated, and immediately the bit was back in her mouth. Helena kept her promise, and they were run around the harbour where the swarthy sailors called out to them and suggested obscene things that shocked even the school-trained

Companions. They were hitched again at GaJa's, where he came out and leered at them, feeling Carria over and commenting that she was in better shape after the school. He even offered Ula money for them to be part of a brothel party and let his clients play with them.

Ula declined the offer, but not before she let GaJa have a thorough inspection of his potential purchase, letting the brothel owner measure her orifices and probe their depth. Ula had his maid wash her now urine scented pussy and legs clean and, with glee, GaJa rubbed sweet oil onto his fingers and slid them into her.

He pinched her clit, and commented on it as if it was a jewel or wine, then made approving noises about the way her cunt would fit lots of different penises well, and how with school training he was sure that she could satisfy at least three men or women at once.

Unable to do anything, Carria had to endure the process, until Ula told GaJa that she was only playing, and that the merchandise, however damaged, had to be returned to the palace dungeon soon.

Finally, Carria felt the weight behind her again, and without waiting for a signal started off as fast as she could, back around the square, where a few people were still gathered and gave a sarcastic cheer when they came into view, then back up the road to the looming form of the Sultan's palace.

On the return journey Ula and Helena made the two carts travel together, so that the two drivers could chat to each other as they made their transports carry them very slowly though the town and then lazily applied their crops to speed them up the road.

When they were close to the palace they were stopped, and Carria had the hood placed over her again as the party made its way through the secret entrances to the school and then across the draw-bridge to the dungeon and the room with the stallion.

Ula dismounted and removed Carria's hood, and bit by bit they had their helmets, bits and boots removed. The waist harnesses keeping their arms by their sides, however, were untouched, and they were attached again to long chains between their legs, secured to the wall. But this time they were allowed some slack.

Ula, Helena and the guards left and, alone, Carria allowed herself to try and untangle her emotions. She felt used, she felt shamed and as if she was a worthless slut; the lowest thing in the world. But she also felt love for J'nie and the Sultan's mercy too, and she felt that she needed to go through these ordeals. She confessed her thoughts to J'nie too.

'I think I really want to be hurt. I want to suffer for all that I've done. I've been bad and I need to be punished,' Carria stated.

'I know. I feel the same. I think we must suffer to be whole again.' J'nie kissed Carria with a long, gentle kiss, letting their lips touch for what seemed like eternity.

18

Butterflies and Beetles

The timeglass rang out the end of the second third with a loud, clear metallic knell, and Helena came for them, opening the door flanked by the black uniforms.

The guards marched in front, then Carria and J'nie, side by side, with Ula behind, holding the long chains and pulling them sharply when she thought they were going to slowly. Ula had said nothing, but the women knew she was unhappy that they had passed the first two ordeals. When they were back in the room they had their first chance to look at Ula, and her face was rigid in its disappointment.

'Not tempted away from the path of love then?' Ula taunted them. 'And in the two? You two have no shame, no decency – you are whores. The whole town has seen you as you really are, and yet you are willing to suffer more. Well that's only the worse for you; you should have quit and had some pleasure. From now on its only going to get worse. Your tight little pussies might have given you pleasure; now they will give you pain.'

She marched off, and Helena came back to check them. Carria noted something had changed about Helena; she seemed to have some care for them in her expression. Whether she had decided that they had been through enough, or that the next ordeal was too terrible, she could not be sure, but she had some sympathy now as she unlocked the chains.

'The Device next,' she sighed. 'J'nie; you know what this thing is. Are you sure you want to experience this?'

J'nie paused, then spoke with a soft, even tone. 'I know what it does – we both do. Nobody has experienced it in our generation, and now I know for certain that I have to, whatever it can or will do to me.'

'Very well.' Helena gave them both a gentle, almost friendly, slap on their exposed cunts, then had the guards frogmarch them over to the third room, with a butterfly inlaid on it. Helena did not enter, but stayed behind as the guards and prisoners entered the chamber. Standing in its centre was the imposing figure of Ula gently smacking a crop into her gloved hand with an impatient air.

Ula smiled, but said nothing. She turned neatly on the high heels of the guards and marched across the chamber, her short, black pleats lifting slightly as the back of her thighs kicked against them.

Two straight, padded benches lay in the middle of the chamber in parallel, the crossed wood legs polished to a bright shine and the red leather surface finished with detailed bronze pinheads. Following Ula to the benches, Carria noticed that the walls were of a different stone that had been carved with intricate designs: swirling forms of butterflies and stag beetles in flames etched into the fine surface that seemed to move in the uncertain light of the wall torches. Carria glanced up to see a high domed ceiling above her, and a thousand thin threads glistening in the torchlight, and fixed to each a butterfly of gold, encrusted with minute jewels and reflecting the flickering light as if they were raining as slowly they drifted in the rising and falling currents of the air just above the benches.

Ula directed them to lie down and, sitting on the bench, Carria awkwardly swung her legs up onto the leather, where one of the guards held them wide, while the other guard next to her pulled her head down until she was flat on her back. Carria was aware that the little golden butterflies were now just touching her still sensitive skin, brushing against her as she breathed and exciting her with their cold kisses. There was a rustling and Carria moved her eyes to see a silk screen with butterflies in flames printed on it had been placed between her and J'nie.

She waited, trembling a little at the thought of the next ordeal, that Helena has promised would be painful. Then she heard a series of sharp little gasps of pain from behind the divide; then silence. She looked up, but the faces of the guards showed no signs of acknowledging the sounds, or even her. When she tried to raise her head, however, the guard firmly pushed her back onto the flat surface of the bench.

The sharp, staccato noise of the other two Guards' heels against the stone floor echoed and faded, then Ula's face was suddenly very close, and the two remaining guards were holding her down hard. She could smell Ula's sweat; her sexual odour and the strong scent of the new rubber guard's uniform. Ula's lips were worked into a smile, but her hard eyes showed a determination that could not countenance pity. Again Carria tried to raise her head, but she was held fast, and then she glanced down at a sudden sensation on her right breast to see Ula had pulled the wings of one of the golden and jewelled butterflies open, revealing a row of rounded teeth under it, and was now allowing it to close like a clamp onto her breast. Carria tried to move away, but could not, the pain grew as the wings opened again and the clamp exerted its full pressure on her. She heard Ula walk down to the end of the bench, and then another stab of pain as another butterfly was closed onto the sole of her left foot. Carria felt a testing tug on the golden thread and could feel both clamps pull upwards; she followed the gleaming line of threads up to the ceiling and saw that it was actually one thread, passed over a small wheel-like pulley high above her.

Ula worked with the skill and attention of a physician, clamping a dozen butterflies and threads, hung from their high pulleys to Carria's breasts and nipples, then moved to her feet and the most tender parts of her legs, the inner thighs and backs of the knees, to secure the other ends with their own butterflies. Each new pinch caused Carria to gulp for air, but the pain was just about bearable, even with the drugs in her still making every slightest touch seem like a red hot iron. It was the fear of what she was being prepared for that nagged at her and made her shake. She tried to stop, but it only got worse, and she cursed her own weakness.

Carria felt the pain more acutely on her stomach for some reason, but it was when Ula clamped her pussy open in five places that she couldn't help but let her pain out in a low sob. Ula ignored her, and attached the threads to her arms, still held rigidly by her sides by her harness.

The guards released her and their heels ticked out of the room. Carria lay in numb shock as Ula went behind the screen. There was a creaking of wood against wood, then a scream of pain that Carria knew was J'nie. Ula returned and strapped a large ball on a thread into Carria's harnessed hand.

'Pull it when you have had enough,' Ula sneered, and then Carria heard the creak of wood again. The lines went taut, and then the support of the bench was gone. The pain amplified a thousand fold. She was hanging in the air, the butterfly clamps biting deep into her flesh.

Ula walked with a clicking of her heels to Carria's taut and spread legs, and stood between them, looking down at Carria's head.

'Just for you.' Ula spoke softly and blew Carria a kiss before placing her index finger on Carria pussy and giving it a hard shove. The power of the movement shocked Carria; suddenly every part of her ached and screamed for mercy as she made shallow swinging and twisting motions.

She looked about wildly: the screen had gone. She saw J'nie hanging as she was, her bench winched down low to the ground. She tried to look down her body and caught Ula leaving the room before the change in balance made her feet and pussy clamps pull up and, in agony, she had to lie flat again. It didn't help. She tried to shift her weight again, this time in a controlled way, but it only made the clamps on her left side pull this time, and in a frantic effort to relieve the pain she tried to push her right elbow out, but this only cased her pussy to sting. Without thinking she tried to pull her legs in, the agony stopping all thought and making her act like a trapped animal, but her breasts and nipples suddenly flamed in intense discomfort.

Helplessly, Carria writhed in the air, hoping to find some position that would give her some comfort, but there was nothing. She looked across to J'nie for some assurance – but she too was struggling to find a less agonising position.

Pain made her loose all idea of the length of time. She tried counting slowly to divert her, but when she managed to block it for even a moment she forgot herself and moved, bringing fresh agony and a little scream of frustration.

But something else kept her focused: she now knew she deserved this punishment. She had involved J'nie in her plans and she needed to be punished for that. Yes, it made sense now; her mixed feelings made sense. It was like being back at the school where any bad behaviour was quickly and severely punished, but then came freedom from its guilt. She had done something terrible to J'nie, the woman she loved; had harboured thoughts of slaying the Sultan, a man she now thought of as kind and forgiving – she had to be called to account. Each and every pain she suffered was only what she really wanted, to feel clean and allow her to start again with the J'nie and the Sultan.

Carria tried to make the pain greater, pulling her legs up so that the clamps bit deep into her, but she finally acknowledged that any move to pull her legs in caused her breasts too much suffering and, excruciating as it was, the only position she could adopt was to attempt to lie flat. Her mind called out for more punishment, but her body would not respond.

'J'nie,' Carria meekly whispered. 'You remember what I said after the cart ride? I mean all of it. I've been wicked and I want to suffer for it. I think the Sultan knew that. That's why he devised these ordeals – to see if we would fail, but also to see if we wanted to go through them. I think he knew we would.'

J'nie was also lying flat. She turned her head a little to the side, letting strands of her flame red hair fall over her face. 'I know. We have dishonoured the school, and ourselves. I have betrayed the Sultan and humiliated my position. But be ready – there will be more pain to come. We must endure this as our reward for treachery, and then be free of it. I deserve the pain, and whatever else she has planned for us, but at the end we will have done penitence and we will start over; you me and the Sultan.'

'For me, J'nie, when this is over we'll fuck all day and night – just think of that.' Carria made her voice sound firm and sure, but inside she was uncertain whether she would make it through the physical pain too. 'It can't be much longer, and if this is the worst I'll endure it for as long as needed.'

As soon as Carria said it, she knew that this couldn't be the end though. It wasn't so much worse than a hard pussy spanking, or the ritual that Yvonne had gone through. Answering her silent question, she heard a faint ticking, growing louder and louder as more ticking joined in; then dozens of ticking noises. Shuddering, she peered up into the ceiling to see where the noise was coming from, but she couldn't make anything out yet, just the occasional sparkle.

As the noise grew louder she felt the threads vibrate slightly causing a fresh wave of agony over her whole body. With a final effort to find the source of the new torment she ignored the pain and craned her head to try and catch sight of what was making the new cacophony. Gradually she made out the source: on each thread a thumb-sized silver beetle was crawling down, their silver metal shells glinting in the light.

Each was an exquisitely crafted machine in the likeness of a stag beetle, whirling with some finely worked mechanism, their pincher heads snapping in unison as they descended. Carria shouted out to J'nie that she loved her, and they should never lose faith in each other, then lay her head back and waited for the torment that was to come.

The beetles did not hurry, but with precise timing landed on all points of her body at once. Each was tethered to its thread by its own fine chain and started to bite in a circle, starting at the butterfly and moving outwards. Carria kept her teeth together and attempted to forget the ball in her hand, the idea of pulling it was too tempting. Then she felt the beetles nestling into her open pussy. Carria realised that she could hear J'nie screaming above the ticking noise and tried to put it out of her head, then she started to scream too as one of the metal animals started to push itself into her, snapping as it made its way deep into her open cunt.

She tried to shake, to throw the creatures off her, but they clinged to her and the pain of the clamps made her stop, exhausted and covered in the sweat of physical effort and fear. Eventually she stopped all attempts to struggled, but lay as still as she could, accepting the punishment and so beaten by the agony that she became almost relaxed.

They stopped biting. Carria thought she might have dreamed it but, raising her head, she saw the little metal shells marching back to the threads and start to climb them. Too exhausted to care, she lay still, letting the pain run through her body and satisfied in knowing that she had endured this test and moved closer to her own salvation through pain.

She lay as still as she could, trying to clear her mind, but something else was happening. She could feel the butterflies warm, and their metal wings flap. The heat increased; suddenly they were hot with a strange tingling sensation, as if little bolts of lightening were being pumped into her. Then it got worse. Her body started to jerk of its own accord. She lost all control over it as it made her move, and the pain of each point got harder to contain as it continued to make her hurt herself on the vicious teeth of the clamps.

She understood the flames on the walls now, and longed for it to stop. After so much pain could she last this final test? Sobbing uncontrollably, she felt herself lose all control: her bladder emptied itself; tears streaked down from her eyes; she drooled onto the floor. He body, soaked in sweat, cried out for mercy, and then she heard the distinct bell of the timeglass.

Carria's face broke into a manic smile – she had lasted through the ordeal and, ignoring the pain, she looked up to see if the doors were being opened. But there was no sign of any activity. The little shocks were getting stronger and, confused, she put her head back.

Was this a cruel trick – a final terror? She screamed over to J'nie, hoping she might know. 'Why haven't they come?'

J'nie answered, her own voice strained and with fear in it. 'I don't know. We should be free. The Device should shut down. Something's wrong.'

Carria was going to ask more, but the uncontrolled jerking of her body was now so great that her head was rolling too and it was impossible to form any words. She must have passed out, but was shaken conscious again by a crash from the door. With the last of her strength she looked up to see the Sultan and Helena running to them followed by the guards.

Carria hardly noticed the guards winch the benches up and remove the butterflies. She lay on the bench until the guards washed her over with scented water and, staggering to her feet, she saw J'nie sat on the opposite bench, a weak smile on her face. Carria noticed that J'nie's body was covered in the tiny red welts of the clamps and pincers, and that together they had tattooed her with the shape of a butterfly over her body.

As Carria regained her senses she became conscious of Helena and the Sultan talking in an animated way.

'I didn't think she'd dare. I mean why should she? She's had everything she wanted. I knew she hated Carria, but to let the device run on that long,'

'Well . . .' The Sultan measured his words with care. 'What we do know is that neither of your subjects attempted to call for help. Therefore I think we can assume they have passed all the ordeals.'

'Yes, Sultan. I will prepare myself to be whipped.' Helena sounded as if she was glad she had failed.

'That won't be necessary. You have proven yourself to be a good headmistress, and you did all you could for these women. You allowed Ula to lock the door – that was an error – but I too have made errors, and we learn from them. That you failed is more to do with their spirit than your failure. I do not wish to see you whipped for that. There is no debt to repay.'

Now fully awake, Carria saw Helena kneel before the Sultan, and in the far corner of the room she saw two guards standing over the trussed figure of Ula.

The Sultan put his hand on Helena's bare shoulder and made her rise. He addressed her warmly.

'Now, headmistress, what I do ask of you are two things. First, to attend to the girl Ula in the traditional way. If she wants to stay here then I want her whipped every cycle in the main chamber before the school for the next season, and maiding at the school until the next term. Spare her nothing; she should sample justice.

'Second, I have some ideas for the school that we must discuss. Certain events have opened my eyes to new experiences that must be considered.'

Carria noticed he even made a small bow to Helena before dismissing her. Helena left with her guards, the passive and bound Ula hoisted upon the guards' shoulders. As they departed, J'nie got up and came over to her, putting an arm around Carria and kissing her gently, carefully placing her hands so that they did not touch any of the raw areas of skin.

'We made it – even Ula's extra treat,' J'nie whispered. 'No mines or plantations.'

'Do you think he would have really sent us to the mines?' Carria asked. 'He hasn't had Helena whipped and Ula's getting a second chance.'

J'nie paused, frowning, then spoke. 'I think he would, at least for a time. But I couldn't have let him – or you – down twice.'

The Sultan came up to them and, bowing to them, kissed their hands.

'You have proven your love and loyalty. We shall retire to my quarters. When you have recovered you shall be my only Companions and help me rebuild the school.'

He carefully removed their harnesses and put his arms around them, helping them to walk from the dungeon and across the drawbridge where more Companions waited to attend to them.

19

New Arrivals

The Sultan stirred at the sound of thirteen cock crows. Beside him J'nie and Carria shifted on the silk sheets of the enclosed bed, its four posts supporting a canopy of gossamer-thin gold netting. Finding each other and embracing, their wrist chains clinking with the motion, the women made low murmurs of sleepy contentment. The Sultan kissed them both in their slumber. It had been exhausting the night before, but he had woken with a massive erection, and the thought of the fun the three of them had had dressing up in his chambers made him eager for more.

Although neither woman was fully awake, he decided to help them, leaning over and kissing J'nie gently on her breasts while letting his hand work between the two women and move steadily to Carria's softest areas.

The Sultan was careful not to go to fast, and coaxed the women's bodies to sexual arousal without waking them. He was very particular to slip their sleeping panties off without tugging, and threw them on the glass floor. In their dreamy state their hands automatically groped for something to touch. Carria started to stroke J'nie's thighs, and J'nie's practised hand wrapped itself around the Sultan's firm cock.

The Sultan felt another hand move onto his balls, massaging them gently. With a sigh of pleasure he rolled over onto his back, knowing that Carria must now be awake, and letting her mount him.

If he had started this, he now relinquished his control, allowing Carria to settle over him, then with aching slowness push down onto his straight cock. She let out a whimper of pain and pleasure and then he felt the hot slippery sides of her cunt enclosing him.

J'nie was awake now as well and, encouraged by Carria, straddled his shoulders. Looking up, he saw the women embrace and kiss, then he watched in anticipation as J'nie's wet cunt moved itself closer and closer to his head, until he could see no more, but his mouth and nose were filled with the sweet musk of sex. Without hesitating he started to kiss and lick, and gently bite the hot flesh, drinking in the juice.

Then they were as one. Every rhythmic push down to his engorged penis made him thrust his tongue deep, and the women kiss more deeply and squeeze their opposite's breasts. There was laughter to start with – a high manic laugh of play – then as the pace quickened and the beads of sweats started to roll off their skin, the smell of sex becoming overpowering, the thrust deep and savage, the laughter turned to sighs of pleasure, then cries of frustration and abandon.

He could hardly breath, but the urgency he had kept his tongue probing, then J'nie started to move up and down. He heard screams, and then stillness. With an effort he arched his back, the silk sticking to it, and thrust deeply in Carria. J'nie rolled off him in time for him to see Carria strain at her wrist chains, her hair flying in every direction as her head shook, then he could not contain himself. Carria yelped and threw herself backward in climax as a long white streak flew from him.

Dazed, he lay on the bed as J'nie kneeled over him and licked his cock clean and Carria picked his semen up on her fingers and licked them one by one.

They all slept, exhausted. When they awoke there was a tray of fresh fruit that a maid must have brought and hungrily they ate.

'That was good. Better than being in the mines?' the Sultan declared.

'Would you have sent us there?' J'nie smiled at him.

'You'll never know, will you?' The Sultan grinned back. 'But you know that is what awaits you if ever you reveal what happens here.'

'I think,' Carria interrupted, 'that you are trying to threaten us. But you shouldn't do that. We're equals now remember? You signed the declaration.' She got off up the bed and wandered over to window, letting the sunlight bathe her naked body.

The Sultan stretched out on the bed, letting his naked frame extend to its full length.

'But I am still the Sultan,' he reminded them.

Before he had time to react J'nie had jumped up from the bed and had held his feet fast and Carria was wrapping silk rope about his wrists. He tried to struggle, but it was already too late. One wrist was secured to the bedpost and Carria was working on the second.

It was pointless and he relaxed as his legs were spread apart and tied. J'nie picked up her panties and stuffed them into his mouth in a large ball. Satisfied that he was no longer capable of any movement they kissed each other and left the room.

When they returned the Sultan could hear the rattle of glass vials and the click of heels. Straining to look up, he saw that were both now dressed in the uniform of the guards, and were carrying black bags.

'Well now, still the Sultan, are we?' J'nie said. 'You know the punishment for disobedience of our agreement. Carria, the oils.'

J'nie was handed a vial from the bag and poured the cool blue oil over the Sultan. When there was enough she started to rub it over his body, massaging it into the skin. The Sultan felt the surge of excitement and knew that he was becoming aroused.

'That's very bad.' J'nie waved a finger in front of his face. 'You are not here for pleasure. Carria, the rings.'

The Sultan looked down to see Carria slip a large, flat metal ring over his member, pushing it down over his balls to the stem. Then, with a jerk, he felt the ring tighten. Carria then took a tube made from amber and screwed it onto the ring. Finally she placed a second ring on the one in front of the balls, then screwed it down into the amber tube. The Sultan took a deep breath to ease the discomfort, but Carria hadn't finished. She then took a small funnel and placed it into an opening on the tube. The Sultan saw clear fluid being poured, then felt the icy coldness as the tube filled. He tried to gulp for air, but J'nie's panties stopped him and he was left breathing in fast and shallow draughts through his nose.

His erection melted quickly, although he still felt aroused and wondered where they had found this device. Carria checked that he was completely limp, then placed a third, short funnel with three small clamps around the foreskin, anchoring them on the metal ring by short wires and letting the ring. She then drained the amber tube and the Sultan relaxed.

'It's done,' Carria, said. 'He's going to be a good boy now.'

J'nie nodded, and took a straight blade from the bag and started to shave the Sultan, starting with his arms and legs, then moving to his chest. The Sultan, mesmerised by the blade and helpless, began to feel blood returning to his cock. The clamps began to bite into his skin and, worse, his exposed tip was growing and now he understood the purpose of the funnel. In it there were a thousand teeth that pricked him and made him squirm on the silk bed.

'Don't move. I might cut you,' J'nie commanded, and he held himself rigid as she continued to shave.

But the vision of J'nie and Carria in their uniforms, the sensation of the oil, the shaving – but most of all the pain itself – kept him aroused, and in an agony of pleasure he realised he had ejaculated.

'Finished!' J'nie announced, and stood back.

'But look what he's done,' Carria protested. 'He's been dirty again.'

'Yes, he needs to understand about being punished. Carria, bring me the red vial.'

The Sultan felt the thin fluid over his shaven body, then every pore hurt as the stinging fluid felt as if it was burning him.

After they had untied him, the Sultan kneeled before his mistresses and thanked them. Then he rose and embraced them. He now accepted that there was a part of him that needed to be dominated, as well as dominate, and in these two women he had discovered his needs and had them fulfilled.

It was odd that J'nie had been his mistress for so long, but that he had never found this out before; nor had she sensed it. But he was grateful. He knew more ways to please her and now regarded that as important and be pleased. Things were different and better now. The events had turned the women on too, and he soon found himself in bed again, this time with unrestrained passion.

As he lay in bed, the women now undressed and next to him, he asked where the amber device had come from.

'Its one of the new devices for the school, to teach pleasure and pain, and self-control. Although you would have been whipped for letting go so easily,' Carria teased. 'Its based on a Far Island design.

'Helena has been very enthusiastic about it. She really is doing a great job there. J'nie and I have talked about it with her a lot. You should see her, and the school today – it's the punishment day.'

'Really?' the Sultan exclaimed. 'The new term must have started. I will. Just one more thing first.' And he slid down the silk and started to lick each of his mistresses' pussies in turn. When they were satisfied, the three of them got up and prepared for the visit. After bathing in rose water and cleaning the chains they dried themselves on the balcony overlooking the harbour. Then the women helped each other with the cosmetics and clothes.

Carria now also wore the deep blue of a full Companion, but the Sultan had decreed that both of the women now wore a distinct new design. They had a double edge of gold on their skirts, which were now tight and straight for, as the Sultan had noted, nobody else now had the right to see what only he should see. For that reason they now also wore tight rubber tops, revealing only their nipples. The wrist chains remained, however, as a mark of their loyalty to the tradition of the Companions, and their heels were even taller than before to give them a more commanding presence when they mixed with the others.

The Sultan rang for the corridor, and his private corridor whisked them down to J'nie's former chambers, now occupied by Helena. She welcomed them, and bowed to all three of them with a long and low gesture which gave J'nie an inner smile as she imagined the trim arse bent over.

Helena led them down the stairs; the Sultan and herself at the front, J'nie and Carria behind. Things had changed. The school was now cleaner and all the torches had been replaced with luminous strips. The air was scented and fresh, and as Helena led them to the podium room she pointed out the new fittings.

'We have, Sultan,' she explained, 'made every effort to eradicate any lessons that are not actually teaching or enjoyed by the pupils. Although that means we have had to be more selective, and test applicants more carefully, the increased intake compensates us.'

'How do you test for our special wants?' the Sultan nquired.

'J'nie suggested the system. We now have a dozen former mistresses out in the town, across the island and even in other dominions scouting for suitable candidates. We have closed the dungeon too; punishments are now strictly performed here, with the same tools as for pleasure. This serves a double purpose: the pupils learn the limits of their endurances and when for each the pain ceases to be enjoyable.

'We can then use that knowledge to devise suitable punishments. You will see some examples today,' Helena added as she showed them into the podium room.

The podium room now had three seats facing the raised platform. The familiar dark figures of the guards lined the back, and the school was assembled in front of them. Yvonne sat in her blue pleated skirt, now a part of the Companions herself. In front of the full Companions, the junior Companions sat in a neat line, proud to have obtained their first skirts, then the new arrivals, occasionally looking about them, and acting nervously.

J'nie looked at these new arrivals closely, for it was odd to her that half them were now male – Carria's most dramatic change – and in their wrist chains and belts they looked every part members of the school.

Helena took the stage, and welcomed the Sultan and his mistresses, before declaring that there were to be two punishments that day. With a flourish she pulled back two silk sheets to reveal two figures tied with rope around their thighs and shins into squatting positions on circular discs. These were held in the air by long ladderlike frames, onto which the helpless figures were also tied, their arms pulled through the ladder like horizontals and fastened together over their abdomens. The discs, upon which their feet rocked, were also covered in small brass studs that made them constantly shift positions.

Although both had full gags in their mouths, with three straps, Carria recognised Ula immediately. The other was a young man; a new recruit. Carria wondered why Ula was being punished – her spanking should have finished with her maiding.

'These two students have been caught,' Helena announced, 'attempting to pleasure each other with their fingers. This is, of course, strictly forbidden for pupils of the school, as it is clear from the pussy and cock chains new pupils are fitted with. It is particularly sad that they were engaged in a very dull form of sexual intercourse, and as such they will suffer the punishment laid down by the new rules of the school.

Helena waved two guards forward and they proceeded to wind ropes, also with brass studs in them, around the man's balls and Ula's cunt, then use small wheels to pull them taut up to the top of the ladders.

'The punishment fits the crime – for using their cock and cunt for unauthorised purposes we shall teach these organs a lesson. Guards, remove the discs!' Helena commanded and the two guards flipped a lever on the side of each device that dropped the discs to the floor.

The two figures swayed, their feet frantically attempting to find purchase on the ladder, but the bonds held them and finally they came to rest. Carria looked hard at Ula's wide fear-filled eyes and felt that she was glad to have seen her enemy finally punished. J'nie too looked at the captives as they gurgled senseless noises of pain and fear from their gags and felt a rush of blood to her cunt. But this time there would be no need to sneak off to her private red room. Now she knew she would experience the shared pleasure. She might, she mused, even have Helena send the equipment up to her for inspection and use. But she would not use the vicious rope that now was driving its victims to jerk their bodies, attempting to find a more comfortable position – a task she knew was impossible.

Helena conducted the punishment for a whole segment before allowing her victims to be released, and made them apologise to the school for their behaviour, before removing three links from their chains and replacing their cock and pussy chained tightly. The Sultan saw that the cock guard was the same device that the women had used to play with him, and whispered a suggestion to Carria and J'nie.

J'nie glanced over to see that the Sultan had attained a hard on that stretched his pants. Looking up she saw that Carria had noticed too, and hiding their mouths behind their hands they giggled to each other.

The school was now flourishing: the scouts had found many people wanting to join, and even Ula appeared to learn her lessons. One evening Carria noticed that the sun's rays were making the room turn the colour of burning coals. A gentle breeze made the canopy of the Sultan's bed flutter over the sleeping forms of the Sultan and J'nie. Idly, she got up silently and found herself wandering over to the Sultan's private terrace.

Carria looked out from the palace and toward the fading light, below her the harbour spread out, a bustling trading day drawing to a close as the sun sank. She watched one of the tall ships slip away from its anchor and, with a cheer from the quay, make its way silently out to sea.

She followed it as it shrank to a spot on the wide ocean, melting into the fiery orb of the sun. And with its parting she felt a little sadness. She had learned so much in Estra; she had come for revenge and found passion. She had wanted to put things right, and in a way she had, but she had also discovered things about herself that she would never have imagined.

She had come to understand herself, and discovered someone different to the closeted princess of the Islands; a wild passionate sexual being that had been trapped. Like a country that had never been explored she was creating a map of herself, from the first time with J'nie to the pleasures of losing control. The pleasure that lay in pain, and the fear of losing love. Yes, the school had trained her well.

Carria glanced back at the sleeping forms of her two lovers on the bed. She had come this far and she was satisfied, but out there, across the water, what new delights might await her?

She walked back to the bed and kissed the Sultan and J'nie as they slept contentedly. They were so happy, she thought. She had allowed them to find themselves too, and when the time came she knew she would leave Estra a better place than she found it. For now, she was content too, but the one day the ocean would call her again, and she would go, seeking new and strange pleasures.

NEXUS NEW BOOKS

To be published in May

CHALLENGED TO SERVE
Jacqueline Bellevois

Known simply as 'The Club', a group of the rich and influential meet every month in a Cotswold mansion to slake their perverted sexual appetites. Within its walls, social norms are forgotten and fantasy becomes reality. The Club's members are known to each other by the names of pagan gods and goddesses, or those of characters from the darker side of history. Two of them – Astra and Kali – undertake to resolve a feud once and for all by each training a novice member. After one month, the one who's deemed by the other members to have done the best job will be allowed to enslave the other, finally and totally, for the duration of the Club's activities and beyond.

£6.99   ISBN 0 352 33748 6

BENCH-MARKS
Tara Black

Continues the stories of Judith Wilson, Kate Carpenter and their boss at the Nemesis Archive, the imperious Samantha James. The Archive is a discreet but global concern dedicated to cataloguing the perverse excesses of errant female desire throughout history. Tara Black is a sophisticated writer of up-to-date erotica who manages to combine a thoughtful look at the conflicts that face intelligent, self-possessed young women who like to spank and be spanked, with taught, horny flagellatory prose.

£6.99   ISBN 0 352 33797 4

THE TRAINING GROUNDS
Sarah Veitch

Charlotte was looking forward to her holiday in the sun. Two months on a remote tropical island with her rich, handsome boyfriend: who could ask for more? She is more than a little surprised, then, when she arrives to find that the island is in fact a vast correction centre – the Training Grounds – presided over by a swarthy and handsome figure known only as the Master. But greater shocks are in store, not least Charlotte's discovery that she is there not as a guest, but as a slave.

£6.99   ISBN 0 352 33526 2

NEXUS BACKLIST

This information is correct at time of printing. For up-to-date
information, please visit our website at www.nexus-books.co.uk

All books are priced at £5.99 unless another price is given.

Nexus books with a contemporary setting

ACCIDENTS WILL HAPPEN	Lucy Golden ISBN 0 352 33596 3	☐
ANGEL	Lindsay Gordon ISBN 0 352 33590 4	☐
BARE BEHIND £6.99	Penny Birch ISBN 0 352 33721 4	☐
BEAST	Wendy Swanscombe ISBN 0 352 33649 8	☐
THE BLACK FLAME	Lisette Ashton ISBN 0 352 33668 4	☐
BROUGHT TO HEEL	Arabella Knight ISBN 0 352 33508 4	☐
CAGED!	Yolanda Celbridge ISBN 0 352 33650 1	☐
CANDY IN CAPTIVITY	Arabella Knight ISBN 0 352 33495 9	☐
CAPTIVES OF THE PRIVATE HOUSE	Esme Ombreux ISBN 0 352 33619 6	☐
CHERI CHASTISED £6.99	Yolanda Celbridge ISBN 0 352 33707 9	☐
DANCE OF SUBMISSION	Lisette Ashton ISBN 0 352 33450 9	☐
DIRTY LAUNDRY £6.99	Penny Birch ISBN 0 352 33680 3	☐
DISCIPLINED SKIN	Wendy Swanscombe ISBN 0 352 33541 6	☐

DISPLAYS OF EXPERIENCE	Lucy Golden	☐
	ISBN 0 352 33505 X	
DISPLAYS OF PENITENTS	Lucy Golden	☐
£6.99	ISBN 0 352 33646 3	
DRAWN TO DISCIPLINE	Tara Black	☐
	ISBN 0 352 33626 9	
EDEN UNVEILED	Maria del Rey	☐
	ISBN 0 352 32542 4	
AN EDUCATION IN THE	Esme Ombreux	☐
PRIVATE HOUSE	ISBN 0 352 33525 4	
EMMA'S SECRET DOMINATION	Hilary James	☐
	ISBN 0 352 33226 3	
GISELLE	Jean Aveline	☐
	ISBN 0 352 33440 1	
GROOMING LUCY	Yvonne Marshall	☐
	ISBN 0 352 33529 7	
HEART OF DESIRE	Maria del Rey	☐
	ISBN 0 352 32900 9	
HIS MISTRESS'S VOICE	G. C. Scott	☐
	ISBN 0 352 33425 8	
IN FOR A PENNY	Penny Birch	☐
	ISBN 0 352 33449 5	
INTIMATE INSTRUCTION	Arabella Knight	☐
	ISBN 0 352 33618 8	
THE LAST STRAW	Christina Shelly	☐
	ISBN 0 352 33643 9	
NURSES ENSLAVED	Yolanda Celbridge	☐
	ISBN 0 352 33601 3	
THE ORDER	Nadine Somers	☐
	ISBN 0 352 33460 6	
THE PALACE OF EROS	Delver Maddingley	☐
£4.99	ISBN 0 352 32921 1	
PALE PLEASURES	Wendy Swanscombe	☐
£6.99	ISBN 0 352 33702 8	
PEACHES AND CREAM	Aishling Morgan	☐
£6.99	ISBN 0 352 33672 2	

PEEPING AT PAMELA	Yolanda Celbridge	☐
	ISBN 0 352 33538 6	
PENNY PIECES	Penny Birch	☐
	ISBN 0 352 33631 5	
PET TRAINING IN THE PRIVATE HOUSE	Esme Ombreux	☐
	ISBN 0 352 33655 2	
REGIME	Penny Birch	☐
£6.99	ISBN 0 352 33666 8	
RITUAL STRIPES	Tara Black	☐
£6.99	ISBN 0 352 33701 X	
SEE-THROUGH	Lindsay Gordon	☐
	ISBN 0 352 33656 0	
SILKEN SLAVERY	Christina Shelly	☐
	ISBN 0 352 33708 7	
SKIN SLAVE	Yolanda Celbridge	☐
	ISBN 0 352 33507 6	
SLAVE ACTS	Jennifer Jane Pope	☐
£6.99	ISBN 0 352 33665 X	
THE SLAVE AUCTION	Lisette Ashton	☐
	ISBN 0 352 34481 9	
SLAVE GENESIS	Jennifer Jane Pope	☐
	ISBN 0 352 33503 3	
SLAVE REVELATIONS	Jennifer Jane Pope	☐
	ISBN 0 352 33627 7	
SLAVE SENTENCE	Lisette Ashton	☐
	ISBN 0 352 33494 0	
SOLDIER GIRLS	Yolanda Celbridge	☐
	ISBN 0 352 33586 6	
THE SUBMISSION GALLERY	Lindsay Gordon	☐
	ISBN 0 352 33370 7	
SURRENDER	Laura Bowen	☐
	ISBN 0 352 33524 6	
THE TAMING OF TRUDI	Yolanda Celbridge	☐
£6.99	ISBN 0 352 33673 0	
TEASING CHARLOTTE	Yvonne Marshall	☐
£6.99	ISBN 0 352 33681 1	
TEMPER TANTRUMS	Penny Birch	☐
	ISBN 0 352 33647 1	

THE TORTURE CHAMBER	Lisette Ashton ISBN 0 352 33530 0	☐
UNIFORM DOLL £6.99	Penny Birch ISBN 0 352 33698 6	☐
WHIP HAND £6.99	G. C. Scott ISBN 0 352 33694 3	☐
THE YOUNG WIFE	Stephanie Calvin ISBN 0 352 33502 5	☐

Nexus books with Ancient and Fantasy settings

CAPTIVE	Aishling Morgan ISBN 0 352 33585 8	☐
DEEP BLUE	Aishling Morgan ISBN 0 352 33600 5	☐
DUNGEONS OF LIDIR	Aran Ashe ISBN 0 352 33506 8	☐
INNOCENT £6.99	Aishling Morgan ISBN 0 352 33699 4	☐
MAIDEN	Aishling Morgan ISBN 0 352 33466 5	☐
NYMPHS OF DIONYSUS £4.99	Susan Tinoff ISBN 0 352 33150 X	☐
PLEASURE TOY	Aishling Morgan ISBN 0 352 33634 X	☐
SLAVE MINES OF TORMUNIL £6.99	Aran Ashe ISBN 0 352 33695 1	☐
THE SLAVE OF LIDIR	Aran Ashe ISBN 0 352 33504 1	☐
TIGER, TIGER	Aishling Morgan ISBN 0 352 33455 X	☐

Period

CONFESSION OF AN ENGLISH SLAVE	Yolanda Celbridge ISBN 0 352 33433 9	☐
THE MASTER OF CASTLELEIGH	Jacqueline Bellevois ISBN 0 352 32644 7	☐
PURITY	Aishling Morgan ISBN 0 352 33510 6	☐
VELVET SKIN	Aishling Morgan ISBN 0 352 33660 9	☐

Samplers and collections

NEW EROTICA 5	Various ISBN 0 352 33540 8	☐
EROTICON 1	Various ISBN 0 352 33593 9	☐
EROTICON 2	Various ISBN 0 352 33594 7	☐
EROTICON 3	Various ISBN 0 352 33597 1	☐
EROTICON 4	Various ISBN 0 352 33602 1	☐
THE NEXUS LETTERS	Various ISBN 0 352 33621 8	☐
SATURNALIA £7.99	ed. Paul Scott ISBN 0 352 33717 6	☐
MY SECRET GARDEN SHED £7.99	ed. Paul Scott ISBN 0 352 33725 7	☐

Nexus Classics

A new imprint dedicated to putting the finest works of erotic fiction back in print.

AMANDA IN THE PRIVATE HOUSE £6.99	Esme Ombreux ISBN 0 352 33705 2	☐
BAD PENNY	Penny Birch ISBN 0 352 33661 7	☐
BRAT £6.99	Penny Birch ISBN 0 352 33674 9	☐
DARK DELIGHTS £6.99	Maria del Rey ISBN 0 352 33667 6	☐
DARK DESIRES	Maria del Rey ISBN 0 352 33648 X	☐
DISPLAYS OF INNOCENTS £6.99	Lucy Golden ISBN 0 352 33679 X	☐
DISCIPLINE OF THE PRIVATE HOUSE £6.99	Esme Ombreux ISBN 0 352 33459 2	☐
EDEN UNVEILED	Maria del Rey ISBN 0 352 33542 4	☐

HIS MISTRESS'S VOICE	G. C. Scott ISBN 0 352 33425 8	☐
THE INDIGNITIES OF ISABELLE £6.99	Penny Birch writing as Cruella ISBN 0 352 33696 X	☐
LETTERS TO CHLOE	Stefan Gerrard ISBN 0 352 33632 3	☐
MEMOIRS OF A CORNISH GOVERNESS £6.99	Yolanda Celbridge ISBN 0 352 33722 2	☐
ONE WEEK IN THE PRIVATE HOUSE £6.99	Esme Ombreux ISBN 0 352 33706 0	☐
PARADISE BAY	Maria del Rey ISBN 0 352 33645 5	☐
PENNY IN HARNESS	Penny Birch ISBN 0 352 33651 X	☐
THE PLEASURE PRINCIPLE	Maria del Rey ISBN 0 352 33482 7	☐
PLEASURE ISLAND	Aran Ashe ISBN 0 352 33628 5	☐
SISTERS OF SEVERCY	Jean Aveline ISBN 0 352 33620 X	☐
A TASTE OF AMBER	Penny Birch ISBN 0 352 33654 4	☐

------- ✂ --------------------------

Please send me the books I have ticked above.

Name   ....

Address   ....

                 ....

                 ....

                 .... Post code...................

Send to: **Cash Sales, Nexus Books, Thames Wharf Studios, Rainville Road, London W6 9HA**

US customers: for prices and details of how to order books for delivery by mail, call 1-800-343-4499.

Please enclose a cheque or postal order, made payable to **Nexus Books Ltd**, to the value of the books you have ordered plus postage and packing costs as follows:

    UK and BFPO – £1.00 for the first book, 50p for each subsequent book.

    Overseas (including Republic of Ireland) – £2.00 for the first book, £1.00 for each subsequent book.

If you would prefer to pay by VISA, ACCESS/MASTERCARD, AMEX, DINERS CLUB or SWITCH, please write your card number and expiry date here:

....

Please allow up to 28 days for delivery.

Signature ....

Our privacy policy.

We will not disclose information you supply us to any other parties. We will not disclose any information which identifies you personally to any person without your express consent.

From time to time we may send out information about Nexus books and special offers. Please tick here if you do *not* wish to receive Nexus information.   ☐

------- ✂ --------------------------